PIZZA 911

PIZZA 911

A Mister Jinnah Mystery

Donald J. Hauka

DUNDURN
TORONTO

Copyright © Donald J. Hauka, 2015

All rights reserved. No part of this publication may be reproduced, stored in a retrieval system, or transmitted in any form or by any means, electronic, mechanical, photocopying, recording, or otherwise (except for brief passages for purposes of review) without the prior permission of Dundurn Press. Permission to photocopy should be requested from Access Copyright.

All characters in this work are ficticious. Any resemblance to real persons, living or dead, is purely coincidental.

Editor: Jennifer McKnight
Design: Jesse Hooper
Cover design: Courtney Horner
Cover image credit: © kb2001/istockphoto.com
Printer: Webcom

Library and Archives Canada Cataloguing in Publication

Hauka, Donald J., author
    Pizza 911 / Donald J. Hauka.

"A Mister Jinnah mystery".
Issued in print and electronic formats.
ISBN 978-1-4597-2807-3 (pbk.).--ISBN 978-1-4597-2808-0 (pdf).--
ISBN 978-1-4597-2809-7 (epub)

    I. Title. II. Title: Pizza nine one one.

PS8565.A774P59 2015   C813'.6   C2014-906778-X
                                                        C2014-906779-8

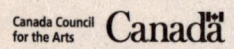

1 2 3 4 5   19 18 17 16 15

We acknowledge the support of the **Canada Council for the Arts** and the **Ontario Arts Council** for our publishing program. We also acknowledge the financial support of the **Government of Canada** through the **Canada Book Fund** and **Livres Canada Books**, and the **Government of Ontario** through the **Ontario Book Publishing Tax Credit** and the **Ontario Media Development Corporation**.

Care has been taken to trace the ownership of copyright material used in this book. The author and the publisher welcome any information enabling them to rectify any references or credits in subsequent editions.

J. Kirk Howard, President

The publisher is not responsible for websites or their content unless they are owned by the publisher.

Printed and bound in Canada.

VISIT US AT
Dundurn.com | @dundurnpress | Facebook.com/dundurnpress | Pinterest.com/Dundurnpress

Dundurn
3 Church Street, Suite 500
Toronto, Ontario, Canada
M5E 1M2

To Margaret and Bartley,
the best writing team anyone could have asked for.

To Dhirendra,
who brought Jinnah to life, and to Salim,
who lives it every day. Much thanks and hugs.

And to the memory of Andy Ross,
my frosty friend and mentor, who has, sadly,
reached the Big 30 of his life.

Chapter One

God is watching, even if no one else is, Jagjit Major told himself as he approached the dark double doors of Commonwealth Pizza. But God's observation didn't stop the devout Sikh from grumbling as he put down his bucket filled with cleaning fluids and cloths. One gloved hand groped for the keys in his faded blue overalls. It was Sunday evening and the pizza parlour was closed — just like almost every other business in the compact strip mall that straddled the edge of Little India in South Vancouver. God was almost the only one watching Major on this warm, overcast nightfall. But that was the reality of things. It was hard times for Little India. Most of the stores that the janitor had passed on his walk to work had not only been closed for business, but boarded up for good. The clothing stores, the jewellery bazaars, the carpet factory outlets were being replaced by pawn shops and cheque-cashing fronts. Everyone was moving from the city to the suburbs and now Surrey, across the Fraser River, had the biggest South Asian community (and the biggest Diwali festival) in British Columbia. His friends and relations like the Gills, the Bains, and Sidhus — all gone. But not the old man. The old man was immovable. He, at least, had not sold out and moved on. It was not for Major to judge, but he thought that as long as the owners of Commonwealth Pizza had decided to stay in Little India, they ought to be open for business. Perhaps this was yet another thing the old man and his son could not agree on. A white smile split his dark beard as the deadbolt slid back with a click. Those two seldom agreed on anything.

Major sensed that something was wrong even before he swung the door open. A scent had faintly reached his nostrils, warning him. Now thick, acrid smoke struck him in the face as he stepped inside. Coughing, he waved furiously at the shifting clouds. Through the haze he could see the shadowy shapes of chairs stacked on the tables. Choking, he buried his nose in his sleeve. There was no crackle of flames, no roar of a blaze raging. Nor was there the smell of burning wood and plastic. This was a far different smell, foul and nauseating. As his eyes adjusted to the gloom, he could see the source of the fumes. The kitchen. He swore, not caring if God was watching or not. The son often left things in the ovens for him to clean up. But never before had there been smoke like this. Or such a stench.

Major made his way half-crouching into the kitchen. Smoke was pouring from the huge blackened stainless-steel commercial oven. He reached for the oven door handle, but recoiled from the heat. The temperature was cranked right to the top. Major glanced briefly around the kitchen. His eye landed upon a large wooden pizza paddle. Just the thing. He grabbed it and jammed it into the handle of the oven, struggling to open it. Finally, he hooked it just right and wrenched with all his might. The heavy door fell open.

A hot blast staggered Major backwards. The stench was now overpowering. Coughing and holding down the bile rising in his throat, he forced himself to approach the oven. The smoke had dissipated, but waves of heat shimmered and danced in the air, making it look like water. He cleared his throat and peered inside from a safe distance. Dark shapes were outlined against the red glare of the oven. Something sat charred and still smoking, heaped on several metal platters, glowing red around their edges. He looked closer. Poking through the pile of ashes closest to him was the distinctive dome shape of a human skull.

It took a few seconds for the information to be fully processed by Major's overloaded brain. It took much longer for him to finish vomiting into one of the sinks in the kitchen. Then he unsteadily groped his way to the telephone and dialed 911.

"Police, fire, or ambulance?" asked the operator.

"All three," Major managed to gasp before he was ill again.

* * *

"I've had it. My bags are packed and I'm going back to Africa. So, Mr. Richard Whiteman, so-called editor-in-chief, you can take your deadlines and your lectures on ethics in journalism and kiss my brown ass goodbye! I'm out of here!"

There was a short pause after Hakeem Jinnah said this. The rest of the Vancouver *Tribune* newsroom hummed with activity as the newspaper gradually gathered momentum, steaming slowly toward deadline. The TV news chattered in the background, copy runners criss-crossed with each other, bearing page proofs and photos for the news deskers laying out pages and rewriting stories. But a hush lay over the central city desk. The soft clack of computer keys ceased and people on the phone asked whoever they were speaking with to hold on for a moment. It seemed an eternity before Ronald Sanderson cleared his throat somewhat doubtfully, filling the vacuum.

"Is that what you're really going to say to him?" he asked.

"Not this time," Jinnah admitted. "But if things work out in Africa, I'll be back in a month and then I can tell him to his face."

It was at times like this that Sanderson regretted sitting next to Jinnah, the *Trib*'s high-strung crime reporter. He studied the slender brown face framed by gold glasses across from him. Jinnah sat, dressed in his traditional "crime of fashion" style (tight black polyester pants, acrylic white disco shirt, too much heavy gold jewellery — a sort of Indo-Canadian Bruno Gerussi), with one hand on his computer mouse, the other flipping through the phone book. He was not exactly the very picture of business savvy and Sanderson wondered if his latest get-rich-quick scheme was finally the real deal.

"It all sounds a little drastic," said Sanderson, "giving up your career and all."

"Ronald, I'm telling you, I'm sick of this place! I'm fed up with my job, my boss, and my life! This month's leave of absence is the smartest thing I've ever done!"

Sanderson suppressed a smile. Up until a few weeks ago, Jinnah had claimed investing his life's savings in a computer dating service called Online Life-Partners Enterprises (or the "OLE," which had instantly earned the nickname the "Orient Love Express") had been the smartest thing he'd ever done. The OLE had subsequently been investigated by the Securities Commission and Jinnah had been forced to sell his interest at a loss. Sanderson was about to remind Jinnah of this, but he never got the chance. Barrelling toward them was the force of nature known as Frosty.

"Jinnah! How old is this guy who robbed a bank wearing only a towel?"

Nicole Frost's voice was the product of thirty years in the business, rough-hewn by hollering questions louder than any other reporter in the scrum, three packs of cigarettes a day, and a fondness for single malt scotch. Acerbic at the best of times, there was an irritable edge to Frosty's voice that rattled Sanderson's West Coast sensibilities. Jinnah, as usual, was unfazed.

"It's in the third 'graph, Frosty," he said reasonably, his deep voice resonating with patience.

"No, it's not. Neither's his name."

Frosty's patience level was zero: unusual with so much time before deadline. But then, Jinnah had that effect on managers, even the ones who admired him, like Frosty. He swiftly called up the story in question on his screen. Staring at it, he cursed loudly in Punjabi.

"Sonofabitch!" he growled, switching to English. "I'll send you an add."

Frosty grunted and turned her sour gaze on Sanderson, who flinched. "Well? Exactly what is your contribution to the *Daily Miracle*, Ronald?"

The *Daily Miracle*. The desk's not entirely inaccurate name for the creation of each edition of the paper. Sanderson, a general assignment reporter, had been given three non-stories to work on that morning. None had panned out. He opened his mouth to explain, but Frosty had already turned away with a disgusted snort and stomped back to her terminal. Ronald slumped in his seat and watched Jinnah pound out his add. He wrote effortlessly, sticking to his tried-and-true crime story formula. The fact that he also read aloud as he wrote was a constant irritant.

"Police have charged twenty-eight-year-old Jonathan Blocks with armed robbery ... and indecent exposure after an incident at the Bank of Montreal on Denman Street...."

Jinnah paused and leaned around the side of the computer he and Sanderson shared. The leering grin on his face told Ronald another tasteless Jinnah Joke was imminent.

"Ronald, you realize that Blocks would have

gotten away with it if he hadn't dropped his towel while fleeing police, hmm?"

"Oh yes?" said Sanderson, not meeting Jinnah's gaze.

"Yes. You might say he blew his cover!"

Jinnah howled with laughter. Sanderson gritted his teeth. The steady stream of bad jokes, horrid puns, and other "witticisms" from Jinnah's corner was undoubtedly one way in which Hakeem dealt with the stress of reporting on death, murder, mayhem, and the darker side of human nature. Sanderson considered it somewhat puerile. He returned to the topic of Jinnah's impending departure.

"Seems to me now is not the time to be taking extended leaves of absence," Sanderson stated as if he were a pre-Charter of Rights judge ticking off a lawyer only recently called to the bar. "Your job may be absent by the time you get back."

"So might be the paper," rejoined Jinnah. "All the more reason to go, hmm?"

"And leave the Wet Coast? What is Nairobi like at this time of year anyway?"

"Fucking hot, buddy. It's always hot. I'm leaving in three days, and when I get there, I'm going to meet with my relatives —"

"And, more importantly, their business connections."

"Exactly. If all goes well, I'll be fabulously wealthy."

"By setting up the biggest chain of Burger Palace fast food outlets in Africa?" asked Sanderson, with just a slight note of scepticism in his voice.

"Beef is where it's at in Africa. Are you going to actually file anything today, Ronald? It is a *daily* newspaper, you know."

Sanderson flushed as Jinnah hit the send key. A paragraph of precisely twenty-seven words made its way to Frosty at city desk. Jinnah leaned back in his chair, feet calmly planted on his desk, stirring a cup of coffee with four creams and four sugars in it. It wasn't much, but it was twenty-seven more words than Sanderson had contributed to date and it rankled him. So did Jinnah's crack about the *Trib* not being in business by the time he returned in four weeks. The newspaper industry was in trouble and the *Tribune*, one of the last independent major daily newspapers in Canada (or just about anywhere else), faced with largely absent advertising revenues, had a credit rating only slightly better than Greece. The thought of Jinnah bailing out at exactly the right moment was too much for Ronald to bear.

"It's not as bad as all that," Sanderson backtracked, as he often did during his arguments with Jinnah. "There are rumours of another buyer. The *Star* chain, for one —"

"Hah! Then I am truly getting out while the getting is good!" cried Jinnah, nearly spilling his coffee. "I have no wish to become an invertebrate."

Sanderson tried hard to smother an infant smile in the bathwater behind his teeth. Jinnah was referring to the back-story of poor Douglas Princeton, the assistant night news editor. In his prime he'd been the city editor of a hip, happening daily in the B.C. Interior that had been bought by the *Star* syndicate and unceremoniously merged with its rival. Both papers had been union shops and layoffs were done by strict seniority. Princeton, not yet thirty years old, had been saddled with a newsroom whose average age was twice his own. No amount of shouting at the deaf-as-a-post reporting crew could prompt them into action. They weren't ambulance chasers, they were passengers. Nothing happened in a hurry. Or with great accuracy. They'd gone down in legend as "Doug and the Slugs." It had been too much for Princeton, who quit and joined the *Trib* as a desker, his career prospects (not to mention his nerves and his own hearing) in tatters.

"Well, we're unlikely to be bought by a newspaper chain anyway," said Sanderson. "It's far more probable we'll be gobbled up by some Google/Yahoo dot-com media conglomerate."

"Fantastic! Then instead of being reporters, we'll be content providers," snorted Jinnah.

Sanderson shifted uneasily in his desk. He was used to Jinnah's get-rich-quick schemes and his endless exit strategies. He had always put it (and his desk mate's eccentric behaviour) down to the stresses of being a police reporter. Dealing with death and the worst in human nature on a routine basis must, after all, be wearing to even the strongest psyche, let alone one as riddled by neuroses as Jinnah. But there was something about this particular venture that made Ronald's guts feel a bit like Hakeem's own digestively challenged intestinal tract. He seemed, well ... *serious* about this one. The presence of Jinnah in the newsroom was, generally, intolerable. The thought of the *Tribune* without him was unthinkable. The idea made Sanderson uneasy. And unusually loquacious.

"But why would you want to leave here?" he hectored his colleague. "You're respected among your colleagues, feared by your competitors —"

"Loathed by my editor."

"That goes without saying at a daily," said Sanderson. "I'm sure under his thick, black, callused heart, in some small corner, Whiteman actually likes you, Hakeem."

"Huh!" snorted Jinnah, stirring the sickly sweet contents of his grande-sized cup. "Fat chance! When I get back from Africa and I'm rich and famous, I'll have some choice words for that old windbag."

"Which old windbag?" asked a voice with an Etonian accent directly behind Jinnah.

Jinnah, startled, leaned so far backwards in his chair to stare wide-eyed and upside-down at his tormentor that he almost fell out of it. Richard Whiteman loomed above him, glasses in one hand, a promotions newspaper box card in the other. Eternally in his fifties, Whiteman ran the *Tribune* the way Tiberius had run the Roman Empire: by being the biggest bully in town.

"Mr. Jinnah, your leave of absence doesn't officially start for several days yet. I think we would all be grateful if until then you take your feet off your desk and at least pretend to do some work," said Whiteman, quite loud enough for the entire newsroom to hear.

Jinnah sat up straight. This time the whole newsroom fell silent. Sanderson seized his phone and pretended to dial a contact. It did not do to get caught in the crossfire of a Jinnah-Whiteman spat. Other, more courageous hacks like Frosty watched brazenly, many with smiles on their faces. Realizing he had an audience's undivided attention, Jinnah rose to his feet, aplomb fully restored.

"You're right, Whiteman. I'll have to file for undertime."

Jinnah reached for his coat. Whiteman thrust the promotion card at him, blocking his escape route.

"I trust you've filed your much-heralded missing biker exclusive? The one I sold to promotions today on your express promise to deliver?" asked Whiteman dryly.

Sanderson risked a quick glance at the confrontation. The card was a mock-up of the front page, featuring a large picture of an Indo-Canadian biker named Moe Grewal who looked about thirty. Over top was a huge, screaming headline: "Missing Biker Mystery Solved? A *Tribune* Exclusive!" In much smaller type under that was Jinnah's byline. Jinnah winced. Sanderson stifled a laugh as he watched Hakeem — his bluff called — switch from braggadocio to begging.

"It's not so easy, Mr. Whiteman," he pleaded. "There is so little to go on in these gangland warfare cases. I've knocked at a thousand doors of silence."

Whiteman stood still, unmoveable — very much like one of Jinnah's doors. Like clockwork, the cop reporter fell back on his habitual hypochondria. He felt his forehead and swayed slightly on his feet.

"I fear I may be coming down with something," he whined. "Perhaps I should go home before I infect the rest of the newsroom."

Whiteman calmly tore the promotional card in half and dropped it into Jinnah's blue bin. He turned to Frosty at city desk.

"Ms. Frost! Plug the hole on page one where Jinnah's 'exposé' is supposed to have gone ..." Here Whiteman glared momentarily at Jinnah, whose eyes were firmly closed, a shaking hand shading his suddenly feverish eyes. "... with the Middle East wire," he finished.

Frosty stared fixedly at her computer screen.

"Right, Chief," she barked.

Whiteman turned and stalked away.

"Unless Jinnah develops something other than malaria in the next hour," he called over his shoulder in parting.

Jinnah collapsed in his chair, eyes still closed, and listened as the noise level of the newsroom gradually returned to normal. Amidst the chatter of voices, clatter of keystrokes, and the hum of printers, he heard something that sounded like a hedgehog choking on a wad of cotton batten. He opened his eyes to find Sanderson staring at him, shaking with suppressed laughter.

"What the hell's so funny?" Jinnah fumed.

"You really showed the old windbag that time!" guffawed Sanderson.

Jinnah picked up the phone, then put it down again.

"Ronald, I am going to set up the biggest chain of Burger Palaces in the world. I am going to make a fortune. Then Whiteman can kiss my brown butt."

"I wonder if Burger Palace's head office knows it's about to have so many new franchises purchased."

Jinnah shook his head.

"We aren't exactly going to buy franchises," he admitted. "We are just going to use the name."

"Isn't that illegal?"

"In Africa everything is legal, as long as you pay the right amount of money to the right people," Jinnah said with a laugh.

"Have you? Paid the right people, I mean?"

Jinnah regarded Sanderson and smiled enigmatically.

"I'm as good as gone, my friend," he said, sipping on his cooling coffee.

"You'll be back."

"Not if things work out in Africa. I've got investors, locations, licences —"

"And a good lawyer? Because Burger Palace is going to sue that brown butt of yours if you use their logo without buying the franchise."

Jinnah snorted.

"You'll see, my friend. Once I've made my fortune, I'm going to come back to Vancouver and rub Whiteman's nose in it. Until then, however, I am trusting you to make sure no one steals my desk."

"You can't just call a new fast food chain Burger Palace and get away with it," persisted Sanderson. "There is such a thing as international law, Hakeem."

Further recriminations over international copyright and franchising jurisprudence were cut short by Jinnah's phone ringing. Recognizing the number on the call display, he grabbed the receiver with the speed and deadly intent of a cobra. It was Sergeant Craig Graham of the Vancouver Police Major Crime Section.

"Hakeem? Are you busy?"

Even if Jinnah had been in the middle of writing an exclusive about an axe-murderer, he would have dropped it to listen to Craig Graham. The lean, laconic cop was his best source on the Vancouver Police. But Jinnah wasn't about to let Graham know that, so he adopted his smart-assed routine. Just to keep him honest.

"You better believe it, Craig," said Jinnah. "Did you know that you have to have twelve different vaccinations to go to Kenya?"

"I mean right now," said Graham impatiently.

"I'm not sure. I think I'm having a reaction to those shots."

"You'll get quite a different reaction if you come down here to South Vancouver and see what I've got for you, buddy."

A very small part of Jinnah's conscious mind clocked the policeman's forced, jocular tone and the use of the word "buddy" to describe a reporter he had recently called "a discredit to yellow journalism." The rest of his intellect and his inherent instincts were focused on the information being handed to him.

"What is it?" Jinnah asked, trying hard to sound nonchalant.

"Murder, I think."

"Is it front page, my friend?"

"Just get down here. Corner of Main and Linder. You won't be disappointed."

"Be right there."

Jinnah hung up. Totally transformed from petulant to blissful. Sanderson watched as he popped a fresh tape into his microcassette. No digital recorder for the Mighty Jinnah-ji.

"Well?" Sanderson asked. "What have you got? User Key One or Two?"

Jinnah smiled happily at his desk mate, ignoring the taunt. Sanderson constantly accused him of writing only two or three different types of stories — stories so similar, in fact, that they were called "User Keys." User Key One was the best: "Why did he/she have to die?" If the victim failed to actually shuffle off the mortal coil (a failing that almost always moved a story off the front page and inside), Jinnah fell back on User Key Two: "Lucky to be alive." His inherent instincts told him that Graham had a User Key One of special variety for him. And that meant the front page.

"I don't know yet," Jinnah told Sanderson truthfully, pulling on his coat. "But it's the line story."

"How do you know?" Sanderson called after him.

"Because that's what Graham always delivers."

At that moment, Jinnah had no idea just how tasteless his remark was, but with this semi-prophetic quip, he was out the door.

By the time Jinnah arrived on the scene a half an hour later, Commonwealth Pizza and the small strip mall in which it was situated was a media midden composed of four successive layers. The first and most permeable layer was the barricade of police cars, fire trucks, and an ambulance. With lights flashing and hoses bulging, the emergency vehicles formed a bright, damp, and potentially explosive (in an aqueous manner) maze. Jinnah gingerly stepped over the hoses, taking care not to scuff his Guccis. The second layer was harder to barge past, being a large, curious crowd composed mostly of Indo-Canadians and the employees of the half-dozen other stores in the mall. They were held back by the third stratum: the yellow and black crime scene tape erected by the police.

Pressing up hard against this boundary were a number of Jinnah's competitors: a few radio reporters looking anxious as the top of the hour drew nearer, one or two newspaper scribes like himself with the luxury of a little more time on their hands and looking bored, and at the very front, several TV news crews. All were hoping to breach the fragile plastic cordon and enter the fourth layer at the heart of the matrix: beyond the doors of Commonwealth Pizza. Jinnah grunted his greetings at those in the pack whom he knew. In his haste to find Graham, he walked right past a TV reporter he'd not seen before. Then she turned and Jinnah caught her profile. He stopped and did a double-take.

To the untrained eye, she was simply a stunning TV blonde — a knock-off Armani girl, smiling at him with perfectly capped teeth. It was her eyes, however, that gave her away. They alone had needed no makeover. And they were beaming at Jinnah.

"Caitlin? Caitlin Bishop?" he gasped.

"Jinnah!"

Caitlin Bishop threw her arms around Hakeem and hugged him, much to the amusement of the rest of the scrum. *To hell with the rest of the scrum*, thought Jinnah, and hugged her back. He stepped back and grabbed Caitlin's shoulders, looking her over.

"My God, Caitlin! What have you done to yourself in the past ... how long has it been?"

"Five years. Elevated my profile — both surgically and professionally," laughed Caitlin. "I, ah, went into TV, you know."

Jinnah's smile faded slightly. He noticed for the first time Caitlin's cameraman standing behind her, one of those tall, beefy shooters who was forever asking print reporters to move over or get out of the shot. Kevin, if memory served. He took this in with a nanosecond's glance and returned to the far more pleasing sight of Caitlin.

"You were in J-school at Ryerson, right?"

"I got a summer job at City TV. Filled in at a CBC station in Halifax for a while. I just started here at CXBC."

There was an awkward pause as Jinnah tried hard to keep smiling. Caitlin had been a summer student at the *Tribune* just five years ago and he had taken her under his wing. She had been totally different then: thin, mousy-brown hair, glasses. Dressed like a devotee of the Black Eyed Peas. Her physical transformation was truly stunning. But that wasn't what bothered Jinnah. Caitlin had the right stuff. She was a natural reporter. Together they had laughed at the shallowness of much of TV news. "Info-tainment," they had sneered. Caitlin looked down at her shoes — rather expensive ones, Jinnah noted — and frowned.

"Don't say it. I know. I sold out."

"Don't be ridiculous!" Jinnah cried, feigning sincerity. "Lots of TV journalists manage to do good work despite, ah, the limitations of their media. What exactly do they have you doing? The weather?"

The smile returned to Caitlin's face as she looked back into Jinnah's eyes.

"Nope. They've given me the crime beat, actually," she said proudly.

Jinnah was revising his opinion of just how useful TV news was and marshalling fresh examples of the limiting nature of the ten-second clip compared to in-depth reporting when Sergeant Craig Graham appeared at the edge of the crime tape. Before anyone could even blink, Caitlin grabbed her microphone from Kevin and had it nearly inserted up Graham's left nostril.

"Sergeant! Is it a murder? Gang related? How many victims?"

Caitlin left scarcely a second between these questions and even Jinnah was awed by the tenacity of her pit bull imitation. *To think I used to have to bully her into asking a cop to spell his name*, he thought. Graham, however, didn't miss a beat. He calmly looked down the length of Caitlin's microphone and smiled.

"I'll have a statement for you later," he said.

Before Caitlin could launch another barrage of questions, Graham motioned to Jinnah to follow him a short distance down the sidewalk fronting the pizza parlour. Jinnah grinned apologetically at Caitlin.

"Personal stuff," he lied. "Likely about the VPD-*Tribune* hockey pool."

Gratified by Caitlin's perfectly sculpted scowl, Jinnah caught up with Graham in front of a video arcade next to Commonwealth Pizza.

"Who's the blond pit bull?" he asked.

"Caitlin Bishop. She was an intern at the *Trib*. Don't ask," Jinnah added, noticing his friend's curious look.

"Well, lose her. Meet me around the back, service entrance. She looks like the type who would make me letting you into the crime scene a big story."

"Oh, you got that right." Jinnah grinned. "Give me ten minutes, my friend."

In the intervening ten minutes, Jinnah traded a few rumours about the *Tribune*'s impending collapse/sale/merger with Caitlin, brought her up to speed on the newsroom gossip — who had quit, been promoted, or died — and then excused himself to "make a call to the desk." Caitlin was naturally suspicious, but diplomatic enough not to say anything. To do so would have broken the unwritten laws of "The Pack." Everyone in The Pack knows his or her competitor will call in any favour, promise, and inducement, or even murder a close relative (and if the story is big enough, perhaps all of the above) to get the story first. But every member of The Pack also has to pretend that every journalist is equal and entitled to the same open access to the information as everyone else. Like many of the polite fictions that sustain small communities, it was sacrosanct, and Jinnah was quite confident even Caitlin would not dare follow him as he quietly slipped around the back and into the alley behind the strip mall. He passed three Smithrites before arriving at the rear entrance of Commonwealth Pizza. The back door was barred by the hulking presence of a constable with dark hair, dark eyes, and brown skin.

"Hello, Bains," said Jinnah cheerfully. "Pulling overtime?"

Bains was one of the original Indo-Canadian members of the Vancouver Police force. His family had been in British Columbia longer than most of the European "pioneer" clans. The only accent discernible in his irritated voice was pure West Coast.

"No. Straight time. Should get extra pay for this kinda crap."

Jinnah laughed as he brushed past Bains into the pizza joint. It had a large, simply furnished dining room. Red-and-white checked tablecloths covered the large, round tables. Chairs waved their legs in the air atop them. Jinnah wrinkled up his nose. The pong was overpowering. The place was crowded with police. His attention was drawn to the kitchen, where a forensics team wearing white gauze masks was huddled over a food preparation table. On it sat five large metal pizza trays. On them were heaps of ashes and bits of something burnt. Jinnah knew in an instant it certainly wasn't pizza. On one of the trays, the skull glimpsed by Jagjit Major was clearly visible. He also knew he would be able to identify other human remains if he looked closely. He wisely decided not to. Standing over the forensics team was Graham.

"Finished, boys?" he asked.

"Almost. Just waiting for the meat wagon," replied an officer.

"Better yet, the dustman," said another.

Jinnah felt sick. Graham grinned, amused.

"Makes you kinda hungry, eh?" he quipped.

Jinnah swallowed his rising gorge and forced himself to smile.

"I am becoming reacquainted with my lunch."

Jinnah moved closer — rather reluctantly — for a better look.

"Janitor arrived to find the place full of smoke and the main oven on high," explained Graham. "The poor bastard looked inside and found our friend here."

Graham indicated the heaps of charred and burnt remains.

"After he was finished being sick, he called us."

"That's really a body?" cried Jinnah, even though he had no doubts. "You're kidding me!"

"Nope. Dismembered, tossed onto those trays, and put in the oven for disposal. Wrong kind of oven, unfortunately for the perp."

"Oh my God," said Jinnah softly.

As revolting as the spectacle was, Jinnah felt himself becoming morbidly fascinated by this most unusual murder.

"No signs of blood? A struggle?" he asked.

Graham shook his head.

"Or of forced entry," he added significantly. "Office upstairs is untouched."

Graham watched as Jinnah's queasiness vanished. It was a sure sign that the body in the oven had ceased to be merely remains to Hakeem and was starting to become an irresistible mystery.

"I have never heard of someone trying to dispose of a body in pizza oven," said Jinnah, unable to tear his eyes off the sight. "Any idea who the victim is?"

"I'm told they think it might have been a male because of the sheer mass," said Graham. "But there are no other anatomical clues left to tell for certain without performing an autopsy, though how even Aikens is going to make head or tail of that mess is beyond me. Definitely a DNA job."

Jinnah nodded. If anyone could sift through these cindery remains, it was Rex "Dr. Death" Aikens, the top forensic pathologist in Vancouver. Unbidden, his encyclopedic mind ran over some of the most gruesome cases Aikens had briefed him on. His lunch started to reassert itself.

Jinnah was spared the embarrassment of hurling at a crime scene by the welcome distraction provided by the meat wagon's arrival. He watched with Graham as the white-gloved forensic staff loaded the pizza trays very carefully into gigantic plastic bags, then into hard-plastic boxes. It was the most unusual body removal Jinnah had ever witnessed. He had quite forgotten he was going to Africa in a few days. His entire mind was bent toward the mystery man in the oven.

"I don't suppose you have any suspects?" he asked.

Graham shrugged.

"The janitor tells us there's a gang of skinhead wannabes who hang around the arcade next door and talk big."

"Might be a hate crime," said Jinnah. "Anything is possible …"

Jinnah's flight of fancy was aborted in mid-takeoff. He suddenly remembered that he was the only reporter behind the police lines. Although his enlarged ego had simply taken this for granted, his inherent instincts smelled a professional rat.

"What do you want of me, Sergeant Graham?" he asked. "You let me in here for some reason."

"Well," said Graham, shifting his weight from foot to foot. "This establishment is owned by one Kabir Shah and his son, Armaan. There's no sign of them."

Jinnah was unmoved. He could now see where this was headed.

"Uh-huh," he exhaled heavily.

Jinnah felt his pockets for a cigarette. He could not possibly imagine anyone objecting to him smoking in here under the circumstances. Then he checked himself. No, no cigarettes. Frosty would find out. It had been a foolish thing to do, challenging her to go without cigarettes for a month. She'd agreed after betting Jinnah $100 he couldn't go cold turkey himself. Well, he was off in three days and there was no way Frosty would be able to tell he was smoking a pack a day in Kenya. Ignorant of this internal, nicotine-charged drama, Graham was still waiting for a reply. As Jinnah remained silent, the policeman started to come to the point.

"Look, Hakeem. Who knows what we got here. Could be murder —"

"What was your first clue?" interjected Jinnah.

"Or it could just as well be a suttee," Graham persevered. "Couldn't it?"

Inwardly, Jinnah sighed. Poor old Craig. At least he tried to take culture into account when dealing with the community.

"Craig, I know of no widow determined to throw herself on her husband's burning ghat who could also chop herself up."

One of the forensic guys who had been poking around the ashes with a pair of tweezers plucked something metallic from the ashes. It was melted around the edges, but Jinnah could make out that it was a belt buckle sporting a lion riding a Harley. He recognized the motif instantly.

"A Young Lions biker buckle!"

Jinnah's inherent instincts started to tingle. Maybe Whiteman was going to get his much-heralded exclusive missing biker story handed to him on a platter after all.

"Could be Moe Grewal. Or Mal Singh. Our missing bikers." Jinnah grinned.

"Could just as easily be one or both of the Shahs."

"Okay, so maybe it's a two-for-one deal, hmm? Or an extra-large biker disposed of without the Shahs' knowledge."

"Can't rule anything out at this point," Graham admitted.

During the infinitesimal pause between those magic words and Graham's next utterance, Jinnah was already composing his story. He had everything he needed, including the blanket permission to speculate wildly provided by that glorious phrase "police are not ruling out anything." He'd be finished early, home ahead of time, and ready to start packing ...

And then Graham said, "That's where you come in."

Jinnah's mental news writing (definitely a User Key One story) came to a shuddering halt. He looked at Graham and smiled. *Ah! That's what he wants! Fat chance, my friend!* He clapped a friendly arm around Craig's shoulders.

"Sorry, pal. I'm leaving for Kenya in three days."

Graham shrugged off Jinnah's arm. But not in an unfriendly manner: he was at his most solicitous. He needed to be.

"I don't want to piss off the community. You can open doors I can't."

There was a pause. Jinnah waited. Graham moved from pleading to playing on Jinnah's sense of guilt — a sure sign of desperation.

"You owe me for the John Fortune case," he said.

Jinnah winced slightly. Graham had been helpful in supplying him with a great deal of information about Fortune, who had a suspicious habit of losing his heavily insured wives. But two could play the guilt game, and few were better than Jinnah himself.

"You owe me for the Sidoo case."

Jinnah's retort stung, but he didn't care: his sense of guilt was about as well-developed as his sense of shame. Besides, had it not been for Hakeem's prying into corners, Graham would never have busted Siddo's people-smuggling ring — one of Craig's biggest policing triumphs. But Graham too had checked his shame at the door.

"It would be a piece of cake for you to use your contacts in the community to dig up some information on the Shah family for us. They're more likely to talk to you than a cop anyway."

Jinnah uttered a stream of curses in Punjabi.

"I haven't got time for this sort of thing!" he added in English.

"C'mon, Hakeem. One for the road!" cried Graham.

"What's in it for me, hmm?"

Graham drew himself up to his full height and assumed that pompous tone he usually reserved for press conferences.

"The eternal thanks of the Vancouver Police Department, Hakeem. That ought to be more than sufficient payback."

There was another one of those awkward silences that punctuated Jinnah and Graham's relationship. A lot of other reporters would have been intimidated, but Jinnah knew he was dealing from a position of strength. Graham needed him more than he needed Graham right now. He let the silence do the talking for him. Finally, Graham broke.

"All right," he capitulated. "You get it first. Exclusive. Deal?"

Jinnah grinned. An exclusive meant the front page was all his. Whiteman would be kissing his brown butt even before he left for Africa.

"Deal," he said, turning to go. "And Craig? You definitely got the short end of the stick on this one."

"What do you mean?" Graham called out to Jinnah, who was making his way out the back.

"You're the one who has to try to make Caitlin Bishop take 'No comment' for an answer."

Jinnah left the building feeling better than he had in days. He retraced his steps back to the front of the mall. Taking care that he wasn't spotted, he looped back through the parking lot to make it appear he was merely coming back from his van. By the time he reached the front door, Graham was already outside, surrounded by the media, attempting to give a low-information interview while being badgered by Caitlin Bishop.

"At approximately 7:30 p.m. we received a call from someone claiming to find human remains inside this establishment —"

"Is the victim male or female?" shouted Caitlin.

Graham looked slightly thrown for a moment before continuing.

"We're still trying to ID the remains ..."

Jinnah was tempted to watch the entire show, but he had work to do and a deadline looming. He scanned the edge of the crowd pressing around the media scrum. To his right, he could see a knot of black-clad, close-cropped punks with piercings and toting skateboards standing in front of a video arcade. Skinhead wannabes. All male. All white. None over the age of sixteen. He figured that a brutal murder and dismemberment were out of their league, but you could never tell what sort of information you could get by talking to the natives. He pushed his way through the onlookers toward the punks. He had his microcassette tape recorder on and discreetly hidden under his notebook. Sizing them up, he settled on a reasonably soft opening question.

"Don't get this much action around here every day, hmm?"

The punks glared at him silently. Jinnah turned his questioning temperature up a notch.

"You guys get along with the owners?" he asked, just a trace of hostility in his voice.

This got their attention. The gang exchanged a collective glance, looking mostly to the tallest teenager — a gangly youth in torn gangster-rapper pants that looked in imminent danger of sliding off his non-existent hips and sporting a fringe of hair on his forehead that was a shade of a red not found in nature. Obviously their leader.

"They're okay. For Pakis," he said, not making eye contact with Jinnah.

Ah, mild racial taunting. They really were wannabes. True skinheads would have just spat at him. Jinnah was also given comfort by their footwear: the punks were wearing DC skateboard shoes. Their appearance was very likely a simple fashion statement rather than a vocation. He pressed on, sure of himself.

"Know anybody who might want to do harm to them?" he asked.

There was an indignant muttering among the punks. The spokesman sounded like any aggrieved teenager accused of breaking curfew.

"You think we did it? No way, man. Could'a been anybody who burnt the toast."

There were a few laughs at this and the punk spokesman appeared well-pleased with his wit. This was fast becoming a waste of time, but Jinnah kept at it.

"Like who? Seen anyone unusual lately?"

The punk spokesman, encouraged by his friends' laughter, grew more belligerent.

"Like they're all freaks, man," he sneered. "Pakis, rag tops, dot heads —"

"And the follicle-challenged, like yourself," Jinnah cut him off. "I'm talking about right now. How about tonight? Anyone suspicious?"

The punk spokesman looked from Jinnah to the scrum with Graham at the centre.

"You a cop or a reporter?" he asked carefully.

"A bit of both. How about it?"

The punk spokesman glanced at his gang. They were looking at Jinnah with a mixture of suspicion and fascination. He was quite used to this reaction.

"Well," said the spokesman slowly. "There was this one dude. In and out a lot. A real clothes rack."

Ah. Now they were getting somewhere. Maybe.

"A sharp dresser? Like me?" asked Jinnah.

The punks laughed derisively.

"Oh yeah," said the spokesman, voice dripping with sarcasm. "Just like you."

Before Jinnah could determine if the punks were dissing his fashion sense or his race, his pager beeped. Glancing at the number, he muttered a mild curse in Urdu for the punks' benefit and switched it off. He hit the stop button on his microcassette with a satisfying "click." The interview was over.

"Thank you, gentlemen," he said, turning to leave.

The skinhead wannabes were not perhaps the sharpest knives in the drawer. It took their spokesman a moment to come up with any sort of parting shot — a lame one.

"Who was that? Your boss, man?" he said derisively.

Jinnah didn't bother to turn around and face them as he answered in parting.

"Someone far more important, my friend."

It was a short drive to Jinnah's house from Commonwealth Pizza. The "Jin-mahal," as Sanderson liked to call it, was an older "Vancouver Special," with a massive wrought-iron balcony clinging to the brickwork at the front and steel bars on all the windows. Jinnah was a nervous, light sleeper and the bars (as well as the alarm system and video-surveillance cameras mounted by the doors) helped him get at least some REM sleep. He unlocked the front door with a feeling of dread. His wife, Manjit, did not page him at work unless she thought it extremely important. And extremely important usually meant something to do with their son, Saleem. Typical fourteen-year-old, and every bit as sharp as his father, although Jinnah hated to admit it when they were in the middle of an argument.

Manjit greeted him at the door, her blue sari floating on a breeze of her own making.

"Hakeem! So quick this time," she said, embracing him.

Jinnah hugged her hard. He could still not believe they had been married for over fifteen years. Her family, being Sikh, had not been terribly happy when she had wed Jinnah, an Ismaili Muslim. They were, in fact, only now slowly extending the olive branch to her and acknowledging Jinnah's existence. *Ah, but patience*, thought Jinnah. *We must be at our most generous when dealing with family.*

"Hakeem," said Manjit softly in his ear. "It's your son —"

The words were hardly out of her mouth before the warm balm of patience dissolved in Jinnah's soul. He broke off the embrace and strode down the hall toward his son's room, bellowing.

"Saleem!"

Manjit, trailing in Jinnah's wake, urged restraint.

"Hakeem! Use reason, not volume."

"How far did reason get you?" growled Jinnah. "Saleem!"

He threw open the bedroom door to find Saleem sprawled on his bed, talking on his cellphone while fiddling with his laptop. Jinnah saw a cocky reflection of his own adolescence in his son's face. Then he noticed the image flickering on Saleem's computer screen.

"Saleem —" Jinnah barked.

Saleem took one look at Jinnah's eyes and cut his friend on the phone off immediately.

"Call ya later, Raj," he said hurriedly, flipping both his phone and his laptop shut and assuming an air of guilty innocence.

"Hakeem," Manjit whispered, pleading with Jinnah. "Remember reason."

Jinnah tried. But then Saleem looked at him as if

nothing in the world was wrong and said with his best feigned coolness, "Hey, Dad."

Jinnah felt his pulse starting to pound harder.

"This had better be bloody important, Son," he said.

Jinnah went over to the bed and opened Saleem's computer. The bright, bold image used primary colours on an LCD screen capable of displaying over sixteen million different hues. Unfortunately, all Jinnah could see was red. He picked the laptop up and held it closer to his myopic eyes.

"Cool, eh, Dad?"

Jinnah stared at the screen. There was a top-end dirt bike, gleaming in high definition. Like Jinnah's blood pressure. Still, his son surfing the net for dirt bikes didn't warrant Manjit paging him at work. Something wasn't quite processing right. He looked sideways at his wife for an explanation.

"Saleem told me he was buying school supplies," she said calmly. "Instead he took money that was meant for his university fund out to put a deposit on this ... device."

"It's a dirt bike, Mom," said Saleem, a note of whining sliding into the bored, persecuted voice.

Ah-chah! Now things were starting to fall into place. A simple case of fiscal malfeasance. And right in the middle of a murder.

"Saleem!" chided Jinnah, his volume dropping like the stock exchange. "Lying about money! You'll end up a politician."

Manjit recognized the tone in his voice. It was Jinnah's "I'll deal with this later" inflection. She tried to stall him.

"Hakeem, this is important."

Jinnah turned slowly, holding Saleem's laptop between himself and Manjit.

"Manjit, did you know you paged me in the middle of a murder investigation for this?"

Manjit said nothing. Saleem leapt into the gap.

"So I can buy it?" he asked eagerly.

Until now, Hakeem had been successfully calming himself down. But in jumping to conclusions, Saleem had fatally trampled on what remained of Jinnah's parental patience. It snapped.

"Are you kidding?" roared Jinnah. "No! You want to die before I have a chance to kill you?"

Saleem was stung into silence. Jinnah saw his face hardening and regretted his outburst. Fighting his anger, he tried the practical approach.

"We can't ship a bike to Kenya, Saleem."

Bad move. Saleem's back went up faster than a leaky condo.

"I'm not moving to Kenya!" he shouted.

Ah! So this is what this is really about. The tense triangle of people around the bed exchanged looks, but no words for a moment. Jinnah was sweating. Name of God, he needed a cigarette. That thought finally broke the Mexican standoff. He tossed Saleem's laptop onto the bed.

"I don't have time for this. I've got a murder to solve."

Manjit knew better than to say anything as Jinnah stormed out the door.

* * *

Jinnah climbed into his van, known to his colleagues as the "Satellite-Guided Love Machine." It was true it had a GPS system, but the legendary Jell-O-filled waterbed in the rear was a slanderous fiction propagated by Sanderson, Frosty, and others. Once again, Jinnah reached for a cigarette and stopped himself. This no smoking thing was killing him! He fumbled in his shirt pocket for his nicotine gum, popped two pieces in his mouth, and drove fast to the *Tribune* building. Why was he always at a loss when it came to dealing with Saleem? Why did the boy refuse to be handled like a crime case? For there Jinnah had no doubts as to his next move. But to achieve it — and secure the front page — he needed Frosty's help. And time was running short.

Moments later, Jinnah was kneeling by Frosty at her desk, pleading his case as she chewed the filter tip of an unlit cigarette. The front page layout on her computer screen had a main story on top. The "line" story was, in Jinnah's opinion, vastly inferior to his own piece. The headline read "Middle East Talks Stalled." Jinnah took a cigarette from his pocket and used it as a pointer, circling the text under the headline.

"Who wants to read about talks in the Middle East when we have an extra large murder with all the toppings, hmm?" he said, giving his voice just a touch of that low cadence that Crystal, the city desk clerk, had dubbed the "Jinnah Tiger Growl."

Frosty smiled and Jinnah's hopes soared. Then Sanderson wandered by and spotted their unlit cigarettes.

"You two aren't going to break a city bylaw and light those, are you?" he said self-righteously.

"If he does, he owes me a hundred bucks," growled Frosty.

"And I'll get almost twice that," said Sanderson.

Jinnah glared at his desk mate.

"What are you on about, Ronald?"

"Your bet. Crystal's running a staff pool. My money's on Frosty."

Although offended, Jinnah dismissed this with a snort. He had more important matters to attend to. He turned to Frosty.

"Well? How about it, hmm?"

Frosty kept her eyes on her screen, highlighting and manipulating text, flowing the edited copy into the appropriate holes.

"Explain to me again why I'm going to risk my job by holding the front page?"

"Twenty minutes, Frosty. Tops, thirty. I can get to Fogduckers and back in time to beat first edition deadline."

"You mean beat Caitlin Bishop."

There was never much affection in Frosty's voice but this harsh pronouncement was especially cold. Jinnah grinned. Frosty had not liked Caitlin as an intern. She'd liked her even less after Jinnah's description of her makeover and new TV job.

"You should have seen her," Jinnah enthused, rubbing it in. "She has blossomed like a lotus."

"Really?" asked Sanderson. "She was such a mouse when she was here."

"Amazing what a little mentoring by the great Jinnah-ji will do, eh?" said Frosty.

Jinnah put this slight down to nicotine withdrawal and carried on.

"Are you going to hold that spot for me on page one or not?"

"Not," said Sanderson, sticking his oar in. "You won't get through the front door of that bar."

There was much Hakeem Jinnah could stomach in the way of cheerful abuse from his colleagues, but this went too far. Sanderson had touched on the raw, red nerve of Jinnah's congenital cowardice. Suggesting he didn't have the guts to walk into a biker bar and come away with a usable interview instead of inside a body bag. Casting Kenya, burgers, and his leave of absence aside, Jinnah straightened up and lobbed Frosty his unlit cigarette as he turned to go.

"Smoke?" he asked.

"After you," said Frosty, a quiet smile playing about her lips.

Sanderson watched Jinnah disappear into the warren of cubicles and partitions that was the *Tribune* newsroom. When he turned back to Frosty, he was surprised to see her screen was black.

"Damn system crashes." She shrugged, sniffing the unlit cigarette in her hand with longing. "Looks like the paper's gonna be late. Let's go get a coffee, Ronald."

Jinnah did not take the direct route out of the newsroom. A self-confessed physical coward, he knew Sanderson was right about the danger he faced walking alone into a bar frequented by missing bikers Mal

Singh and Moe Grewal. The memory of what had happened to Michel Auger in Montreal over a decade ago was still fresh in his mind. But he had no intentions of braving this ordeal by himself. To that end, he approached the photo editor, Dennis Lumsden, whose desk was on the far side of the office.

Lumsden was idly flipping through colour images on his computer. He was in his fifties and well past busting his butt to cover too many assignments with too few bodies. He had gone through a phase where he had tried to screw up as many things as possible so the company would give him a buy-out and it hadn't worked. Now he was coasting, having embraced the management philosophy of employee empowerment, which, roughly translated, meant his photographers did all the assigning of jobs, downloading of images and videos, and liaising with the other departments, leaving him free to simply flip through the wire photos and attend meetings. He liked meetings. He didn't like Jinnah.

"I have a job for one of your boys, Dennis, my friend," said Jinnah cheerfully.

"Forget it," said Lumsden without looking up from his browser.

"What sort of attitude is that?"

"The right attitude. You want a ride somewhere, take a cab. We're not a taxi service."

"Listen, this is for the line story!"

"That's not what the list says."

Lumsden tapped his keyboard. The photos vanished and were replaced by the city desk news list.

His dull eyes flickered with a touch of malicious delight. He spoke in a monotone that made deadpan seem exciting.

"Why, what's this here? The city list. And what's at the top of it? Ah, a story. Hmm ... don't see your name on it, Jinnah. Oh well. *C'est la vie.*"

Jinnah grabbed Lumsden's mouse and shook it, clicking the "exit" button. The list vanished. Lumsden remained unmoved.

"This is going front page, buddy, I guarantee it!"

"Funny," said Lumsden, voice professionally bored and devoid of emotion. "Didn't come up at the meeting."

"Come on, Dennis!" pleaded Jinnah. "Have I told you about the mystery man in the oven?"

"Does he come with extra cheese?"

"That's not even remotely funny!"

"Look, I have three city desk jobs in Surrey in the middle of rush hour. Fashion has my best lensman at a show that features models wearing clothes that remind me of my high school graduation photo. The new video cameras they've foisted on me don't work for crap and sports wants another body —"

"Right now, downtown Vancouver," said Jinnah. "Thirty minutes, that's all. Maybe less."

Lumsden grunted and punched some keys on his terminal. He had tried indifference and pleading a lack of resources. These having had no effect on Jinnah, he reverted to a surefire defence: the bureaucratic imperative. A photo request template popped up on screen.

"Have you sent me an email form?" he asked dully. "You have to fill out the forms, you know."

Jinnah came very close to quite voluntary — hell, enthusiastic and quite justifiable — homicide. Lumsden was spared swift strangulation by the sudden and quite random appearance of Clint Eastward. The youngest photographer on staff, in his mid-twenties, he was fond of extreme sports and had an expressed desire to climb Mount Everest without oxygen. His last name sounded very much like "Eastwood" and he was always being ribbed by *Trib* staff. Jinnah was no exception.

"Ah, Clint Eastward, my friend!" he cried. "How'd you like to make my day? Come with me to Fogduckers."

Eastward regarded Jinnah warily.

"I'm not a taxi service. What's Fogduckers?" he added.

"A biker bar. We need a picture."

"Bikers already have pictures. Front and side view. ID numbers."

"The question you have to ask yourself is, 'Do I feel lucky?' Well? Do ya, punk?"

Eastward groaned, but Jinnah had piqued his interest. Besides, it beat another dog story assignment. He grabbed his camera bag and cast an inquiring eye at Lumsden, who had his nose back in his photo browser.

"Just get back on time for the hockey game and don't file any OT, okay?" the photo editor said, thus giving his tacit blessing without his actual permission.

The man was, Jinnah had to admit, a master, and he glowed as he checked his watch. There was still time. He followed Eastward down to the company's underground parking lot where the photographer's car was parked. It was a compact model, painted the newspaper's blue and yellow colours and an absolute pigsty. Eastward had to shove a midden of old newspapers, assignment sheets, candy wrappers, mouldy sandwiches, and other things Jinnah dared not try to identify into the back so the reporter could sit (somewhat reluctantly) on the seat. It was a short drive to the Downtown Eastside where Fogduckers sat amidst the other strip bars, hotel saloons, and "lounges" in a neighbourhood known as "The War Zone." Eastward only spoke once during the drive.

"So, too scared to go by your lonesome?" he said with that studied nonchalance peculiar to *Tribune* photographers.

"Of course not!" lied Jinnah, indignant. "It's just that we need a picture."

"The last time I tried to take a biker's picture, I nearly had to have a camera-ectomy, understand?"

Jinnah understood. He was beginning to get the shakes himself. Name of God, what had he gotten himself into? They pulled up a half-block away from the bar. Eastward's car stood out painfully on the edge of the sea of Harley-Davidsons out front that proclaimed the establishment's clientele. Jinnah felt the knots in his stomach twist and tighten as Eastward shut the engine off.

"Out," he said.

"Aren't you coming?" asked Jinnah, his voice soaring toward a most undignified squeak.

"Nope." Eastward shook his head. "I'll try to shoot inside with a great big be-Jesus zoom lens, but that's as close as I get."

The knots in Jinnah's stomach had now become completely Gordian. Worse, his malaria was reasserting itself. And he was having a nic-fit.

"Come on, Eastward! Are you a coward?" he blustered.

"No, just smart. Go on in. I'll be watching."

"Are you kidding? Go in there by myself?" said Jinnah, masking his panic with as much outrage as he could muster.

"What? You a coward?" replied Eastward, unmoved.

"Of course not —"

"Then get out of my car," said Eastward, reaching over and opening the passenger-side door.

It took a great deal of begging and cajoling, but in the end Jinnah finally got Eastward to agree to come inside on the condition he keep his cameras in his bag. As they walked toward the doors, two men in business suits walked out of the bar. One was a slender Asian man with a goatee. The other was a hulking, blond, body-building type who looked as if he was about to explode out of his suit. Jinnah, feeling slightly less malarial with Eastward at his side, managed a grin.

"Bet they didn't make the dress code," he said as the two men passed.

Eastward frowned.

"You mean their suits?" he asked, opening the door.

"That too," smiled Jinnah.

Fogduckers had a dark, musty interior. It was one of those drinking establishments where the *eau de beer* and a wide variety of essence of tobacco had co-mingled and produced a fragrant blue-grey paste a half-inch thick on the ceiling. Faded and torn posters of motorcycles with half-naked women draped over them adorned those portions of the wall not dedicated to displaying either Harley parts or animal skulls. It was the skulls that prompted Jinnah to pause briefly in the doorway.

"Those are *animal* skulls, are they not?" he whispered to Eastward.

"Humans are animals too."

Jinnah walked toward the bar, a sturdy-looking edifice gaily decorated with the carvings of various patrons' initials and not a few death-heads. The rows of bottles stood, as usual, on shelves in front of a vast mirror. But the owners had thought it best to add a bullet-proof glass case and irons bars to cut down on wear and tear.

To Jinnah's left was the main room, divided in two by a line of pool tables. On one side of this divide, beefy men with long hair leathers wore red bandanas. On the other, the patrons had a similar dress sense, but sported blue head coverings. They were the sort of happy, cheerful customers with nicknames like "Snake" and "Ace." Some fortunate tattoo artist was obviously doing a booming business.

Thirty pairs of eyes swivelled in Jinnah's direction. Jinnah in turn glanced over at Eastward, anxious to see his reaction. He knew the photographer would expect to see rough, unshaven faces and large, hulking bodies. But it was obvious from the look on Eastward's face that he hadn't expected to find that every biker in the bar was, like Jinnah, of South-Asian origin. *Maybe now he knows what I mean by "dress code."* The reporter grinned inwardly. The thought that Eastward might be uncomfortable as the only white face in a sea of brown frowns cheered him immensely.

The collective eyes of the patrons followed them as they made their way to the bar. The bartender, Jinnah knew, was the gatekeeper. He might be a font of information, even introduce them to the people Jinnah needed to talk to. Or he might just throw them out without further ado. He bellied up to the bar, Eastward alongside him.

"Excuse me, my friend," Jinnah said to a back. "I was wondering if you could help us —"

The back turned around. The front was a large, muscular man wearing a black leather vest and Harley-Davidson T-shirt. The face attached to the front was white. Jinnah was so surprised he stopped mid-sentence.

"Whaddaya want?" demanded the bartender.

The voice that issued from the man seemed to come straight from his bowels and was just as garbled: low and menacing. What Jinnah wanted was to turn and run while Eastward held the pursuing hordes back, but he had come here for a story, damn it, and he was going to get one.

"My name is Hakeem Jinnah, and this —"

"Don't give a rat's ass what yer name is," said the bartender. "Whaddaya want ta drink?"

"Drink?" said Jinnah, startled.

"Yeah, drink," said the bartender. "In my bar, you drink or I toss yer sorry ass out."

There was an agonizing pause while Jinnah's Ismaili brain tried to process this information. Eastward leaned over and whispered in his ear.

"Order a beer or something, for God's sake," he hissed.

Jinnah turned to his colleague and pronounced, rather too loudly, that he could not.

"I'm a Muslim, for God's sake," he added.

The bartender glared at Jinnah.

"Don't care if ya can drink it or not," he rumbled from the depths of his intestinal tract. "But ya gotta buy one to sit down! Raj or Kingfisher?"

This was too much information for Jinnah.

"Beg pardon?" he asked.

The bartender gritted his teeth. He pointed to the pool tables.

"See those tables? That's the 'Green Line.' Guys on the left are the Young Lions. They drink Raj. Other side's the Phoenix Club. They drink Kingfisher. Now what'll it be?"

"You got Molson Canadian?" asked Eastward.

The bartender grunted and turned to Jinnah.

"And you?" he asked menacingly.

Jinnah briefly considered arguing that he just wanted to talk to someone about Moe Grewal and Mal Singh — a move that probably would have proven fatal. Fortunately, he was rescued by a knight in shining black leather.

"He can buy me a beer," said a leather-clad man sliding onto the barstool next to Jinnah.

The bartender's lips curled into a look of distaste

as he grabbed three Rajs from the cooler and opened them with what Jinnah thought was undue violence.

"I'll need a receipt," Jinnah called to the bartender as he moved down the bar.

Eastward gave him a nudge in the ribs for that. Jinnah didn't have time to reprove him. He had to deal with this doubtful saviour beside him. The man was pleasant-looking enough: a young Indo-Canadian with a broad, handsome face, wearing a red bandana and dressed rather too neatly for a real biker. Or so Jinnah thought.

"My name's Billy," said the man.

"Hakeem Jinnah. This is Clint Eastward, my —"

"Colleague," Eastward cut in before Jinnah could say the dirty word, "photographer."

"I know who you are," said Billy, indicating Jinnah. "Heard your name. Read your stuff too."

"Really?" asked Jinnah, slightly flattered.

"Yeah. It's bullshit," said Billy casually, finishing his beer in one long pull.

Jinnah felt his heart racing. Damn! I knew I should have taken a phenobarbital before coming in here.

"What exactly is the bullshit you're referring to?"

"The bullshit about Moe Grewal and Mal Singh being involved in drugs, rip-offs ... that bullshit," said Billy, making a good start on Jinnah's beer.

"Mal Singh was a member of the notorious Phoenix Gang," said Jinnah. "He had a rap sheet a mile long. So did Moe Grewal of the Young Lions gang."

Billy took down another third of his beer and belched delicately.

"It's the Young Lions Indo-Canadian Motorcycle Club. And what you have just repeated is police bullshit."

"According to whom?"

"Me," Billy said, smiling. "I'm the president."

Eastward calmly sipped his beer as Billy chugged Jinnah's Kingfisher. The biker's 'tude was working: it was evident the reporter was having the piss scared out of him. Billy turned sideways to face Jinnah full-on.

"Stories like yours *hurt* the club," he said seriously. "They *hurt* the families in the club, and they *hurt* our individual business pursuits. Get my drift?"

Jinnah did. He had talked to enough of these hoodlums to know the code. Billy had used the word "hurt" three times. That was a three-alarm blaze. Cursing his lack of foresight in regards to sedatives, he stalled furiously for time, looking for either a way into the interview or a back exit to the bar. Neither were immediately presenting themselves.

"I can understand your point of view, my friend," he said as smoothly as his gelatinous bowels would allow. "That is why I am here — for your point of view."

"Sure." Billy laughed. "My point of view. You'll print that without a lot of police bullshit folded around it?"

It was at this point Jinnah happened to look down and notice Billy's belt buckle: identical to the one found in the pizza oven. The image of the lion restored his courage — or perhaps, more accurately, tipped the balance away from his congenital cowardice in favour of his inherent instincts. He knew in an instant the buckle was the way out of his present discomfort and into the interview he needed. It could also be the equivalent of telling Billy what size of sleeping bag he took and what brand of cement he preferred. But he took in a breath and dove into the deep end of the rhetorical pool.

"Nice buckle, Billy," he said, choking back the bile rising in his throat. "What can you tell me about Commonwealth Pizza?"

Billy, who had been smiling a ferocious smile, looked blank for the first time.

"What are you talking about?" he asked, eyes narrowing.

Ah! Out of his comfort zone at last! Jinnah had finally regained the conversational initiative and decided to hit hard — metaphorically speaking.

"A body was found in a pizza oven there tonight. Topped with a Lions belt buckle. I wondered if it might belong to Moe Grewal."

Billy's face hardened. His jaw was a rigid line and his nostrils flared. All in all, a pretty good imitation of a bull, Jinnah thought. The professional in him rejoiced at the reaction. The congenital coward wondered what form his goring would take. This unworthy thought vanished when Billy stood up, turned around, and shouted across the bar in a voice that cut through the tinny music like a scimitar.

"Hey, Mindy!"

The conversation in the bar died instantly. In a corner, a very large, very ugly biker in a blue bandana raised his head.

"What?" he asked coldly.

"Got a question for you!"

The very large biker stood up. Jinnah would have followed suit, but he discovered his knees had turned to jelly. Eastward had finished his beer and was now clutching the empty by the neck like a cudgel. Just in case.

"Listen, Billy," whispered Jinnah. "Don't you think —"

"Know who that is?" snapped Billy.

Jinnah shook his head.

"That's Parminder Singh, head of the Phoenix gang."

"You mean *club*, surely," said Jinnah quickly.

Parminder Singh slowly walked toward them. Eastward edged closer to Jinnah and gauged the distance to the door.

"Look, we don't want to cause any trouble," said Jinnah. "I mean, if we're creating all this tension —"

"Don't flatter yourself, buddy," said Billy.

Mindy Singh stood nose-to-nose with Billy. The two men glared at each other, breathing beer and cigarettes into their opponents' face.

"What do you want, Pretty Little Billy?" asked Mindy.

"My reporter friend here wants to know if you toasted Moe Grewal in a pizza oven."

"Don't bother on my account —" Jinnah protested.

"What if I did?"

Billy's frame stiffened. Jinnah's bowels nearly loosened.

"If you did, you die," Billy said.

Despite being nearly catatonic with fear, Jinnah felt moved to prevent bloodshed — especially as it was likely some of his own blood would be part of the mix.

"I think there has been some mistake —" Jinnah began.

Mindy looked down on him in a manner that would have done Whiteman proud.

"You said it, pal."

Mindy took a step back and a switchblade appeared magically in his hand. He flipped it open and began to trim his fingernails with an exaggerated insouciance. Nobody moved, not even Jinnah's bowels, which were by now paralyzed along with the rest of his nervous system.

"One, I haven't seen Moe for two weeks," said Mindy, not looking up from his delicate task. "Two, if I did off him, would I put him in a fuckin' pizza oven where every dipshit in the universe could find him? Three, why don't you tell your reporter friend what happened to Mal Singh while we're talkin' missing persons?"

The part of Jinnah's brain not completely focused on whether or not he would not only *make* the front page of tomorrow's paper but *be* the front page of tomorrow's *Tribune* pried itself away from his reptilian complex and sat bolt upright. Oh-ho ... maybe this *is* a two-for-one deal....

"Mal was your little rat," spat Billy.

"Moe was playin' the same game," said Mindy with a dangerous calm.

Jinnah had by now nearly forgotten his life was in danger. In this context, there could be only one meaning for the term "rat."

"You're saying that Grewal and Singh were police informants?" he asked.

Billy turned toward Jinnah, face livid.

"You print that and you're —"

"He's what?" cut in Mindy. "Haven't you got enough blood on your hands, pretty little Billy?"

There was a pause customarily referred to as the calm before all hell breaks loose. The bartender used it to pick up the telephone and speed-dial 911. Eastward used it to step back and grab Hakeem by the arm. Jinnah's reptilian complex used it to remind him why it had remained unchanged for millions of years — if it ain't broke, don't fix it. So he was prepared for flight when, in the next instant, Billy (who had also miraculously sprouted a switchblade) sprang at Mindy and the bar erupted into a melee of shouting, brawling, knife-wielding gang members. Jinnah and Eastward were a full fifty feet from the door.

"Come on, Hakeem."

Eastward jerked Jinnah to his feet and dragged the reporter through the bar toward the front exit. They had to duck and weave past several snarling combatants and, at one point, a beefy hand reached out and grabbed Jinnah by the collar. He yelped as Eastward calmly took the legs out from under the assailant by hurling a chair at his lower limbs. The biker lost his grip as he went down and the reporter and photographer scuttled through the doors, racing toward their car and safety. The cool night air slapped Jinnah in the face as they ran up the street. He turned to see if they were being pursued, but all the action was still inside the doors of Fogduckers.

"Shit!" spat Eastward as they reached the car.

"What's wrong?" gasped Jinnah, breathless.

What was wrong became instantly apparent when Jinnah stopped looking at the passenger door and shifted his gaze downward. The car was on blocks and all four tires were missing. Jinnah almost fainted. He was revived by a fresh dose of adrenaline when the bar doors burst open and several bikers spilled out, clutching at each other, throwing punches and grabbing hair. Eastward was already on his cellphone, calling for help, when the wail of a police siren split the night. Jinnah turned to see the approach of flashing red and blue lights. *Name of God, not the police too!* Eastward had also spotted them. His cellphone slowly dropped to his side.

"How you gonna explain this one to the cops?" he asked in a low voice.

Jinnah didn't fancy trying to persuade the police he hadn't really provoked a gang fight in a biker bar. Running was out of the question. But then, what the hell were he and Eastward doing there in the first place? Two cops were scrambling out of the car. Jinnah recognized one of them as Bains. The other was a white guy he'd seen before. Lyall, was it? An inspiration hit Jinnah. He clicked on his microcassette and started taking verbal notes. Loudly.

"Police arriving at biker bar brawl at nineteen-hundred hours," he said above the din. "Three cars responding in record time —"

Eastward looked at Jinnah as if he was mad for a moment, then caught on. He ripped a camera from his case and started clicking away. For all intents and purposes, they looked like any pair of journalists covering a bar fight. Bains slowed just enough to call to Jinnah before entering the melee.

"Hey, Jinnah. How'd you get here so fast?"

Jinnah forced himself to look nonchalant.

"We're improving our response time," he said with a smile.

Bains and Lyall began dealing with the combatants outside as other police cars roared up and more officers arrived on the scene. After a few minutes, Jinnah dropped the charade and motioned to Eastward that it was safe to leave. It was imperative they exit the scene before the police noticed the state of their vehicle and started asking awkward questions about arrival times. They hustled south toward Georgia Street where they could hail a cab.

"How am I going to explain my car to Lumsden?" wailed Eastward.

"You think you got problems," said Jinnah. "How am I going to explain an expense claim for three beers without a receipt?"

In the end, Frosty only had to put off the news desk for about fifteen minutes past the city desk deadline to move copy off the floor. Jinnah helped by dictating his new top of the story to her as she hammered it directly onto the front page layout.

"Alleged police informant Mal Singh is missing," Jinnah read his near-illegible scrawl off his notepad.

"His fellow accused 'rat,' Moe Grewal, may have been lured to his death at Commonwealth Pizza ... by unknown assailants. Period, new paragraph. A well-dressed Indo-Canadian man has been seen lurking near the establishment by witnesses. Period. Thirty."

Frosty, chewing on a licorice stick, typed almost as fast as Jinnah dictated. The words flew from her fingertips and onto the screen. The headline about the Middle East had vanished and been replaced by "Pizza Oven Corpse Enflames Biker Brawl: A *Tribune* Exclusive." Frosty finished and ran a quick spell-check. Jinnah anxiously looked from her inscrutable face to the screen.

"A perfect fit," he observed.

Nicole Frost had earned her nickname honestly. She was fifteen minutes late getting the line story off the floor, the news editor had been screaming at her all night, and now, in the face of delaying the entire paper irreparably, she paused, staring at the screen while Jinnah fidgeted in his chair.

"Unnamed sources. Speculative. Not a lot backed up. And overwritten," she said dryly. "Hardly Webster Award–winning stuff."

Jinnah snorted dismissively and waited for Frosty to pronounce final judgment.

"Sure you didn't Rambo this sucker just to rub Caitlin's surgically trimmed little nose in it?" she asked.

They shared a wicked laugh as Frosty hit the "send" key. It had been a helluva day, but Jinnah had ended it on top of the world. He might live to be the Kenyan King of Burgers yet.

Chapter Two

Jinnah awoke with Manjit nuzzling at his ear. Music floated from the clock radio into the room like a warm balm. He kept his eyes shut and basked in the moment. He felt good. He had scooped the front page despite Whiteman and Caitlin Bishop, and with (for a change) the full blessings of the Vancouver Police. In a couple of days, he would be boarding a flight to Kenya and laying the groundwork for a whole new life that didn't involve charred remains in pizza ovens (he made a mental note to not include pizzas on the Burger Place chain's menu). Unless, of course, he succumbed to a reaction to that damned hepatitis B vaccination, which had hurt like hell. No, life was pretty damned good at the moment. He had no idea it was the beginning of one of the longest days of his life. Things started to go wrong almost from the second his eyelids fluttered open to see Manjit's face smiling down at him.

"Hakeem, you promised to help me with my problem this morning."

Jinnah groaned. He'd been too tired last night to deal with Manjit's latest issue. For a change, it hadn't been about Saleem. It was something about a mysterious malady afflicting several patients at the community health clinic where she worked as a volunteer translator. Jinnah's brain was still a bit foggy. *To hell with the public health system*, he thought, and instead of answering with mere words, gathered his wife in for a kiss. After a moment, Manjit broke it off.

"Jinnah! I have to find out what's making everyone sick," she said, pulling away.

Jinnah pinned her down on the bed and hoisted himself over top of her.

"No fair!" cried Manjit. "You're supposed to be giving me a lesson in sleuthing!"

Jinnah kissed his way up one brown, smooth leg.

"I am. From the *Kama Sleuthra*," he murmured. "No charge."

"Jinnah —"

"Don't worry, I'm all in favour of probing this mystery deeper...."

He kissed Manjit again. Things were just starting to get interesting when the music on the radio was replaced by the news. A voice in Jinnah's head told him to ignore the newsreader and turn the bloody radio off, but since his story was right off the top of the package, it was already too late.

"... a published report linking the body found in the pizza oven last night was dismissed as 'wildly speculative' this morning by the Vancouver Police," the newsreader said in erudite CBC tones. "In a statement, Sergeant Craig Graham —"

"Sonofabitch!"

Jinnah was disengaged and out of bed in a flash. As he grabbed for his clothes Manjit, who was used to being usurped in her matrimonial bed by the likes of the disembodied newsreader, clicked the radio off and sighed. She pulled on her robe. There was no time to shower first — she knew how fast the inveterately lazy Hakeem could move when motivated.

Moments later, Manjit made one more attempt to talk to Jinnah in the kitchen as he gulped down his coffee and struggled to tuck his shirt into his pants. She met with limited success.

"Hakeem, please, about this outbreak —"

"Wildly speculative!" Jinnah howled for the fifth time.

That bastard Graham! Craig had stabbed him in the back and the shiv between his shoulders felt distinctly Bishop-like. The double-crosser! He would get even before the day was over....

"Sonofabitch! Sorry, darling?"

Jinnah's subconscious had finally got his attention. Manjit had been speaking to him for several minutes, taking his grunts and suppressed oaths for attention. Name of God, after all these years, didn't she know better?

"This outbreak," Manjit persisted.

"Probably just the flu," said Jinnah absently, finishing his coffee.

"That doesn't explain the rash," Manjit protested. "Everyone had flu-like symptoms *and* this awful red rash."

Jinnah looked at his wife as if she'd just been conjured up by a djin. He'd been so preoccupied by his own thoughts of getting even with Graham that he hadn't even been listening. He put his hands on her shoulders softly.

"Manjit, a good detective looks for the connecting threads. What do all the patients have in common, hmm? Besides their symptoms, I mean. Okay? Call me at work if you find anything."

It wasn't much, but it was a start. Manjit smiled tolerantly as Jinnah pulled on his jacket.

"Go easy on Graham," she said.

She's been reading my thoughts all along! Jinnah popped two pieces of nicotine gum in his mouth and scowled.

"He's gone too far this time," Jinnah growled. "Sergeant Craig Graham is about to undergo trial by Jinnah!"

Graham had already undergone trial by fire that morning. The chief arsonist wasn't his boss, however, but Superintendent Frank Capulet of the RCMP was. Capulet had thrown the door to Graham's office open without knocking and thrown a copy of the *Tribune* on Craig's desk by way of saying hello.

"What the hell sorta crap is this!" he bawled at Graham as if he was some rookie constable.

But Graham was no rookie and he didn't work for Capulet. He glanced coolly down at the headline: "Pizza Oven Corpse Enflames Biker Brawl." Then he looked up at Capulet, who had once been in good shape and was now, frankly, a little past it.

"Good morning, sir," said Graham. "What can I do for you?"

"Explain this, for a start."

Capulet threw a black-and-white photograph down on Graham's desk. Graham instantly recognized it as an RCMP surveillance photo. It showed Jinnah and Eastward in front of Fogduckers, passing the two men who had left just before they entered. Graham's indignation at being screamed at vanished as he picked up the eight-by-ten.

"You got Fogduckers under surveillance?" he asked, voice neutral.

"Yeah, I do. And now I got six months of a drug investigation hanging by a thread thanks to this reporter pal of yours."

Graham had known Jinnah had blundered onto something totally unrelated to the body found in the oven the second he'd seen the *Trib*'s front page. But his conscience was clear: he'd never asked Jinnah to go to Fogduckers.

"What exactly is the problem, Superintendent?" Graham asked in a far more helpful tone.

Capulet rested both hands on Graham's desk and leaned into the Sergeant's face.

"The problem is your buddy has named Moe Grewal and Mal Singh as police informants, that's what. If he was wrong about that, would I have a problem?"

Graham's stomach went acidic in an instant.

"And what were they helping you with, sir?"

"None of your goddamn business. The real question is who helped Jinnah get this particular bit of information into print?"

"I didn't tell Jinnah about Singh and Grewal because I didn't know they were your guys. He must have got it from the bikers."

Capulet tapped the newspaper significantly.

"I know who his unnamed police source is. I am reliably informed that you even let him into the crime scene."

Graham was on his feet now. Capulet wasn't the only one who had turf to protect.

"Hey! I've made more collars with Jinnah's help than with your gang of cowboys!" he shouted.

Capulet straightened up. He assumed the voice of the senior law enforcement agency dictating to the local gendarmerie.

"Unless you want me to raise this with your superior officer, I suggest you find a way to control Mr. Jinnah."

Graham smiled for the first time that morning.

"Control Jinnah? What do you suggest?"

Capulet made a suggestion. Several, in fact. Issuing a statement to the press calling Jinnah's story "wildly speculative" was step one. And by the time Jinnah charged into the police station looking for him, Graham was already closeted with another journalist, busily spinning the police line as part of step two. Jinnah sat fuming outside Graham's door, unaware of what step three was. After a half an hour had elapsed, the door finally opened and Jinnah leapt to his feet — only to see Caitlin Bishop being escorted out of the office by Graham.

"Thanks for the chat, Craig." Her perfectly capped teeth smiled at him. "Later."

Jinnah was practically nose-to-nose with Caitlin. He was so startled that he didn't see Graham slip around behind him and beckon to two uniformed cops hanging around the duty desk. His entire event horizon was filled by Caitlin's polished white teeth.

"Nice scoop, Jinnah." Caitlin smirked.

"What garbage is he feeding you?" asked Jinnah, voice shaking.

"Just the facts. Remember facts?"

Normally, Jinnah would have dismissed this as professional trash talk: envy and venom spewing from a TV reporter — a mere meat puppet, for God's sake — who had been beaten. But Caitlin was no ordinary meat puppet. She was what passed for a protégé. Something in Jinnah's large and complex psychological makeup called pride was pricked to the quick.

"I remember teaching you ethics!" he roared. "Justice. Upholding the law —"

Jinnah's polemic on the majesty of the law was interrupted by the arrival of three policemen. Graham stood in front of him. Behind and on either side of Jinnah were Bains and Lyall.

"Hakeem Jinnah?" said Graham in a manner that suggested he'd never laid eyes on his reporter friend before. "You're under arrest."

Jinnah froze. Arrest? What the hell for? Then the memory of the brawl at Fogduckers came flooding back. So did his habitual hypochondria.

"You can't arrest me!" Jinnah cried. "I have Asian Chicken Flu. Highly contagious." Jinnah coughed a few times, unconvincingly.

"I'll take my chances," said Graham as Bains slapped the cuffs on him.

"What the hell are you arresting me for?" Jinnah demanded.

"Assault, inciting a riot, and obstructing a police investigation. How's that for a start? Take him down," he ordered Bains.

And as Caitlin Bishop and Craig Graham watched, Jinnah was led away to a holding cell. After he disappeared (coughing and whooping vaguely like a chicken), Graham turned to Caitlin.

"Like we agreed. All this is off the record. Right?"

Caitlin Bishop nodded.

"Right."

As holding cells went, it wasn't bad. At least Jinnah didn't have to share it with anyone else, which had been his prime fear. That and his urgent need to use the toilet. But his bladder would have had to burst before he used the stainless steel fixture in the corner of the cell in plain view of the guard. So he sat on the cell bunk, chewing his Nicorette furiously, waiting. It only took Graham fifteen minutes to show up.

He was carrying a plain brown envelope and a file folder. Jinnah hoped it wasn't the start of his criminal record.

"So," said Graham, "when I said go into the community, I didn't mean scope out its biker bars."

Jinnah looked up sharply. Rule One of interrogation: never admit to anything.

"What makes you think I was in Fogduckers?" he asked.

Graham slid the RCMP surveillance photo from out of the envelope and held it under Jinnah's nose. Rule Two of interrogation: rail against the injustice of it all.

"Since when did Canada become a police state? Is Big Brother watching my every bowel movement?" he cried.

Graham's cheeks coloured.

"You don't get it, do you?" he said, voice tight as he fought a flash of anger. "They want me to issue the equivalent of a police *fatwa* against you. Cut you off from every cop in the city."

"What the hell for?" demanded Jinnah.

"You trod on some Mountie toes down at Fogduckers."

This was bad. It explained a lot, however: the mock arrest, the holding cell, Graham's somewhat conflicted fury. Which brought Jinnah to Rule Three of interrogation: when faced with an ugly truth, blame someone else. After all, a reporter was only as good as his sources, and his source had been Graham.

"You yourself said you couldn't rule out the biker connection," he said, a shade defiantly.

"I never said Moe was an informant. I never mentioned Mal Singh."

This was not going at all well. Time to play the freedom of the press card.

"Since when is it a crime to print the truth?" he asked indignantly.

Graham exploded.

"When the truth could get someone killed, Hakeem!"

The fierce shout so close to his ear sent a bolt of pain through Jinnah's head. He felt ill. He *was* having a reaction to that damned hep-B vaccination. He tried to think. He felt it wise not to reply directly to this last point. Graham was right. If the Mounties were this pissed off, then he must have blundered into an undercover operation that involved more than a few bags of BC Bud passing hands in the washrooms of Fogduckers. He adopted a contrite tone.

"Okay, so let's drop the offending line of inquiry. If the man in the oven wasn't an extra large biker with anchovies, who was he, hmm?"

Apparently Jinnah had finally played the right card, for Graham calmed down — almost. At least, he appeared to be breathing normally. He sat next to Hakeem on the bunk and opened the file folder, his manner much more businesslike.

"That's for you to find out. Here."

Graham held up another photograph. Jinnah squinted in the dim light. He saw two Indo-Canadian males. One was sixtyish, distinguished, smiling. The other was a younger man, very handsome. Father and son. Standing in front of a pair of dark wooden doors that looked familiar.

"Kabir Shah," said Graham. "Owner of Commonwealth Pizza. Missing. And his son, Armaan. Also missing."

Jinnah took the photo and studied the two men. From their body language, he could see the picture was posed, not spontaneous. Armaan's smile was somewhat forced-looking. Tension between father and son? He looked over at Graham.

"Victims? Or suspects, hmm?"

"Could be either," admitted Graham. "What do you think?"

"I thought my name was Salman Rushdie around here."

Graham cracked a grin for the first time since entering the cell.

"More like Rupert Murdoch, actually."

"Easy!"

"I need you to find out where the Shahs are."

Jinnah's embryonic sense of bonhomie evaporated. He did a swift mental calculation of the legwork involved. He also forgot entirely that he was, technically, in police custody.

"Craig. Kenya. Two days. Burgers," he reminded the sergeant.

Graham looked at Jinnah and closed the file folder. His smile widened as he stood and walked slowly toward the door.

"Your choice," he sighed.

Jinnah leapt off the bunk and stood in the middle of the cell.

"You're not going to keep me in here! You have no basis for these so-called charges. I'll be out in hours. Won't I?" he added.

The guard unlocked the cell door. It swung wearily open, framing Graham in a heavy, metal rectangle. Which struck Jinnah as ironic.

"The wheels of justice spin slowly sometimes, Hakeem."

Graham held the door open with one hand and the file folder like a sort of hall pass in the other.

"Coming?" he asked.

Jinnah considered the chances of Whiteman posting his bail even in the best circumstances.

"Sonofabitch," he muttered as he grabbed the file folder from Graham's hand.

The Shah residence in South Vancouver was elegant. As Jinnah walked down a seemingly endless driveway, he marvelled at the well-kept grounds and gardens. They spoke of wealth and taste.

"I should get into the pizza business," he muttered, wondering if he'd be able to afford a modest mansion like this if Burger Palace was a success.

Jinnah noted no cars in the semicircular driveway. He rang the doorbell. No answer. He listened carefully. Faintly, he heard the muffled whine of a lawnmower.

Judging it to be coming from the side of the house near the back, he walked around to the left. Down a side yard that was as wide as a tennis court and looked about as long as a football field, Jinnah saw a young woman of about fourteen years old mowing the back forty. She was Indo-Canadian. He walked on the carpet-like grass and shouted above the mower's noise as he drew near.

"Hey! Are you by chance Ms. Shah?"

The young woman looked at Jinnah and switched off the mower. In the stillness of the morning, birds could be heard chirping in the fruit trees in the vast expanse of the backyard.

"No," she said sulkily.

Ah, hired help! Usually a font of information, especially if they weren't overly fond of their employers. Jinnah gave her his most winning smile.

"My name's Hakeem. What's yours?"

The young woman eyed Jinnah critically. *She's wondering what my business is and whether I am to be trusted*, he thought.

"Jasjeet," she finally said. "I cut the Shahs' grass."

Without thinking, Jinnah offered Jasjeet some gum.

"Seen either one of them lately?" he asked, holding out the package.

Jasjeet hesitated momentarily, then took a piece.

"The old guy's always away. Armaan's surgically attached to his girlfriend."

Jasjeet's tone was derisive — jealous, even. Jinnah smiled.

"Do you know this girlfriend's name?"

"Shauna. A real estate agent. Wears her blazer to the house. No class."

Jealous. Fancies the son, likely. Jasjeet popped the gum into her mouth. Jinnah was about to ask a follow-up when she gagged violently and spat the wad out.

"What the hell kinda gum is that?" she choked out.

Name of God! Jinnah had forgotten. The only gum he carried these days was Nicorette. It took several minutes of profuse apologies and coaching to placate Jasjeet and get the name of the real estate firm Shauna worked for out of her. Jinnah took his leave hastily and set out for West End Properties at once.

Perhaps it will stop her from taking up smoking, he thought, trying to put a positive spin on the incident. *At least it will teach her never to accept candy from strange men.*

West End Properties was in Vancouver's densely populated western peninsula, an upscale office just off the main drag of Denman Street and only a few blocks from where Jonathan Blocks, the Towel-Toting Bank Bandit, had "blown his cover." When he saw Shauna standing in front of a listings board, Jinnah understood why Jasjeet had been jealous. A tall redhead in her early twenties, Shauna was gorgeous. And her jacket, he noted, was immaculate: she did look classy. It was all Jinnah could do to stop himself from kissing his way up her arm when she shook his hand by way of introduction. Maintaining control of himself, he decided to skip preliminaries and go straight to the heart of the matter.

"So, Shauna, have you seen Armaan lately?" he asked.

"He was with me last night. All night," said Shauna firmly.

Jinnah could tell Shauna was rehearsing a line. She and Armaan had obviously talked. Presumably Armaan knew by now there was a body in his pizza parlour's oven. So Shauna was to be his alibi, eh? Jinnah knew better than to try to bully or browbeat such a woman. He turned his charm up to maximum and oozed sincerity.

"You know, I am deeply, deeply concerned for him." Jinnah gave Shauna his best "Tiger Growl" voice. "He has told you, of course, about the body in the oven?"

Shauna's fawn-like eyes grew wide. She nodded. Jinnah pressed on.

"Why didn't he call the police?"

"He thought the cops would blame him," said Shauna. "But I said, 'You're innocent, get a lawyer.' Y'know?"

Either Shauna was telling the truth or she was a better actor than Meryl Streep. Jinnah continued with his sympathetic line.

"Does he have any idea who did this?"

Shauna's creamy, oval face looked pinched with worry. She lowered her voice.

"He said no. But he seemed really scared —"

"Is there a problem, Shauna?" an unfamiliar voice asked.

Jinnah turned around and saw trouble approaching

in the form of a man in his mid-thirties: tall, barrel-chested, and going prematurely bald. Oh-oh — the boss....

"It's okay, Mr. Miller," said Shauna.

Miller gave Jinnah the once-over. He didn't bother introducing himself. He put a hand on Shauna's arm, filling Jinnah with a jealousy of his own.

"You're not doing your boyfriend any favours here. I don't think you should be talking to the press," Miller said. *Damn, recognized. Still, it proves he reads my stuff....*

"Aren't you with the police?"

Shauna's tone was mingled with a touch of anger (which made her all the more attractive) and just a hint of scorn (which stung Jinnah's inflated ego to the quick).

Busted. He smiled lamely.

"They, ah, asked me to make a few inquiries. Did I not mention I was a reporter?"

"The police asked you that, eh?" said Shauna, now downright suspicious. "Armaan and his lawyer are meeting with the police right now."

Miller raised his eyebrows as if to say "I told you so." Jinnah muttered a few apologies and fled the office. *Sonofabitch!* While he'd been out beating the bushes looking for the Shahs, at least one of them had flown right into Graham's office. He walked quickly to the alley where he'd parked the Satellite-Guided Love Machine. Now he had to hurry over to the police station — right back where he had started. He could only hope no one else had tracked Armaan Shah down first.

* * *

Jinnah's worst fears were confirmed when he came around the corner to the front of the station to find a small scrum of reporters waiting outside. Parked right on the curb was a satellite news truck and pacing in front of it, cellphone glued to her ear, was Caitlin Bishop, an unlit cigarette in her mouth.

"No, he's in there with his lawyer," she was saying. "We're gonna goon him on his way out."

As Jinnah approached her, Caitlin said a quick "g'bye" and shut her phone off. The full megawatt of her carefully constructed smile beamed at Jinnah.

"Hey," she said.

"*Salaam alaikoom*," Jinnah replied.

They stood at the foot of the station steps. They both knew why they were there, but etiquette dictated they feign ignorance. Caitlin lit her cigarette. She took out a pack and offered one to Jinnah. Tempted as he was, Jinnah shook his head.

"No thanks. I don't smoke."

Caitlin's plucked eyebrows arched upwards.

"Since when?" she asked doubtfully.

"Frosty and I have a bet going."

The mention of her former *Tribune* tormentor temporarily chilled Caitlin's warmth.

"Oh, Frosty. Still alive, is she? Give her my love."

This put their conversation in the deep freeze. Jinnah shifted uncomfortably, trying not to breathe in Caitlin's second-hand smoke. He could see she was itching to bring up the events of earlier this morning outside Graham's office. He was wondering why she hadn't gooned him, let alone Armaan Shah. Perhaps a pre-emptive strike was in order....

"Ah, Caitlin, about this morning —"

Caitlin waved her cigarette at Jinnah.

"Forget it. Craig swore me to secrecy."

Jinnah let out a gust of breath. That was a relief. Although Caitlin was getting rather cosy with *Craig* Graham awfully quickly. And she was in a playful mood with Jinnah himself.

"So, who posted your bail?" she asked, eyes gleaming with amusement.

"It was all an unfortunate misunderstanding. They mistook me for a TV reporter."

They laughed. Jinnah remembered the days when he and Caitlin had shared many laughs in the *Trib* newsroom. They'd had many serious debates as well. His mood swung abruptly toward the serious. Their relationship had changed profoundly. He was no longer the Great Jinnah-ji, mentor supreme. Caitlin was a pro in her own right now — no longer a neophyte.

"You know, Caitlin," he said, trying not to sound like a father figure and failing miserably. "If you'd stayed with the paper, you'd be a senior reporter by now. Doing meaningful stuff."

There was the briefest flicker in the blue eyes. Regret? Resentment?

"Not everyone shares your idea of what's meaningful," she said.

"You used to. Didn't you?"

"Of course. Only now I share them with two million people a night."

Caitlin seemed almost apologetic. But not quite enough for Jinnah's taste.

"But you only get sixty seconds. What can you do with that, hmm? Except confirm opinions they already have. I sometimes get sixty inches. A documentary a day. I can change their minds. Which would you rather have: sixty seconds or sixty inches?"

Caitlin took a very deep drag on her cigarette and looked at Jinnah sideways.

"Are you sure you want me to answer that?" she asked dryly.

Whoa! The old Caitlin would never have said that! Time to change the drift of this conversation.

"So," said Jinnah, voice squeaking only slightly as he made a 180-degree conversational turn. "First CBC. Now CXBC. What's next?"

"I don't know. CNN, maybe, or FOX. You want to help me plan my life? Have a drink with me. The Off the Record Club. Say five, five-thirty?"

It was quite an invitation. Before Jinnah's moral barometer could be pressurized any further, two figures emerged from the police station escorted by Bains. One was a white man in his late thirties. The other Jinnah recognized instantly as Armaan Shah. The subject of drinks evaporated as Caitlin scrambled to get to the front of the scrum, which had already formed around the two men descending the steps. Armaan Shah was letting the white guy, his lawyer, do the talking.

"Mr. Shah, who was inside the oven?" barked Caitlin.

Armaan looked at Caitlin with big, soft, dark eyes: rather like a puppy. His lawyer put one hand on Armaan's arm and the other in the small of his back as he propelled his client through the media gauntlet.

"Where have you been hiding?" Caitlin persevered.

"He was at his girlfriend's," said the lawyer in a high, nasal tenor. "He knows nothing about this. He's very upset."

Jinnah was already familiar with this undercover story and ignored it. From his vantage point four steps above the milling throng, he focused on Armaan. He looked genuinely scared, but of what? The consequences of his actions? The media? Something Graham had said to him? Armaan and his lawyer had reached the sidewalk and were pushing the scrum ahead of them toward a waiting car. Caitlin made one last attempt to get a sound bite from Armaan.

"Mr. Shah, don't you want to tell your side of the story?" she cried above the general baying of the pack.

At that moment, Bains stepped in front of Caitlin and her cameraman. The lawyer had Armaan halfway into the car before Jinnah, choosing his moment perfectly, shouted out above the scrum from his perch on the steps.

"Armaan! *Aap ke pitta kaha hai?*"

Startled by Jinnah's words, Armaan froze.

"*Oh abhi tak ma hai*," he said quickly, eyes darting up to Jinnah's for just a second.

The lawyer shoved Armaan into the car and climbed in after him. They roared off, cameras recording their departure. The scrum broke up in the usual order: radio reporters desperate to beat each other to air by five seconds first. TV people second. The print guys, as usual, hung around. But Caitlin Bishop still had the heart of a newspaper reporter. She looked at Jinnah with a mixture of awe and suspicion.

"What the hell was that?" she demanded.

Jinnah smiled.

"That? That was Hindi, my friend," he replied with a grin.

Jinnah walked away, humming happily and absolutely certain he was, yet again, miles ahead of Caitlin Bishop. Caitlin stared after him for a moment, then spied Bains behind her. She whirled on him.

"So what did he say? Jinnah, I mean?"

Bains shrugged.

"Ask my grandmother. I only speak English."

Which was a lie, of course, but as much as Bains disliked Jinnah, he had even less time for TV reporters — especially pushy, presumptuous blondes.

It was nearly noon when Jinnah arrived at the newsroom. Replaying the exchange with Armaan over and over in his head. And chuckling every time he thought about the look on Caitlin's face.

"Armaan! Where's your father?" Jinnah had asked in Hindi.

And, startled perhaps by hearing a tongue from the Mother Country, one he'd been raised with, Armaan had automatically replied, "He's in his home country."

The home country in this case was Tanzania, Jinnah knew. So both Shahs were accounted for. Armaan had probably told Graham the same thing. And that meant Jinnah was off the hook. All he had to do now was while away the rest of his shift writing his story and then he was out of there, hopefully never to return.

Unfortunately, others had arrived in the newsroom earlier that morning. Two of those others were sitting in Whiteman's office even as Jinnah breezed into the city desk and slung his jacket on the back of his chair.

Whiteman sat behind his considerable oak desk, which he used like a shield during difficult meetings. Imposing as it was, the desk was no protection at all from the two well-dressed, soft-spoken, but very unpleasant men on the other side of it. Spread out between them was a copy of the *Tribune*.

"Stories like Jinnah's are *bad* for our club's reputation. They're *bad* for our families' images. And they're *bad* for our businesses."

Mindy tapped one beefy brown finger on the desk three times as he spoke, emphasizing the word "bad" each time. He spoke quietly enough, but the threat in his voice was unmistakable, even to one uninitiated in gangland parlance like Whiteman. Beside Mindy sat Billy, looking very businesslike in his suit.

"Well, ah, Mr. Jinnah is our top crime reporter —" Whiteman began.

Mindy leaned his mass across the desk and Whiteman stopped in mid-sentence.

"And they're bad for your business too. Do you realize how much advertising revenue you get from us?"

Whiteman looked at the dark, bearded face just inches from his own and tried to hide his incredulity.

"We, ah, don't advertise gangs, actually," he said.

"Not our club," said Mindy. "Our members. We're business owners."

Mindy placed a sheet of paper with a lengthy list of business names, addresses, and figures on it in front of Whiteman and sat back down. Whiteman gazed upon it uncomprehendingly at first. Mindy helped him to understand its import by pointing out a few of the better-known firms on the list.

"Gujerat Auto Glass, Korma CompuTech, Madras Fine Fabrics, to name a few. We get the preferred rate from your ad department. Because we're such good customers. Loyal, if you get my meaning."

Whiteman forced himself to focus on the figures in front of him. They represented a not insubstantial amount of revenue to the paper. It was one thing for two gorillas in suits to try to intimidate him. But now Mindy and Billy were hitting Whiteman where it really hurt. Worse, the paper could not afford any adverse publicity at the moment, not with the high-level corporate negotiations at such a delicate state. It would put the ownership of the *Tribune* at a disadvantage and editors-in-chief who put their employers in awkward positions found themselves looking for work in the boonies. Whiteman cleared his throat nervously.

"*If* there was an error —" he conceded.

"We want a front-page apology or we launch a libel suit," said Mindy.

Whiteman did a quick calculation: cost of even a specious libel suit (in terms of dollars and reputation) and lost advertising versus the cost of one carefully worded apology. The sum on the apology side of the equation was a nice, tidy zero, save for a substantial chunk of Jinnah's ego. It had the makings of a winning formula.

"Just what would this hypothetical apology say, gentlemen?" Whiteman asked.

The discussion on the wording was interrupted by Whiteman's secretary, who announced over the intercom that a certain Superintendent Capulet was waiting to see the editor-in-chief.

A few moments later, Mindy and Billy left Whiteman's office and crossed with Capulet. The bikers and the Mountie exchanged looks that read "What the hell are you doing here?" Words were unnecessary. Capulet entered Whiteman's inner sanctum while the secretary escorted Mindy and Billy to the door through the newsroom.

Jinnah had witnessed part of the tableaux. Now he was slumped in his seat, praying Mindy and Billy wouldn't spot him. Beside him, Sanderson, wearing a headset, was furiously typing notes at the terminal he and Hakeem shared. Hardly breathing, Jinnah watched as the two bikers made their way toward the doors. He was just sighing with relief when a tray of coffee slammed down on his desk.

"Sonofabitch!" Jinnah yelped, sure he had suffered a constriction of his left ventricle.

He looked up to see Crystal Wagner, the city desk clerk, staring balefully down at him. A smart-mouthed member of the demographic sometimes referred to as "Generation Next," possessing major attitude (expressed partly in tattoos and body piercings), she was the object of much of Jinnah's harmless flirting. But he was hardly in a flirtatious mood.

"Looks like you've already had too much coffee," said Crystal.

"You nearly gave me a heart attack," Jinnah whined, taking one of the grande-sized cups from the tray.

"You say that to all the girls. And men who wear leathers."

Jinnah poured four creams and four sugars into his coffee and blew a raspberry at Crystal. She drifted off to deliver her wares elsewhere and Jinnah was left to guess just how much influence Mindy and Billy had been able to exert over Whiteman. Then there was the matter of what the Mountie wanted. Graham would have some insight into that. Jinnah reached for his phone, but it rang before he could pick it up. He recognized the number on call display immediately. It was the community health clinic where Manjit volunteered.

"Manjit, I haven't got time —"

"Jinnah! I've found a thread!"

Manjit's voice was so excited, so full of triumph, that Jinnah didn't have the heart to cut her off. But it didn't stop his stomach from wishing she'd just call back later.

"Great, my love," he said. "Listen, could —"

"I went through the patient files," Manjit carried on brightly. "All the adult cases were farm workers."

"Tremendous, darling. I'm just a little —"

"The only thing is," Manjit plowed ahead, voice growing heavy with concern. "I can't see how it links with the children who are patients."

Jinnah muttered a brief prayer to Allah for patience of his own.

"Manjit, I'm glad you found a thread. But I'm up to my ass in gharials right now."

"But Hakeem! I need just a little help!"

Jinnah, at a loss, looked about the newsroom for any object, article, or person that might be of assistance to his wife. His eye came to rest on Ronald Sanderson, still hammering away at the keyboard while talking into his headset.

"Darling, I do know someone who's doing nothing at the moment. Hang on —"

A second later, Sanderson's call-waiting light flashed.

"Just a minute, Your Worship," said Sanderson into his headset. "I'll just get rid of this other line...." Sanderson put the mayor of Vancouver on hold and punched the second line. "Ronald Sanderson here — Manjit?"

Sanderson looked over to Jinnah, baffled. Jinnah took the opportunity to reach around the terminal, grab the keyboard, and whirl the tube around, separating Ronald from his notes.

"Manjit needs your help. It's a small sacrifice, Ronald."

Sanderson's finger was poised over the hold buttons like the ass dithering between the two bales of hay. Jinnah made good his escape by walking over to the city desk. There he found Frosty, nursing a hangover, reading the paper wearing sunglasses, and trying to eat a yogurt with limited success.

"Feeling fragile, are we?" said Jinnah, a tad too loudly.

Frosty winced.

"Not as fragile as your job security. Lot of activity in Whiteman's office today."

"I saw Mindy and Billy." Jinnah nodded. "He's got some Mountie in there now."

"There were two women in there with him earlier," grunted Frosty. "If I were you, I'd get ready for a full-fledged management shite-attack."

"The best defence is a good offence," said Jinnah softly. "If I deliver a line story for my last shift in this miserable place, Whiteman can hardly complain, can he?"

"What do you have for a follow then?"

Well, she had asked for it....

"Found out the body was dismembered at the scene. Makes an abattoir look like Martha Stewart's kitchen."

Frosty groaned and pushed her yogurt aside.

"I'm trying to eat my breakfast," she gasped.

"You Christians," Jinnah chided. "You believe you are eating what you think of at that moment. All that transubstantiation stuff."

"That's not enough for a line story. Got an ID on the body yet?"

"Police think he could be a large Hawaiian," said Jinnah, deadpan.

Frosty refused to dignify this with an answer, so he hit her with another joke.

"Know how to order from Commonwealth? Dial Pizza 911."

As Jinnah laughed, Frosty slowly removed her sunglasses, revealing two watery, bloodshot eyes. She chewed thoughtfully on one of the arms. Schooled in all of Jinnah's moods, she knew he was trying to distract her from the question at hand: who was it in the oven? Which meant he had a suspicion he wasn't willing to share. Well, Frosty had ways of making Jinnah spill before she did. She mentally steeled her cast-iron stomach.

"Could it be one, both, or bits of both Shahs?" she mused aloud.

"No," said Jinnah quickly. "Son's alive. Dad's in Tanzania."

Frosty caught the "wallpaper" tone in Jinnah's voice. A tone he adopted when he was trying to wallpaper over little cracks in his stories.

"And who told you this?" she demanded.

"The son. Armaan."

Frosty levelled her raw, red eyes on Jinnah. It made him hurt just to look at them.

"How convenient for him," she said. "Are you sure he's telling the truth?"

Frosty had expressed the doubt that had been nibbling at Jinnah's mind since his exchange in Hindi with Armaan. Ripping the wallpaper off the crack. Hearing it repeated set his inherent instincts tingling.

"No," he admitted. "But I think I know how I can find out —"

Jinnah and Frosty had been so absorbed in the question of transubstantiation and pineapple-topped pizza that neither had noticed Capulet leave Whiteman's office. They were taken completely off guard when Whiteman suddenly materialized in front of them, trembling. In his hand he clutched two sheets of paper. The entire newsroom went quiet. All that could be heard was a gentle wheezing from Jinnah's nicotine-starved lungs.

"Mr. Jinnah. You will be writing a retraction for tomorrow's paper —"

"For what?"

"Any number of inaccuracies and omissions —"

"Omissions?" cried Jinnah. "What sort of omissions?"

Whiteman stared at Jinnah as if willing him to dissolve into a puddle.

"Could you explain to me why, pray tell, Jinnah," Whiteman said, trying to keep control of his shaking voice. "I have had hysterical women parading into my office all day?"

"Let me guess: Mrs. Mal Singh and Moe Grewal's girlfriend, right?"

"Of course! Who else do you think —"

"I would hardly say two women constitute a parade," interjected Jinnah.

"Jinnah —"

"Unless it was a very small parade, say for a tiny nation like San Marino or —"

"Jinnah!"

Whiteman had shouted. That was bad — Whiteman rarely shouted. Jinnah abandoned his "baffle 'em with bullshit" tactics.

"So, what did these women want?"

"They wanted to know why our newspaper printed the ghastly news that their significant others had been incinerated in a pizza oven when the police had not informed them of the sad news, Jinnah."

"The police did not rule out the possibility!"

Whiteman put on his glasses and held up one of his sheets of paper. He waved it in front of Jinnah like the Black Spot. Hakeem glimpsed the letterhead of a Vancouver Police press release.

"I find that statement at variance with the information transmitted herewith by the constabulary," Whiteman said, waxing pompous.

"Could you be speaking English for me, please sahib," said Jinnah, adopting his "Fresh off the boat from Bombay" accent. "I am not understanding you."

"The police say you're a bloody liar!" bellowed Whiteman like a stricken wildebeest. "And I say you're the most incompetent, slothful, indolent, lazy reporter it has ever been my misfortune to employ!"

"Yeah, yeah — if all if this is true, what do we have to retract? Come to the point, Whiteman. It's a daily newspaper, you know."

The newsroom was now absolutely silent. Magically, every TV monitor had been muted, the radios turned down, and even the jocks from the sports department had stopped arguing about the Canucks' Stanley Cup chances to listen to this one. For Whiteman's forehead was now covered in sweat and the veins beneath the flushed flesh were throbbing. *He's either gonna drop dead or kill me*, Jinnah thought. *Allah, perhaps I can take him with me at least.*

"I'll tell you what my point is," said Whiteman, regaining some semblance of composure. "You are going to write a full retraction. We are going to put it on the front page —"

"You've got to be kidding!"

"And furthermore, it will name you. None of this 'due to a reporting error' nonsense! It will clearly place the blame where it is due — on your shoulders."

"You have got to be joking!" cried Jinnah. "What did we publish that's wrong?"

"Read the police statement and you'll find out!" thundered Whiteman.

Jinnah read the statement while Whiteman tried to get his breath back. Irresponsible, yellow journalism … speculation of the worst kind … unfeeling to the family members …

"It doesn't say we were wrong," Jinnah insisted, and, from his perspective, quite reasonably.

"Jinnah," said Whiteman quietly. "You will write that correction or I will personally cancel your leave of absence."

"You can't do that!" shouted Jinnah, producing a reasonable facsimile of a wildebeest himself.

"I can," said Whiteman. "Watch me."

Jinnah looked over at Frosty, who shook her throbbing head a fraction of an inch to either side. It was a heroic effort to warn Jinnah to back down. It failed.

"You caved!" Jinnah fumed. "Caved to a bunch of bikers!"

Whiteman had by now recovered most of his

aplomb. His voice was calmer, his manner almost cool and collected.

"Have you forgotten what happened in Montreal? Fancy six in the back, Jinnah?"

"This isn't Montreal, Chief —" sputtered Jinnah.

"Fine," snapped Whiteman. "Risk your own life. But we're running a retraction."

Jinnah had composed himself. His reply was soft, but firm.

"I'm on my way to Africa."

"A retraction. Or I cancel your leave."

"The union will grieve."

Whiteman actually smiled at this. He knew just how hollow a threat that was for two reasons. First, the union's policy was "work as usual until the grievance is settled." Second, Jinnah had been the only reporter to sign the decertification petition that had been circulated several years previously. Everyone knew just how hard the union would fight for Jinnah's rights. Jinnah knew it too and, certain that he would predecease Whiteman if this kept up any longer, collapsed in a chair next to Frosty.

"Sonofabitch," he muttered.

Whiteman's smile widened. He could hardly wait until the next issue of the paper. He would order extra copies. No! He would have a front page framed! He was so excited that he gave Jinnah both pieces of paper in his hand.

"You'll find the suggested wording on the back of the police release," said Whiteman. "Ms. Frost? I'm making you personally responsible for seeing to it that this correction runs."

"You got it, Chief," said Frosty.

Whiteman marched triumphantly into his office, accompanied in his mind to the ring of the trumpets, the cries of the senators, knights, and plebeians, and the soft whisper in his ear of the boy holding his crown of laurels: "Remember, thou art not a god ..." But by Jove, in this newsroom, Whiteman knew he was the closest thing to it.

Jinnah and Frosty sat silently for quite some time after Whiteman left. Then Frosty put her sunglasses back on and returned to business.

"You were saying you knew how to check out Armaan's story?" she prompted.

Jinnah snapped to. He glowered as he folded the sheets of paper Whiteman had handed to him and stuffed them in his pocket.

"Yes, I do," he growled. "That bastard!"

"Get over it," said Frosty. "How?"

Jinnah looked up abruptly.

"Where's Ronald?"

Sanderson was not at his desk. Frosty looked about, but he didn't appear to be in the newsroom.

"Probably changing his trousers in the men's room," she muttered. "He's scared shitless of Whiteman."

"In which case," Jinnah clucked disapprovingly, "he would hardly need to change his trousers, would he? We must be charitable, Ms. Frost, to the vertebraeically challenged."

"The what?"

Jinnah stood up and retrieved his jacket from his desk.

"Those lacking spine," he explained, heading for the door.

"Mind telling me where you're going, Mr. Front Page Retraction?" Frosty called after him.

"I have to see about my tickets to Kenya," he said loudly.

Frosty watched as Jinnah left. She couldn't blame him for fleeing. She slowly reached a trembling hand out toward her yogurt. It occurred to her that Jinnah was emulating one of his own stories: User Key One-A.

"Why did he have to fly?" She laughed.

Then she winced and cast about her desk for her aspirins.

Chapter Three

Jinnah spent a considerable amount of the short drive from the office to his destination ruminating over the inequities of the world. It was not fair that pompous asses like Whiteman had all the power. Nor was it just that other assholes had all the money. On the other hand, no one had Jinnah's inherent instincts, save Jinnah, and those instincts were leading him to Main Street and Little India.

Turning right off King Edward Avenue, Jinnah roared down Main toward the heart of Vancouver's Indo-Canadian community. Despite the exodus to the suburbs, the stretch between 49th and 60th Avenues still held the Punjabi Market with its shops, theatres, restaurants, and offices, and, potentially, the answer to Jinnah's nagging doubts about Kabir Shah. He was lucky to find parking right on the main drag. The market was crowded for a change. Saris and turbans flashed by in a kaleidoscope of colours and textures. As he walked along the sidewalk, Jinnah passed dozens of brown faces, some of whom he knew, and relaxed a little. It could never be home to him — not even a home-away-from-home. Home was Kenya and Africa, not the Punjab. But the market was full of scents and sounds that transported him to a different time and place, and that was good.

He had walked just over a block when he spied the bright orange awning of Subcontinental Travel. The windows of the small storefront were crammed with posters of Tanzania, Zanzibar, Mount Kilimanjaro, and other destinations that proclaimed their specialty: Indo-African travel. Entering the office, Jinnah found an attractive travel agent in full sari sitting behind the counter, her dark eyes focused on her computer screen. He automatically smoothed his hair and adjusted the gold chain upon his chest as he approached.

"Gupta," he cried, lowering his voice to what he fancied was an irresistible baritone. "Come with me to Kenya and be my Burger Queen."

Gupta calmly closed the file she was working on and opened her top drawer. With a face as composed as a temple carving, she presented Jinnah with a bulging envelope from inside its depths.

"You already have a queen, Jinnah," she said. "Here's your tickets. Such an old-fashioned client — paper tickets!"

Ah! She is playing hard to get! thought Jinnah, ignoring the slight emphasis Gupta gave to the "old" in "old-fashioned." He took the tickets and used the opportunity to enfold Gupta's hand in his.

"All thanks, my goddess of the bookings," he growled. "How many others have you transported to paradise, hmm?"

Gupta smiled and gently removed her hand.

"What are you after, Jinnah?"

"Sadly, just information. Do you handle travel arrangements for Kabir Shah?"

Gupta's mask of consummate professionalism slipped. A distressed frown clouded her face.

"For years," she said, nodding. "A nice man. Such a mess to come home to."

The impact of those words on Jinnah was mixed. One part of him groaned as the wallpaper was torn right off the crack in his story like a Band-Aid off a fresh cut. The other part felt the quickening of nerves, the beginnings of joy at having uncovered a hidden truth.

"He's back from Tanzania? You're sure?" he asked.

Gupta flipped through the Day-timer on her desk.

"I called his friend to pick him at the airport. Here it is. Mr. Puri. You know him, perhaps?"

"Slightly."

Jinnah's bonhomie vanished as he uttered this lie. He pocketed his tickets and stood up to take his leave. Gupta saw her customer to the door.

"Still want to take me to Kenya?" she asked, smiling.

"Ah, mademoiselle, for you I would cover the Serengeti in french fries, but let me attend to some urgent business first, hmm?"

Gupta allowed herself to laugh only after Jinnah was safely out the door.

Ram Puri's shop was in a building two blocks south toward the river. Jinnah half-ran there, mind frantically working out the possibilities. Maybe Kabir Shah was staying with Puri. Or maybe he had already gone off on some other business jaunt. He paused, gasping politely, to open the door of the building for three women dressed in black and heavily veiled. Sunlight streamed through the three-tiered windows of the mini-mall. Bhangra music blared from a store. Jinnah drifted along behind the three veiled woman, rubbing shoulders with other shoppers, some in traditional dress, some in Western clothes. He listened to the chatter in a half-dozen different dialects. Puri's shop was near the back on the ground floor. Several young Indo-Canadian men were gathered in front. They greeted Jinnah warmly.

"Hey, Jinnah. What's news, man?"

The bearded man making this salutation was dressed in a black leather jacket, but he was no biker. Jinnah smiled.

"Hey, Rajvir, my friend!" he cried.

Rajvir put an arm around Jinnah's shoulders and placed a small piece of paper under his nose.

"I sold three more Burger Palace units for the chain," said Rajvir proudly. "See?"

Rajvir handed the cheque over. Jinnah tucked it in his inner jacket pocket and beamed — until he noticed the dark cloud next to them. Rajvir's cousin, Probir, didn't show the same unbridled enthusiasm. His dark face glowered at Jinnah.

"Haven't lost our investment money yet, have you?" he demanded.

Doesn't trust me with his money. Never has. One bad experience with the Orient Love Express and now you can't please him. Well, let Probir mistrust his latest business investment. He had a right to; he'd paid for it.

"No, but I've been spending it."

Jinnah whipped out his new tech-toy. It looked like a cellphone on steroids. The guys crowded in for a closer look.

"Satellite phone. More reliable than cellular in third-world countries."

The guys — save Probir — laughed and slapped Jinnah on the back as he brushed past them and into the shop. Puri's emporium was a dry goods shop with a wide counter, where he slung chai along with the Coca Cola. Jinnah was greeted by a genial, immaculately dressed man with the air of an *eminence grise*.

"Mr. Jinnah. A pleasure to see you, sir," said Ram Puri.

Jinnah liked Puri — on the whole. He was Hindu and like Jinnah, a minority in the predominantly Punjabi Indo-Canadian community of Vancouver. And he had helped Jinnah out of a jam during the ill-fated Orient Love Express business. Of course, it had been to Puri's advantage to do so, but he had never rubbed it in. Jinnah salaamed.

"Do you have a moment of your valuable time to spare, Mr. Puri?"

"Of course. Will you take some chai?"

Puri motioned Jinnah to sit at the counter at the back. Then he poured two steaming cups of tea into delicate china mugs, handed Jinnah one, then took his seat across from him. The two men sat, sipping their steaming brew.

"How can I help you, Mr. Jinnah?" Puri asked after a decent interval had passed.

Normally, Jinnah would have backed into this interview, sparing Puri the brutality of a short, business-only conversation. But he was in a desperate hurry. Better to get it over with, for both of them.

"I was wondering if you knew if Kabir Shah is still in Tanzania," he said, coming right to the point.

"Oh, no." Puri sipped at the lip of his cup. "I picked him up at the airport two nights ago."

"Did you drop him off at home?"

"No, at Commonwealth Pizza."

Jinnah's stomach started to contract. He forced himself to take a mouthful of tea and swallow it before asking his next question. Both tasted bitter in his mouth.

"Do you see him there often, hmm?"

"Yes. Kabir still keeps an office there. Even though he's turned the pizza business over to Armaan."

This was not sounding at all good.

"So Mr. Shah is retired?" asked Jinnah, hoping, perhaps, that Puri was about to reveal that Shah had taken his fifth wheel off to Scottsdale or some such thing.

"Mostly. But he had some files he needed to pick up."

Jinnah carefully poured some of his hot tea onto his saucer to let it cool. He rolled it gently back and forth as he spoke.

"You haven't talked to him since?"

Puri's smooth and cherubic face was suddenly riveted by worried wrinkles.

"No," he said, lowering his voice. "He was quiet. He seemed troubled. He said he had vital business to discuss with Armaan."

Jinnah could tell that Puri shared the same awful thought that had now formed in his own mind. He slurped some tea from his saucer. Perhaps the delicate path was the best one after all, given the circumstances.

"How do they get along? Armaan and Kabir?"

Puri smiled sadly.

"Like Delhi and Islamabad."

As Jinnah had expected.

"Ah-chah! Different generations?"

"Different values. Kabir keeps his money in the community — as far as anyone can tell. Certainly, his charitable works do not appear to stray far from Main Street. But Armaan is young and his spirit wishes to roam the globe."

"In this economy, smart boy."

Puri shook his head.

"Not so smart. Every deal he tries to make is risky. High-risk partners."

"Partners?" Jinnah looked at Puri sharply. "Within the community?"

"Some less-than-savoury members of our community. And others."

Jinnah's mind flashed on the image of the well-dressed Mindy and Billy exiting Whiteman's office. Could one of them have been the well-dressed Indo-Canadian "businessman" the arcade punks had seen hanging around the pizza parlour?

"Has, ah, Armaan lost a lot of money?" he asked slowly.

Puri nodded, a shade reluctantly.

"His father's money."

Jinnah's inherent instincts were tingling at full volume. He kissed the fantasy of writing a simple news story goodbye and twiddling his thumbs during his final shift at the *Tribune* adieu. He finished the tea on his saucer. Carefully replacing the cup on it, he leaned across the counter and closer to Puri.

"You know that the police have been unable to contact Kabir, Mr. Puri?" he asked gently.

Tears were slowly forming in Puri's eyes. He put a hand on Jinnah's.

"Find my friend Kabir, Jinnah. Please," he whispered.

Ronald Sanderson stared out at the expanse of green fields in front of him and felt like an extra in *Gandhi*. Indo-Canadian pickers in traditional dress, both men and women, shimmered like white flames in the reflected heat as they laboured among the bushes. At the edge of the fields children played, chasing each other, playing tag. A few older men wearing turbans were gathered around a lunch truck, chewing samosas and drinking tea. It was a blueberry field in Richmond, but Sanderson could imagine he was somewhere in the Punjab or Pakistan. Except there, the farmer would not have been white, like this one. He was a tall, scarecrow of a man who looked about forty, but he might have been younger. Sanderson was there ostensibly helping Manjit track down the source of the mysterious sickness. But she appeared to need little help.

"So you sprayed these fields just recently?" she asked.

The farmer, like most tillers of the soil, gazed out at the fields as he spoke. Looking perhaps for the answers from the earth itself.

"Well, we try to use as little pesticide as possible. But this time of year, we get infestations. Not as if we're certified organic or anything, y'know …"

His voice trailed off. Sanderson guessed the man to be of Dutch extraction by his faint accent. He decided to make himself useful.

"What have you been using? Anything new or untested?"

The farmer looked right at Sanderson this time. A nerve had been hit.

"Look, we don't do the spraying ourselves," he bristled.

"Who does?" asked Manjit sweetly.

The farmer looked at Manjit with an arched eyebrow.

"A group of us hired a firm. Zephyr Aviation. Gave us a good deal."

"And where might we find the firm and the pilot?"

"Boundary Bay Airport, lady," said the farmer. "Now, if you don't mind, I got work to do."

"Not at all," said Manjit. "You've been most helpful."

The farmer grunted and strode off toward the lunch truck. Manjit turned her dark, sparkling eyes on Sanderson.

"Well, Ronald?"

Sanderson had a story to write. The clock was ticking on Whiteman's attention span. And so far, he and Manjit had uncovered nothing worth justifying his time away from the office. Besides, Boundary Bay Airport was a hell of a long way away.

"Manjit, I —"

"It's okay, Ronald. Just drop me off at the nearest pay phone. I'm sure I can get a cab."

A small part of Sanderson's mind protested internally that there were no pay phones left in Greater Vancouver's busy streets, let alone a farmer's fields. The rest of it was seized by panic.

"I can't do that!" he squawked. "Jinnah would kill me!"

"Oh, I don't think so," said Manjit. "He's leaving for Kenya in two days, you know. He's almost certain to wait until after he gets back."

Sanderson felt his free will slowly ebbing from his bones. His liberal conscience wrestled briefly with his enlightened self-interest. It was a clear decision for liberal guilt.

"Okay," he said, fishing in his pockets for the keys to his SUV. "Let's go."

* * *

The smell of bone being sawed was not quite as nauseating as the stench of burnt human flesh, but it was enough to make Jinnah feel quite queasy. Not that his stomach needed much olfactory stimulus when he was in the lair of Doctor Death. Dr. Rex Aikens, police pathologist, had earned that nickname long before Kevorkian had come along. He was a tall, slender, balding man who, in Jinnah's opinion, looked too dapper to be so well-versed in the ways of death. At the moment he was working with a forensic rotary bone saw, preparing a sample. And giving a running commentary on the shortcomings of pizza ovens as a means of body disposal.

"You see, a pizza oven will only reach three hundred and fifteen degrees Celsius. It chars the soft tissue, but not the bones," he said in the lilting tones that hinted at his childhood in Dublin.

Aikens scooped dried, flaky marrow out of the bone. Jinnah looked away. The pathologist raised his bushy black eyebrows.

"Come, come, Jinnah," he scolded mildly. "It's the only way I have to get an ID now."

"And when are we going to get an ID?" asked Jinnah, carefully averting his gaze.

"Ah, with the state of things at the lab, I fear DNA could take days," said Aikens sorrowfully while meticulously placing the marrow sample on a slide. "There's the problem of finding family members, getting comparative samples …"

His voice trailed off. Jinnah jumped into the conversational gulf.

"Come on, Aikens!" he cried. "You've got to give me something."

Rex Aikens looked over the top of his silver-framed glasses at Jinnah. They had an excellent working relationship. Aikens gave Jinnah information, strictly off the record, which he then confirmed elsewhere. In return, Jinnah helped Aikens answer the one question the victims who fell under his care asked: "Why am I dead?" But Dr. Death didn't have much to give Jinnah on this occasion.

"I can tell you, unofficially, that we have only one body here. A male."

Jinnah chewed his nicotine gum noisily. Aikens sighed. Fine. He would throw the reporter another metaphorical bone.

"A cursory glance of the dental records indicate this is not Moe Grewal. Nor is it Mal Singh. Have you any other suggestions?"

Jinnah did. But he wasn't ready to share them. Not yet.

"I'll get back to you, Doc," he said.

Vancouver's beauty is also its curse. A city surrounded on three sides by water looks gorgeous, but it's hell to drive around in. If you are content to travel on foot, however, there is an alternative. The Aquabus takes pedestrians across False Creek from the West Side to the downtown peninsula. And since West Side terminus was but a few blocks from the Vancouver Police headquarters, the Aquabus was a natural, neutral meeting place for Graham and Jinnah. They sat at the far end of the nearly round vessel as it dodged sailboats and power craft bound for Granville Island or points farther afield. Jinnah whipped out a pack of nicotine gum and offered it to Graham. The policeman pulled out a pack of cigarettes.

"No thanks," he said, lighting up. "I'm trying to quit. Like you're trying to quit the business."

"For health reasons," said Jinnah, cramming several more pieces of gum into his already swollen mouth. "Too many murders. It's making me sick, I'm telling you."

Graham took a deep drag and exhaled, sending a small cloud of blue smoke floating over the green water.

"How are you going to get away with setting up a Burger Palace chain in Kenya?"

Jinnah, who had been looking morose, cheered up.

"Simple, my friend. My uncle owns a cafe in Kenya called 'Burger Palace.' It predates the North American franchise operation. Technically, we're just expanding that restaurant."

"Can I get in on the action?" laughed Graham.

"You have plenty of action to keep you busy right here, buddy," said Jinnah, cutting to the chase. "Listen, if Armaan Shah claims his father is still in Tanzania, he's lying."

"How do you know that?" demanded Graham.

"A friend of the family told me. He also told me that Armaan and his father have been fighting."

"Over what? The white girlfriend?"

The Aquabus cut through the wake from a large power boat. The vessel bobbed up and down like a bathtub on the rolling waves. Jinnah felt slightly sick to his stomach. Gravol! That was the answer to these sea voyages.

"Business," he admitted. "And family. Family business."

Jinnah chewed while Graham puffed, both of them turning over the information.

"So," said Graham slowly. "We have a rich dad ... and a lying son ..."

He left the rest unspoken. Jinnah picked up the sentence.

"Who resents wealthy dad and now Dad's missing."

Or maybe not. There was a corpse lying in the morgue. Jinnah and Graham knew they were both thinking the same thing. Graham spoke first.

"Know what it takes for me to get dental records thanks to the Privacy Act? Affidavits, court orders —"

"What's the rush?" protested Jinnah.

"Hakeem: burgers? Kenya? Two days? Besides, Armaan might just flee and I have no way to stop him at the moment. We need to act fast."

"We, white man?"

The Aquabus had reached the dock. Jinnah sighed, weary. Why was everything about this case so bloody labour-intensive? Especially on his part.

"I'll see what I can do," he promised.

Jinnah gave Graham a pat on the shoulder and left with the other passengers. The sergeant remained aboard, bound for the other side of the creek and his office. He waved as the boat pulled away, sending an erratic smoke signal into the sky. Jinnah stood on the seawall watching the Aquabus slide across the water. Then he took out his cellphone and called Puri. He didn't like doing this to the gentleman, but there was no other way. Puri answered on the first ring.

"Mr. Puri? Jinnah. Do you happen to know who Kabir Shah's dentist is?"

In the end, it didn't take much more than an hour for Jinnah to find himself back at the Shahs' front door. Kabir's dentist, Dr. Lalani, had been only too happy to help and had given Jinnah copies of the pertinent x-rays. It had taken Aikens only a few moments to render his preliminary (and very unofficial) verdict. He'd politely asked Jinnah not to do anything with the information until he'd given it to Graham, and Jinnah had just as politely assured him he'd do nothing rash like rushing such sensitive information into print. But he hadn't said anything about not hammering on the Shahs' rather expensive oak door or attempting to interview Armaan (where, quite naturally, the topic might just come up). Jinnah's tape recorder was already rolling inside his jacket pocket as he rang the bell.

Armaan opened the door and gasped.

"About your father's dentist —" Jinnah began.

"Go away!" Armaan cried, half-choking.

Armaan tried to slam the door shut, but Jinnah's seasoned left foot was already in the jam. Armaan leaned on the door, trying to crush the reporter's foot. He was surprised to see Jinnah smiling at him. He pointed down to his impervious shoe.

"My boots are steel-toed. Your father's bridge-work was gold, was it not?"

Armaan flinched as if he'd been slapped across the face. His grip on the door slackened. Jinnah stared at the young man gravely.

"I think we need to talk, hmm?"

Armaan slowly opened the door. Jinnah nipped inside before he could change his mind. He noted that the entranceway was simply but elegantly furnished. The living room was huge. Expensively decorated, but not garish. Jinnah's trained eye took in *objets d'art* from Africa and India, including, of all things, a tiger-skin rug on the floor in front of the fireplace. Armaan sank, numb, into a sofa. He stared into the black square of the empty fireplace, silent. Jinnah picked up an African artifact — a statue of Edshu, the African trickster god. He wondered if Armaan was a disciple of this clever deity.

"Ninth century. African," said Jinnah turning the statue over in his hands. "Very expensive. And all yours now."

Armaan looked up sharply.

"My father bought that," he said quickly.

Jinnah slowly put Edshu down and turned his gaze on Armaan, who was, he reflected, not a very good trickster.

"You know your father's mortal remains were in that oven."

He said it as a statement of fact, not a question. Armaan froze. His eyes assumed that "deer-caught-in-the-headlights" largeness. Jinnah's own eyes bored right into them.

"Have you considered where his soul is now?"

Armaan, when he spoke, sounded as if he'd been physically winded by this metaphorical one-two punch.

"The police ... haven't said ... anything," he gasped.

"They will when they get his dental records, my friend. They'll be all over you, hmm?"

Armaan didn't respond. *He's cracking*, Jinnah thought, pacing in front of the couch like a tiger and wishing to hell he could smoke a bloody cigarette. *Try a little more pressure ...*

"Know what the police will say, buddy? They'll say you fought with your dad over business. He cut you off —"

"That's not true!" cried Armaan.

"Maybe he attacked you," Jinnah went on, merciless. "You had to defend yourself. Is that how you killed your father?"

Armaan was on his feet now. The fawn-like eyes were blazing.

"No! That's not how it happened."

"Then you tell me. How did your father end up in that oven?" demanded Jinnah.

In the ensuing silence, Jinnah forgot the aching need for nicotine, his arrest that morning, Caitlin's surgically altered appearance, his lessons from the *Kama*

Sleuthra with Manjit — everything he'd been through this day. Inherent instincts screeching, his heart racing, pores sweating. Everything, all the humiliation and legwork, hung on Armaan's next words. When they came, they were painfully soft-spoken.

"I put him there."

As much as he had wanted to get a confession out of Armaan, Jinnah was thrown. He hadn't actually expected this. Armaan stood before him, hanging his head, the very picture of guilty misery. And yet, for some reason, he felt like hugging the poor young man.

"So ... you did kill him," said Jinnah quietly.

Armaan raised his head, eyes swimming.

"No. He was alive when I left ..."

Armaan trailed off, struggling to control the tears, to be coherent.

"After the fight ... I came back to try to explain ... and I found him ... dead."

Armaan collapsed back onto the sofa, racked by sobs. Jinnah felt tears welling in his own eyes. Suddenly, he was at a loss. What the hell do you do when the suspect blurts it out just like that? Where's a cop when you really need one? He put his hands gently on Armaan's shoulders, the way he used to comfort a crying Saleem when his boy had been younger.

"Armaan, hey ... it's okay," Jinnah fumbled.

This lie simply prompted a fresh, violent outburst of tears from the younger Shah. The couch and the carpet were getting soaked.

"You don't understand," wept Armaan. "He hanged himself."

Jinnah gave a start.

"Suicide?"

Armaan took in a long, shuddering breath and tried to regain his composure.

"He was disappointed in me. It was in his note. I had to cut him down."

Armaan buried his head in his hands and cried, but less fiercely now. Jinnah was completely thrown. The young man was clearly in torment. But Jinnah's bullshit-detector was ringing.

"But why didn't you call the police?" he stuttered, trying to think clearly.

"I was ashamed. My reputation. My family's good name. You understand."

Jinnah did understand — to a point. Pride. Face. A very important thing in the community. But something didn't add up.

"What happened to the note? The rope?" Jinnah asked.

"I burned them," said Armaan. "I wasn't in my right mind, Mr. Jinnah. All I could think of was to carry out his wishes...."

The last few words came out as a strangled squeak. The pain, at least was real.

"What? What did he want of you?" asked Jinnah.

Armaan finally looked directly at Jinnah, face damp, eyes rimmed with red. His voice was flat, almost emotionless. It sent shivers through Jinnah's being.

"To cremate him," Armaan said.

Chapter Four

The *Tribune* building's underground parking lot was dark, tomb-like, and smelled bad. As such, it was the perfect match for Jinnah's thoughts. He'd had two meetings since leaving Armaan's house. Neither had been pleasant. He hadn't really expected Graham to greet his news with enthusiasm — hell, not even gratitude. But outright hostility? The reporter's mind boggled almost as much as the Great Jinnah-ji's ego shuddered at the recollection.

"I should have left you in jail!" Graham had shouted, rattling his office windows. "You tipped off our prime suspect!"

"You asked for my help — I gave it!" Jinnah had protested.

"I asked for your help with some teeth! I didn't ask you to take the information to Armaan and help him come up with a crazy cremation story."

Jinnah had passed up the obvious pun about having made an ash of himself (somehow the moment didn't feel quite right) and had switched from the role of bungling investigator to that of expert cultural advisor. It was pretty much his only card in the circumstances.

"What's so crazy? Could be the truth."

Walking around a fetid pool of seep water mixed with motor oil, Jinnah smiled at the recollection of the look of mixed outrage and astonishment on Graham's face after he had lobbed this at him. And how he had pressed his advantage.

"You were raised on hockey and Nanaimo bars — what do you know from *barfi*?" Jinnah had insisted.

"I know murder and this is bullshit," Graham had said with just enough doubt and hesitancy that Jinnah had plowed straight ahead.

"Craig, preserving your family's good name is crucial in the community."

"But a do-it-yourself cremation?"

"Well ..."

Here Jinnah's vestigial conscience had forced him to be cautious. He'd been on shaky ground to begin with and Craig had touched on a topic that had been gnawing at him.

"It depends on his religion. Muslims don't cremate. But if he was a Hindu, cremation is mandatory — the sooner the better. Don't forget your notion of a suttee."

Graham had shifted uneasily in his chair. He had calmed down somewhat and Jinnah had seen the wheels of the investigator whirling behind his eyes as he had asked the key question.

"So which was Kabir Shah?"

Jinnah had enough professional pride to kick himself mentally before answering with a touch too much righteous indignation.

"Shah is one of those tricky, either/or kind of names, Craig. Anyone from the subcontinent knows that."

Graham had leaned back in his chair and had managed to crack a smile.

"But you're from Africa. What — you forgot to ask? The Great Jinnah-ji forgot such a basic question?"

Whatever slight advantage Jinnah had had vanished at that moment. It was only by promising to find out and report back right away without telling anyone (especially Armaan, Manjit, or Frosty) that Jinnah had avoided being arrested for obstruction of justice for the second time in twenty-four hours. In return he'd managed to get Graham's word that he would not, under any circumstances, breathe a word of this to Caitlin Bishop.

The parking lot's elevators were just a few metres away. Jinnah passed a vintage 1952 Bentley Mark VI. Whiteman's car. He noted the stall number for future reference. Depending on how his next interview with the editor-in-chief went, he'd need it — as well as about a pound of sugar.... Sugar! With an involuntary wrench Jinnah remembered how he'd mixed six lumps of the stuff into his tea while talking with Puri just a short while ago. Of course Ram had known what faith his friend Kabir had been. And of course Jinnah had had to break the bad news to Puri in person.

"My dear friend for twenty years," Puri had said over his teacup, seated at the back of the shop. "He helped me set up in business when I first arrived here. Myself and many others."

Jinnah had found Puri's dignity and fortitude in the face of what was obviously a moment of great grief almost unnerving. But not so unsettling that he had forgotten about his mission.

"Mr. Puri, will Kabir's funeral be at a mosque or a temple?"

"You will feel at home, Mr. Jinnah."

The answer had soured the taste of the tea, six sugars or no six sugars. Jinnah had been of the impression that the Shahs were Muslim. Which meant that Armaan's story about cremation had been bullshit. Even worse, that Graham had been right ... he'd almost missed Puri's detailed description of how Kabir would have wanted to be buried and how his soul would not find rest unless the rites were observed carefully. Jinnah had responded with one of the standard phrases he used in such circumstances without remembering who he was talking to — and immediately regretted it.

"It is eternal torment for the souls of all murder victims until their killer faces justice, Mr. Puri, no matter what their faith."

Puri had given Jinnah a sharp, shrewd look. Silently he'd finished his tea and stood up slowly, ending the conversation.

"Then we must pray that Kabir's torment will be brief, Mr. Jinnah," he had said quietly. "Go with God."

Jinnah had cursed himself silently as he made his way through the shop. Puri deserved better than his pat aphorisms. He'd been further upset by the distinct cold shoulder he'd received from Puri's customers on leaving. His inherent instincts told him he'd offended many in the community with his stories on the Shah case. The stony looks on the faces of the people in the shop confirmed those instincts. He'd brushed past hurriedly and was already congratulating himself on a quick getaway when a voice had stopped him dead not ten paces down the sidewalk.

"Mr. Jinnah!"

Name of God. Jinnah had pivoted on his Gucci-clad heel and faced Mr. Puri, anticipating the well-deserved tongue-lashing. He'd been surprised to see the old man actually smiling at him from the shop door.

"If you will be kind enough to return after dinner, I may be able to provide you another piece of this puzzle."

Jinnah had been so astonished he'd been completely self-absorbed during the drive from Main Street to the *Trib* building, trying to guess what Puri's puzzle piece was. So self-absorbed that it was far too late by the time he registered the footsteps behind him in the darkness of the parking garage. He stopped, took a swift look over the left shoulder, and obeyed his congenital cowardice's urgent instructions to duck behind one of the massive concrete support pillars just a few metres from the elevator and safety. Heart pounding, lungs starved for nicotine and oxygen, Jinnah forced himself to hold his breath and listen carefully. Silence. The only thing he could hear were the stifled and stressed sounds of his respiratory, circulatory, and endocrine systems interacting at high gear. Cautiously, he let out a breath.

"Name of God, I'm imagining things," he gasped aloud.

Jinnah had just taken a step toward the elevators when a burly tattooed arm shot from behind the pillar, grabbed him around the mouth, and hauled him into the dark shadows. His congenital cowardice was superseded by base survival instincts and he struggled to break free. He might as well have tried to crawl out of the belly of a boa constrictor. One well-muscled arm had reeled him in. Jinnah felt the other shove something hard, cold, and metallic into his back.

"Scream and you're dead," a deep, harsh voice whispered into his ear.

Jinnah was petrified, but managed a feeble nod against the thick, puffy fingers that held his mouth prisoner. He wasn't at all sure if he could scream if he wanted to. A very small part of his brain that wasn't being flooded by adrenaline and being ruled by the amygdala registered that his assailant's breath had a sour, bilious smell — like undigested butter chicken. It also registered the feathery tattoo on the iron arm holding his head near-motionless. Somewhere deep inside his brain, Jinnah had a handful of perfectly calm neurons telling him who his attacker was even before the unseen man removed his hand from his mouth.

"I'm Mal Singh. Thanks for blowing my cover, asshole."

Sonofabitch! Jinnah should have remembered the Rule of Three. As in bad things happening. First Graham, then Puri. Now Mal Singh: Bad Thing

Number Three. And perhaps three-zero, i.e. "30" — the number every reporter put at the bottom of a story to mark its end. Jinnah called on the handful of normally firing neurons deep inside his supramarginal gyrus to plead his case.

"I went with the information I had —" he managed to squeak before the sharp object was nudged into his upper back.

"Listen, I've read your stuff …"

Jinnah braced himself for the "most if it's bullshit!" part of this well-known sentence. It never came.

"… you got most of it right. But you only got part of the picture."

The number of neurons under the direct control of the amygdala dropped steadily as Jinnah took this in and he began to dare to hope that death might not be imminent.

"But Billy and Mindy —" he croaked.

"Are small-time. A little grow-op, some numbers."

It would be going too far to describe Jinnah's thought process as clear, but it was at least capable of sudden, blinding insight. He hoped it wasn't a final burst of inspiration as he screwed up his courage.

"It took you six months to figure that out?"

Instead of the expected jab between the shoulder blades, Jinnah found himself thrown none too gently against the concrete pillar.

"Hey! Easy! My suit!" he cried.

Singh was right in Jinnah's face and the reporter's momentary indignation died in his throat under the glare of the biker's eyes.

"That took about six minutes. I spent six months scoping out their connections. There's some new kids on the organized crime block."

Jinnah nodded. That made sense.

"Bikers?" he whispered.

Singh shook his head.

"Corporate dudes. Serious dudes. Drugs. Prostitution. Weapons. All hiding behind legit business fronts."

Jinnah was now composed enough to start trying to put some of the missing pieces together. Maybe the well-dressed Indo-Canadian businessman described by the Pizza Punks was part of this new organization.

"Serious?" he asked Singh. "How serious?"

Jinnah was surprised to be slammed against the pillar again — harder. Oops. Touched a nerve.

"Serious enough to ice Moe two weeks ago. They showed me his body. Figured he was a narc. They weren't on to me. Then."

Jinnah braced himself for another session with the concrete pillar. He wondered if having your back ruined by a berserk biker-informant was covered by the *Tribune*'s extended health benefits. Instead, Singh grabbed him, spun him around, and reacquainted the space between his shoulder blades with the hard metal object.

"Then your story comes out. Now I have to leave the country, understand?"

"I'm very, very sorry for the trouble I've caused you Mr. Singh —" Jinnah began.

Singh's face pressed up against Jinnah's cheek, choking off his apology.

"Don't worry about me, Jinnah. You got a wife? A kid?"

Jinnah swallowed hard. Perhaps this was going to be his Big 30 after all. Well, might as well go down in style....

"Yes, my friend," he said with as much bravado as he could muster. "And your knife in my back."

The hard, cold object and its pressure was removed from Jinnah's spinal column. Singh grabbed Jinnah's hand and pressed something into it, then gave him a shove away from the pillar. Jinnah stumbled, then risked a glance at the object. It was a belt buckle: a Phoenix Motorcycle Club buckle.

"You're gonna need all the help you can get. If your cop friends fuck up or aren't there for you, take that to Mindy."

Jinnah stared at Singh, flabbergasted. He had handed him a passport to Bikerland. The RCMP had chosen their informant well.

"Now you're gonna close your eyes and count to ten. I'm gonna disappear."

Jinnah closed his eyes. He counted in his head as far as four before muttering "screw it" in Pushtu and opening them. Singh was gone. Jinnah staggered over to the elevator doors and fumbled for a cigarette. He didn't care if they arrested him for breaking the sacred no-smoking bylaw. Right now it would seem like protective custody. A maelstrom of thoughts raged in his head about Singh, Mindy, Billy, these new, serious corporate dudes. And about Manjit and Saleem. Name of God, he would have to get Graham to have them watched — he was going to Tanzania in another day. The thought brought Jinnah screeching back to the present. And the fact that he was just a few metres away from his desk. And all that was waiting for him there. Disgusted, he threw his unlit cigarette onto the concrete paving and crushed it underfoot.

"I'll say one thing about Mal Singh," Jinnah growled as he hit the "up" button. "At least the son of a bitch didn't ask for a page one retraction!"

The front page retraction hovered over Jinnah's subsequent conversation with Frosty at city desk. Jinnah tried batting it away up toward the ceiling every time the senior assistant city editor raised it, which, given the circumstances, he considered was far too often. Not that Jinnah was doing himself many favours.

"So you're telling me that there's been a major development in the Shah case, but you can't tell me or anyone what it is. What am I supposed to put on the front page? Twenty questions by Hakeem Jinnah? Can't tell you what the story is, folks, but trust us — it's really big?"

"If you give me a few more hours, it will be too big for the front page to contain, Frosty," Jinnah insisted. "Trust me."

"I seem to remember trusting you the other night and having been threatened with a letter of reprimand on my file as a result. And having to place a certain FTR on the front page. Speaking of which —"

"What if I was to tell you Shah may have been the victim of a deadly new organized crime operation moving into Vancouver?"

"What I always say, Jinnah: quotes, names, dates — charges!"

"You know I can get them! What's with you today? Is nicotine withdrawal really that hard, hmm? Look at me —"

"Oh for God's sake, Jinnah!" Frosty snapped. "Do you have any idea what's going on at your own paper?"

Given all he'd been through that day, Jinnah might have been forgiven for missing the rather obvious nervous vibe in the newsroom. But Frosty's unreasonableness seemed to him to be excessive and somehow unrelated to the story in question. He looked up and glanced around the newsroom. Normally chatty deskers were silent. The televisions were on mute. Even the jocks in the sports department were subdued and, like everyone else in the newsroom, darting furtive glances toward the corner boardroom.

"Did someone die?" he asked.

Frosty looked at him with the precise mixture of exasperation and pity she knew would penetrate Jinnah's crowded consciousness. She'd had years of practice.

"Just your paycheque, Jinnah. And maybe the last independent daily newspaper in Canada. No biggie."

The word "paycheque" cut through Jinnah's complex mixture of neuroses and possible crime scenarios and hit the big red button in his brain marked "financial security." The Shahs, Graham, and even the dreaded FTR vanished in a puff of panic.

"They haven't closed the paper?" Jinnah squeaked. "They can't do this to me —"

"To you?" cried Frosty. "You think this is about you?"

"Everything about this paper revolves around me, Frosty!" Jinnah proclaimed. "I am the hub of this great wheel of information."

"Is that so? Well, this gives a whole new meaning to the phrase 'spin on it,' my friend —"

The doors of the corner boardroom opened, cutting Frosty off in mid-rant. Every set of eyes in the newsroom swivelled in unison to watch, unabashed, as a gaggle of executives issued forth. Jinnah was impressed. There were enough power suits there to light a large village in Kenya. There were at least a half-dozen execs he didn't recognize as the assembled suits performed a corporate mitosis, dividing into two distinct groups. On one side, Jinnah clocked Whiteman, Dale Sherman (the head of HR), and ... Name of God! The publisher. The only time Jinnah had seen the *Trib*'s publisher in the newsroom had been five years ago when he had announced a round of layoffs. He started to sweat. What a time for his malaria to flare up again.

"The other guys are some of the top brass from Candle Communications," said Frosty softly, anticipating his question. "They've been in with our execs for about two hours."

"Candle? The cellphone company?" asked Jinnah. "What the hell are they doing here?"

"Buying us," growled Frosty. "And they're not just a cellphone company. They're one of the biggest telecommunications corporations in North America. Anything that Bell or Telus doesn't own, they do. Including our competition."

"But if they buy us —"

Jinnah's protests — and his visions of a merger with the *Clarion* and layoffs done by strict seniority without regard to ability or fashion-sense — were choked off by the orderly parade of the Candle executives down the far wall of the newsroom toward reception; escorted, ominously enough, by just the publisher and Sherman. Whiteman was rooted to the boardroom doorway, his face filled with corporate novocaine (an essential element to executive survival). Silence fell on city desk as the publisher ushered the Candle delegation out, then turned to look at the newsroom. Jinnah half expected him to do a MacArthur, but words to the effect that he would return never came. The boss simply nodded at the staff as if to say "carry on" and was gone.

In the explosion of noisy conversation that followed, Frosty leaned close to Jinnah and whispered urgently into his ear.

"Go get the goods, Hakeem. Don't stick around here. If Whiteman sees you, he'll have you chained to your desk writing your FTR from now until the end of your shift."

"But the paper! Candle!" Jinnah protested.

"If this is the *Trib*'s last front page, Jinnah, make it a good one. An exclusive. Okay? I'll cover for you."

Jinnah was prepared to argue, but then saw Whiteman (who had been surrounded by anxious employees, especially the business department, all asking questions about a possible merger/sale/bankruptcy) cast his eye in the direction of city desk. With an undignified "eek!" Jinnah crouched down beside Frosty and proceeded to move out of the newsroom as fast as his knees could carry him. He thanked Allah that his colleagues were too preoccupied with Whiteman and the post-Candle Communications summit reaction to pay any attention to his craven departure.

All but Ronald Sanderson.

"Jinnah!" he hissed as Hakeem hobbled past their desk. "What the hell are you doing?"

"Lost a contact," muttered Jinnah, redoubling his speed at the expense of his ligaments.

"You wear glasses!"

"I didn't say it was mine, Ronald. Gotta run."

"But Manjit —"

"Will tell me all about it at dinner."

Jinnah dove beneath the desk divider and wriggled under it to the hallway that led to the *Trib* library and freedom.

"But we found something incredible!" Sanderson shouted after the now upright, fleeing form of the *Tribune*'s finest crime reporter.

"Can't hold a candle to my story, Ronald, but file it anyway — under the heading 'Swan Song.'"

And, rubbing his knees while simultaneously dusting off his scuffed Guccis, Jinnah disappeared into the library stacks.

* * *

Jinnah had scarcely guided the Satellite-Guided Love Machine into the blessed daylight when his cell went off. Blatantly ignoring the law against distracted driving, he hauled the phone to his ear and barked, "Jinnah. Speak, infidel!"

There was a strained silence on the other end, punctuated by short, sharp intakes of breath. Jinnah risked a quick look at the call display while executing an illegal left turn off Granville Street. Shit! It was Graham.

"Would it kill you to speak nice to me once in a while, Hakeem? Listen, we gotta talk."

Graham's tone told Jinnah that he was upset about rather more than being called an infidel. Still, he was surprised when Craig named the designated rendezvous. Luckily, he was on the perfect street to get there. So it was that for the second time that day he found himself aboard the Aquabus with Graham across from him. Only this time, they were going the opposite direction. And despite his summons, the sergeant wasn't talking. Jinnah was reluctant to start the conversation. He was searching for a diplomatic way of telling Craig about Mal Singh's warning without giving Graham an aneurysm, but hesitated. Singh hadn't seemed too confident in the Vancouver Police Department's abilities, and it was on this reef the conversation was hopelessly grounded. Finally, he decided on a neutral approach.

"Twice in one day," Jinnah finally broke the silence when they were halfway across. "What's up?"

"My blood pressure," said Graham. "Whatcha got?"

Jinnah gave it to him straight, knowing it could have unpleasant consequences.

"Kabir Shah was Muslim, so Armaan's cremation story is crap."

Graham exhaled for what seemed the first time that day.

"Great. I'm bringing him in."

Jinnah's inherent instincts were at odds. Part of him rejoiced that Graham would provide him with a solid news hook for an exclusive front page story — perhaps the last one the *Tribune* would ever run or that he would ever write. But the greater portion of his being told him this was the wrong move.

"No! Armaan didn't do it! He couldn't have."

"You've got cultural blinkers on, Jinnah. The kid's —"

"No choir boy! But do you really think he has it in him to strangle his father, butcher him, and then bake his body in that oven?"

"Ordinary people do extraordinary things all the time — as you're fond of reminding me. You're just too close to the community —"

"Which is why you asked me to help in the first place, Craig!"

Graham looked away through the port windows at the mouth of False Creek and its sailboats, yachts, and luxury condos. His gut was telling him that Jinnah was right. Armaan really didn't have the stuff it took to commit such a crime. But there were other, far more urgent considerations. Like his career. And other things....

"I'm sorry, Hakeem, but sometimes things are as simple as they seem."

"Armaan's protecting someone."

"And doing a piss-poor job of protecting himself."

"Then I'll go with what I got — 'Dad's Dying Wish: Oh, bury me not!' A *Tribune* exclusive."

"Don't print that! I'm warning you, Jinnah! You don't have the whole picture."

Why do people keep telling me this? Jinnah thought. By now, the Aquabus had made it to the north terminal at the foot of Burrard Street. Jinnah knew that in a matter of seconds the conversation would end.

"Then give me something else!" he pleaded. "*Anything* else! At least tell me when you're making the arrest."

"Can't," said Graham. "You're cut off."

Jinnah stared at his friend, shocked. Name of God, he really meant it this time.

"Is Caitlin Bishop cut off?" he asked suspiciously.

The Aquabus had tied up to the pier. Graham stood and clambered out of the vessel. He didn't look Hakeem in the eye.

"Have fun in Kenya," he said.

"Who's squeezing you, Craig?" Jinnah shouted after the policeman as he walked hurriedly up the dock.

Graham walked straight on. The Aquabus operator cast off and turned his boat around, headed for the far shore. "Gaté, gaté — I am headed for the far shore where there is no remembrance …" The lines floated through Jinnah's mind. But the *Pali Sutra* had never met Nicole Frosty Frost. Now there would be nothing to remember Jinnah by on his newspaper's last front page, save an empty skanda. And that, quite frankly, was not the Jinnah way.

The niceties of Buddhist philosophy were, as Jinnah had expected, quite lost on Frosty as she chewed like a wolverine through his professional hide shortly thereafter at the city desk in front of Clint Eastward and Crystal Wagner. Jinnah could handle Frosty's wrath. But his ruffled professional pride did not appreciate the comments made by the non-reporter chorus.

"You're telling me you wasted an entire shift and have no story to file?"

"Frosty, I have drunk at a thousand wells of silence —"

"After you said 'Trust me, Frosty — just give me a few hours' —"

"One little arrest and he caves. Coward," said Crystal.

"You walk a mile in his Guccis before judging," said Eastward.

"Thank you, Clint —"

"Even if he's an idiot. Hey, I think Armaan did it, Jinnah. It's obvious."

"Armaan didn't do it!"

"Then who did?" demanded Frosty.

"There are larger forces at work here —"

"If Armaan did it, how does that explain the biker belt buckle?" Crystal asked.

Jinnah could have kissed Crystal for hitting the

factual nail on the head, and perhaps a decade earlier might have ventured to do so (in a perfectly politically correct, colleague-like way, of course), but Frosty spoiled the party.

"Jinnah, if you've nothing else to do, I really need that FTR."

Without a word, Jinnah walked over to his terminal like it was the guillotine platform in Paris and sat down. He steeled himself, then typed the dreaded words "For The Record." He stared at them for a few seconds.

"*Apre moi, le deluge*," he muttered.

Before his fingers could further besmirch his professional honour, the television news gave its celebratory fanfare signalling an exclusive story. Jinnah shot a look at the clock on his terminal. Shit! The top of the six o'clock news! He scrambled as fast as his strained ligaments (were they perhaps torn? He should have that checked before he left.) would allow to join Frosty and the rest of city desk as they watched Caitlin Bishop's carefully coiffed hair framed against Vancouver Police headquarters. The subtitles below proclaimed a CXBC exclusive.

"CXBC has learned that new blood evidence has been found that links Armaan Shah to the murder of his father, Kabir Shah …"

Jinnah was acutely aware of every set of eyes in the newsroom burrowing into his back. And the sensation was much sharper and more painful than the Phoenix belt buckle that Mal Singh had given him and was still in his pocket. He was still trying to spin this and figure out exactly how much of what Armaan had told him he could write without Graham hauling him off his flight to Africa for obstruction of justice when things suddenly got worse — way worse.

"... and that set the scene for earlier this afternoon when police moved in ..."

Jinnah and the rest of the *Tribune* newsroom watched as Caitlin's live stand-up dissolved into footage carefully edited to show Graham looking almost tall against the doorway of the Shah mansion, perfectly angled so that when the massive door swung open, Armaan was framed in it. Hakeem knew at a glance that Caitlin had had a great deal of advanced warning to get everything set up so perfectly.

"Armaan Shah. You're under arrest for the murder of your father, Kabir Shah."

Armaan had meekly submitted to the handcuffs, like a lamb to the slaughter. Well, there was no way Jinnah was going to follow suit. He grabbed his leather jacket and microcassette and blasted out of the newsroom. Frosty had just enough time to shout "Jinnah! The retraction!"

"To hell with my retraction!" Jinnah shouted down the hallway. "Caitlin Bishop has a helluva lot to retract right now!"

Frosty and Sanderson watched him go. There was an awkward pause. Everyone knew that Whiteman watched the news in his office and would be out in a moment demanding to know why the *Trib* didn't have this story. In the interim, Sanderson asked, "Does Jinnah realize that Candle owns CXBC?"

Frosty shook her head.

"Jinnah's like a greyhound; when he's on the chase, all he sees is the rabbit running in front of him."

Until the newscast, Jinnah had anticipated his meeting with Caitlin at the Off the Record Club with some pleasure. He liked the club. Its dark wood panelling was festooned with framed cartoons and front pages from Vancouver's print journalism history. The bar itself was like a throwback to Fleet Street, with English bitters and ales prevailing over modern Canadian lagers and the like. Jinnah called it "the bar that time forgot," a place where dinosaurs could (and indeed, metaphorically in the news sense, did) lurk. And he was feeling a bit ancient and fossilized himself when he spotted Caitlin Bishop by the bar, surrounded by admiring fans. He made a beeline for her. She beamed at his approach.

"Jinnah! You didn't forget!"

"No," said Jinnah coldly. "I never forget. Not kindness, nor betrayal."

The corner of the bar where Caitlin had been holding court fell silent. Caitlin's expression changed from shock to hurt to steel so fast Jinnah hardly had time to catalogue them. He steered her into a quiet corner away from the throng. Then unloaded on her.

"Did it ever occur to you that you don't have the whole picture?" he demanded.

"What picture? Armaan's been arrested. I recorded the event. You know what's going on outside of frame? Tell me."

Jinnah had just enough generosity of spirit left to appreciate that it was he who had fed Caitlin that line when she had been a green-behind-the-ears intern afraid to ask a policeman his name. But that's as far as his charity went.

"You realize you've just convicted a man in front of two million viewers?"

"I'm not convicting anyone, as you used to tell me. I report the facts as I find them —"

"Your facts," said Jinnah, remembering the cold shoulder at Puri's shop, "are casting a shadow over an entire community. Remember that."

"Come on, Jinnah —"

"A community wracked with gang and social violence. A community where over one hundred young men have died in gang warfare. Where the scars of the Air India bombing have never healed. And you waltz in there, ignorant of the background —"

"Hakeem, come on — you always taught me that beyond race and culture, everyone is the same! This isn't about ethnicity! It's about a simple case of a spoiled rich kid who wanted to get rich quicker and offed his daddy to spend it on a hot white girlfriend —"

Jinnah found himself running through Armaan's cremation excuse, Mal Singh's information, and his own theories as to how it all fit together, and wondering why he couldn't bring himself to tell Caitlin even a fraction of what he knew the truth was to save his professional credibility. It was not as if he wasn't leaving for Kenya the next day. Or that the *Tribune* might not even exist by the time he got back — if he got back at all. God, he wasn't developing a moral spine at this stage of his career, was he? If so, it was as inconvenient as his recurring malaria. Was it as simple as having been beaten and outmanoeuvred by his former protégé, or was there something more to his objections? And then the line that Graham had used came back to him.

"Caitlin, do you remember me telling you that the truth is a simple thing?"

"Yes. About a hundred times."

"Well I was full of shit. The truth is complicated and depends on where you're standing. Right now I'm standing in the middle of something that is so tangled up I can't even begin to unravel the knots. Yet."

"You're saying the off-screen's that big?" said Caitlin, amused.

"You need an OMNIMAX to capture half of it," replied Jinnah. "You did your job — fine. Same thing I would have done yesterday or the day before. But I'm telling you, my friend, to dig a little deeper while I'm away in Kenya. There are more lives at stake than Armaan's."

"Is yours one of them?"

For the first time since their initial meeting at Main and Linder outside the police tape, Jinnah felt he was talking to his friend Caitlin rather than the TV personality Caitlin Bishop. All pretence had been dropped and she had asked the question with such a quiet voice Hakeem knew he was getting the real goods.

"Look in on Manjit and Saleem while I'm gone, hmm?" he said sliding off his barstool. "And don't be too surprised if Armaan walks."

Caitlin was rooted to her seat.

"Jinnah — don't go! What are you talking about?"

But Jinnah had slipped out the door, leaving Caitlin alone in her seat, a cone of professional silence around her more invulnerable than all the yellow crime scene tape in the world. The ambient noise level of the Off the Record Club returned to normal, but all Caitlin Bishop could hear was a white noise filling her ears.

Manjit was used to Jinnah's moods, God knew, and they had shared many a meal while Hakeem had watched the evening news. Most of the time her husband would be crowing about how he had scooped the electronic media yet again and was even ahead of the Twitterati. But tonight Jinnah simply flipped from channel to channel, watching the arrest of Armaan Shah over and over again. To Manjit, it was exactly the same set of images, the same edit, the same series of interviews repeated endlessly. Caitlin had, after all, got an exclusive, so it wasn't as if there was a different angle from another camera operator to look at or a competing reporter's stand-up to listen to. But to Jinnah, the repetition gleaned important clues as to what had happened. He'd been too upset the first time he'd seen the footage to take in the nuances. Now he saw them: the fact that Bains and Lyall had been there to assist in the arrest and had helped Armaan to the car. The fact that Armaan was completely alone at the time — where had his lawyer been? Or Shauna for that matter? Every camera angle was perfect, as if Caitlin had had time to pre-scout the Shah residence. This had to be linked to what Mal Singh had told him and the RCMP operation he and Graham had stumbled upon — clearly the New Corporate Kids on the Block were involved. But why would Graham do this to him? Why hadn't Hakeem told his best police contact about Mal Singh's warning? Did Manjit and Saleem need police protection while he was in Kenya? Name of God, did Jinnah himself need a bodyguard? He was still trying to construct a logical scenario when Manjit broke his chain of thought.

"Hakeem, I don't know if you have had time to talk to Ronald about our story —"

"Story?" cried Jinnah. "Since when does Sanderson write health news?"

"Since you assigned him to assist me. Threads — remember?"

Jinnah did remember, but that seemed like a very long time ago. He knew if he didn't give Manjit at least part of his attention now, he would have to give most or all of it later. So he switched to a sort of obsession auto-pilot, pushing the Shah case and Caitlin Bishop not precisely to the very back of his mind, but at least far enough for Manjit to sit in the front row of his frontal lobes.

"I remember threads," he admitted, "but it takes more than one to weave a story, Manjit."

"We have found a second," said Manjit proudly. "We have found the source of the pesticide that is making the farm workers sick."

"Fantastic!" said Jinnah with genuine enthusiasm. "Was it Dow Chemical? Dupont? Monsanto?"

"No. A local firm called Black Sea Imports."

Jinnah tried hard to control the look of disappointment mingled with amusement that threatened to sweep across his face. Black Sea Imports? Who would sue them? When it came to chemical poisoning, a page one story demanded one of the big players screwing up, not some small-time local supplier. Still, it might be a good enough yarn for the six-inch hole around page twelve known as "city-one," which Sanderson pretty much owned. He tried his best to look supportive.

"And did you get a sample of this pesticide?"

"No," frowned Manjit. "They refused. I even told them I was with the public health system. But Ronald called the agriculture ministry and they have promised to look into it."

"Well that is a very good start, my love."

Jinnah forced himself to utter this pronouncement with a sort of strangulated enthusiasm. In his care, even a routine promise to "look into it" could be carefully nurtured into a full-blown government investigation into a shocking misuse of a dangerous pesticide. Sanderson would qualify everything, back into the lede, and produce the careful, correct, but ultimately bland prose that would result in poor play or far more likely Frosty spiking the story with a single derisive snort. Considering his familial duty done, Hakeem slipped back into his tortured theorizing on what had happened to turn Sergeant Craig Graham against him and allow Caitlin to scoop him. He was making absolutely no progress when he became aware of Manjit standing in front of him.

"Hakeem, you know if you gave Ronald some coaching, he could produce a much better story …"

"Manjit —" Jinnah growled in warning.

"… one that might make the authorities actually do something about this problem."

"I am not going to waste my time trying to make Ronald a better writer!" snapped Jinnah. "It is like trying to teach a hyena to roar like a lion: he will try his hardest but the best he will do is cough up a hairball."

"People's lives are at stake, Hakeem," said Manjit with extreme patience.

"I don't care! My leave of absence has started as of now and nothing is going to stop me from becoming Kenya's burger king. I'm not leaving this couch until it's time to head for the airport."

"Nothing?" said Manjit sweetly.

"Nothing and nobody," insisted Jinnah. "I've had enough bad things happen to me for one day for God's sake. There isn't a man alive who can pry my bony brown butt from this sofa!"

These words sealed Jinnah's fate. The phone was ringing even as he spoke them. Saleem (who, as the household teenager, claimed a monopoly on the phone, even though he had his own cell) entered holding the cordless device with a scowl.

"Dad. For you."

"If it's the city desk they can kiss my —"

"Hakeem!"

"It's Mr. Puri, Dad!"

The defiant roar died in Jinnah's throat and dissolved into something like a hyena with a hairball. He stared at the phone in Saleem's hand like it was an owl from Varanasi. Whatever Puri wanted of him couldn't be good. But of course he snatched it from his son and tried to sound cheerful. After a moment, he hung up and abandoned all such pretences. Slowly, he rose to his feet and grabbed his jacket off the back of the chair.

"It's awfully early to be heading for the airport yet, isn't it Hakeem?" said Manjit, suppressing a smile.

"I have to see Mr. Puri," said Jinnah resignedly.

"I thought —"

"I am a man of my word," said Jinnah, kissing her on the forehead. "Don't wait up," he added, slipping out the back door.

Jinnah *was* a man of his word. No living man had pried him from the couch. But he hadn't counted on the last wish of a dead man rising up to bite him on his bony brown ass.

The gauntlet of hostiles outside Mr. Puri's shop this evening included Probir and his mates. There were no good-natured jokes about franchises and shares, just cold disdain as Jinnah approached. Probir turned up his ghetto-blaster, blaring bhangra music at top volume to drown out any possible conversation. Jinnah had simply pushed past them and into the store. He found

Puri at his table at the back, but this time there was no hot, steaming cup of chai upon it. Instead, there was a small, curious aluminum case that Jinnah's inherent instincts took an instant dislike to. Puri looked grave on the surface, but there was a twinkle in his eyes that suggested no small part of him was enjoying this — whatever "this" was.

"Mr. Puri, *namaste*," Jinnah salaamed. "You spoke of vital business?"

Puri handed Jinnah a printed email. It was from Kabir Shah's cousin Mohammed.

"As you can see, Mr. Jinnah, Kabir's final wish was to be buried in Tanzania."

Jinnah didn't like where this was going. But his inherent instincts were tingling — a sure sign that, however unlikely it might appear at the moment, he was on the right track.

"I am sure his family has the capacity to fulfill his wish, Mr. Puri," he replied, stalling.

"That is true. But as a Muslim, you know that the deceased must be interned as soon as possible. Fortunately, both the police and the airlines are very understanding in these cases."

Puri patted the aluminum case gently. Name of God, he can't mean it.... Jinnah gave in and asked the question that his instincts demanded and his greed dreaded.

"Mr. Puri, did Kabir Shah's business in Tanzania have anything to do with his murder?"

"Who knows?" Puri sighed. "There is only one way to find out. The family will be happy to meet with you personally should you choose to call upon them on your way to Kenya."

Jinnah's self-interest genes were on red alert.

"On my way? Tanzania is not exactly on the way to Nairobi, Mr. Puri. Besides, surely the police should interview Mr. Shah's family."

"Ah, but they already have their murderer, do they not?"

There was an awkward pause. Jinnah's flight-or-flight instincts were debating among themselves, paralyzing him. In the interval, Puri simply picked up the case and handed it to him.

"It is but a small detour. Kabir won't mind."

Jinnah goggled at the case he was holding, trying desperately to block the image of what it contained from his mind's eye — and failing miserably.

"But Mr. Puri — I couldn't —"

"Do not worry, Jinnah," said Puri, smiling openly now. "All has been arranged. It is, as you would say, a small sacrifice."

Jinnah closed his eyes and did a quick calculation. The old proverb said bad things happened in threes. By his count, this day alone had already brought six and it wasn't over yet. Jinnah muttered his thanks to Mr. Puri and left before a new set came around and unlucky number seven could catch him.

The aluminum case was sitting on Jinnah's kitchen table late into the night like a bag of live cobras, its dull metallic surface dimly reflecting Hakeem's figure as he paced back and forth, unlit cigarette in his hand, wad of nicotine gum in his mouth, and a vortex of conflicting emotions running through his mind. For perhaps the tenth time, he stopped in front of the case and addressed it directly.

"I am not chasing all over Africa with your ashes just so your soul can rest in peace!"

The suitcase's silence seemed to be a rebuke. He stabbed his cigarette at it to underscore his point.

"Listen! I am going to Kenya! I'm the African Burger Palace king!"

It was all too much: Armaan's confession, Graham's treachery, Caitlin's cupidity, and the prospect of the *Tribune* being bought out and merged. Through it all, Jinnah had clung to the one straw keeping his bundle of neuroses afloat: his leave of absence and trip to Africa. And not just Africa, but Kenya. It was a good six hundred kilometres from Nairobi to the Tanzanian capital of Dar es Salaam — a distance that would have to be travelled using small, regional airlines, unreliable buses, and over dangerous terrain. It would take days — possibly even weeks. He would lose his one chance at wealth and success. Every nerve in his body was crying out for a soothing hit of nicotine to calm them. Then he would be able to think and find a way out of this predicament. But what of Frosty and the bet?

"To hell with Frosty!" he grunted.

Jinnah fished inside his pockets and found his lighter. A flame leapt eagerly from the flint. He was just about to light up when Manjit glided silently into the room, plucked the cigarette from his mouth, and flipped his lighter closed in a single, graceful motion.

"Is this a séance, Hakeem?"

"In the sense that I am communing with what used to be my so-called career, yes," said Jinnah, collapsing onto a kitchen chair and staring hatefully at the aluminum case.

Manjit sat next to him.

"Your career is not over because there was one shift when you didn't file a story."

"It's more than that, my love," said Jinnah miserably. "The *Tribune* —"

"Isn't sold yet. It must stay in business long enough for Ronald and I to get to the bottom of this pesticide business. And for you to come home with the answers to why Mr. Shah was murdered."

Jinnah looked at his wife, amazed. She was so calm, so serene, so … certain! How did she do that?

"Even if by some miracle the paper is still publishing when I return, after today I'm not certain I want to go back. Did I tell you even Probir snubbed me at Puri's shop? And the looks I got at the market! Don't they understand I am just the messenger here?"

"They blame you for the message, Hakeem. You know that."

Jinnah looked longingly at the cigarette Manjit was twirling around in her lithe brown fingers. He popped yet another piece of gum into his bloated mouth.

"After fifteen years, you'd think I'd learn. Fifteen years of cloak and dagger and covering my ass. I don't want to play anymore."

Manjit put her arms around his shoulders. She whispered softly into his ear.

"Hakeem, you know you won't be at rest until you solve this case. You can't let an innocent man go to prison. Isn't catching a murderer worth more than all the Burger Palaces in Kenya?"

Jinnah wavered. His vestigial conscience was beginning to develop real spine (or at least something akin to a Pikaia). He made one last attempt at a plea bargain with his own private Portia.

"But what if the *Trib* does close, hmm? If I miss out on the burger business opportunity, we could be ruined. Lose our house, my van...."

Manjit lifted her head and fixed Jinnah firmly with her eyes.

"Hakeem, do you remember the quote from Hafiz?"

Jinnah knew exactly what quote she was talking about. He had used it on his wife often when he considered her anxieties over Saleem's marks or when her own aging process went beyond the bounds of reason (or, even worse, interfered with his own, very real hypochondria). *Now that all your worry has proved such an unlucrative business / Why not find a better job?* Ah curse that Persian poet. He was too smart for the Mighty Jinnah-ji. He tenderly lifted Manjit's arms from around his neck and stood up. He reached inside his pocket and pulled out the Phoenix Gang buckle Mal Singh had given him and placed it on the aluminum case like a talisman.

"What is that?" asked Manjit.

"Something else I have to bring with me to Dar es Salaam," said Jinnah.

Chapter Five

Jinnah stepped off the somewhat unsteady stairs of the battered Hawker Siddeley that had carried him from Nairobi to the crumbling, weed-choked tarmac of what was rather optimistically called Morogoro International Airport in Tanzania and into a furnace. Rust-coloured dust kicked up by the aircraft formed a ragged column rising into the brilliant blue African sky. Still sweating nicotine from every pore, the habitual hypochondriac walked through the gauntlet of goats, chickens, and other barely domesticated animals that had wandered back onto the landing strip the moment the airplane's engines had stopped coughing oil from their cowlings. He was entering the land of onchocerciasis, schistosomiasis, soil-transmitted helminthiasis, and trachoma. If he was really lucky, he might catch the near-fatal Tanzanian Laughing Disease.

Peering through the blazing sun, he took in the airport buildings. A run-down collection of wooden shacks with faded signage in English, Swahili, and German. The people milling about in the scant shade offered by the structures looked like locals: some in white *kanzu* robes, coal-black women dressed in brightly coloured *kanga* wraps, and men in traditional *kikois*. Sprinkled among them were stationary brown cows, studiously ignoring the white cowbirds flitting from bovine back to back. It was, together with the heat, an assault on the senses and neuroses of the primary patient of the *Tribune*'s sick leave program, overwhelming smell, sight, hearing, and taste. It would have conquered touch as well, had Jinnah dared to handle anything other than the holy aluminum case containing Kabir Shah's remains, which he clutched to his chest like an amulet. He took all of this in and did the only thing he could think of that felt appropriate, given the circumstances.

He smiled. He was home.

The contradiction was not lost on Jinnah. Here he was, in defiance of his ancestral avarice, far from his business meetings in Nairobi, in a country where he was almost certain to contract lymphatic filariasis, and he felt happy. He was being driven by two interrelated promises: one to a dead man's best friend and the other to Frosty. In delivering Mr. Shah's mortal remains, he hoped to unearth a truly killer front page story — one that, if the *Tribune* was to be sold/merged/swallowed up by Candle Communications, would be worthy of the paper's Great Big Three-Zero. Here in the region of his childhood, his inherent instincts told him he would get the goods and return to the newsroom in triumph.

This feeling of optimism and hope carried Jinnah right through customs, where there was a minor hurdle to overcome. Hakeem had eyed the tall, imposing customs officer as the line had moved closer and closer to the official, taking him in, trying to judge his character. Unlike almost everyone else in the airport, the gateway guardian was not smiling. So Jinnah was prepared when he got to the counter and was asked in perfect English (laced with just a hint of bureaucratic suspicion) whether he had anything to declare.

"No," he said, his own voice carefully neutral, betraying none of his inner anxiety.

"What have you got in your carry-on, sir?" the customs officer asked, eyes narrowing with suspicion at the aluminum case.

"This?" said Jinnah in mock surprise. "A dead body, actually."

Jinnah laughed at his own audacious honesty. The ploy had the desired effect. The customs officer smiled for the first time since Jinnah had seen him. He looked Hakeem in the eye in a time-honoured and knowing way. Now his voice too was carefully neutral.

"Are you sure, sir? It is illegal to bring 'dead body' into Tanzania. If you have human remains in that case, you would be fined."

Here too Jinnah found himself on familiar ground. Certain he knew what they were really discussing, he pulled out his wallet.

"How much would this hypothetical fine be, officer?"

"How much 'dead body' are you bringing in?"

"About two kilograms."

They settled on a fine of one hundred dollars (U.S. dollars, much to Jinnah's chagrin) before the customs official smiled, stamped Hakeem's passport, and said with every appearance of sincerity, "Welcome to Tanzania, Mr. Jinnah!"

It was only when he reached the terminal's arrivals area that Jinnah had finally started to feel a little overwhelmed. Things started out well enough. He was used to the humanity, the chaos, and unrestrained hustling that went on just outside the building's doors and the soundscape created by the hucksters competing for his attention by shouting in Swahili, Arabic, and English. He brushed past a woman trying to sell him a carving of Zanzibar's Stone Town and another offering slightly used postcards of the Serengeti. Then he was propelled past a group of teens who were cooking *senene*. The savoury, meaty smell transported him back to his childhood, when he had devoured the fried grasshoppers by the pound while playing the Italian card game *Scopa* in Hashmi's restaurant. Hakeem and his fellow *Muhindis* were a mix of Hindus, Sikhs, Muslims, and Christians, but they all got on well enough. Happy times. He was so transported back in time that he didn't notice the swarm of children around him until it was too late.

"*Kubeba mfuko wako*, sir? Carry your bag sir? *Tragen sie ihre tasche, mein herr*?"

A small black hand tugged at his suitcase. Another made a grab for the aluminum ossuary. Startled out of his nostalgia, Jinnah bolted through the crowd, only to come face-to-face with a boa constrictor.

"Beautiful pet, bwana — for wife missus!"

Jinnah froze. The snake flicked its tongue at him. He barely registered the vendor, a man wearing a white turban. The pause gave both the baggage kids and the stone-carving woman time to encircle him. So this is how it ends — not by schistosomiasis, but by boa constrictor. He was an island amidst a swirling knot of people poking and prodding him, unable to tear his gaze from the reptilian eyes, when he heard a voice boom over the din.

"Taxi! Taxi, sir!"

Jinnah instantly recognized the French-tinged accent of a Burundian. He turned to see a hulking cabby in dusty khaki shorts cutting through the crowd like a guardian angel. Hakeem instantly took a liking to the man, who scattered the mob before him like King Cambarantama. His shining white smile was reassuring and Jinnah allowed him to take his luggage and lead the way, slicing a swath through the throng.

"*Nini jina lako?* What's your name?" Jinnah asked.

"Egide," rumbled the giant Burundian.

"Egide, take me to the Hotel Tanganyika."

Egide merely grunted and led Jinnah to his cab. To Hakeem's surprise, his enormous cabby's vehicle was an ancient Austin Mini which sank almost to the road surface when he wedged himself behind the driver's seat. Crammed into the back, Jinnah was oblivious to scenes of rural life unfolding outside the dirty windows. He wanted to assess the situation he was entering and was desperate for information. So as they drove, he worked his satellite phone, hoping his local contact

(Mohammed Shah, Kabir's cousin) had left at message for him at the front desk. No such luck.

"Are you sure?" Jinnah shouted into the phone as the cab rattled along a road composed almost entirely of potholes. "I'm expecting a message from Mohammed Shah —"

Egide had been eying his customer through the rear-view mirror while discreetly listening to his conversation. If his fare had no immediate need to check in to his hotel, he had an alternative.

"I will take you to Zanzibar first. Everyone must see Zanzibar," he declared.

"I don't want to go to Zanzibar! Take me to my hotel!" Jinnah shouted.

Egide had merely shrugged, but it had taken Jinnah five minutes to convince the front desk of the Hotel Tanganyika that he wasn't going to Zanzibar and would indeed be checking into his room very soon, Allah willing. As he hung up, Egide hit a pothole so vast it threatened to swallow the cab whole and shook Jinnah's teeth to their roots.

"Can't you get shocks for this thing, for God's sake?" he complained.

Egide laughed.

"Shocks? I can't even get brakes!"

Jinnah's knuckles tightened around the handle of the aluminum case.

"Tell my wife I died with her name on my lips," he muttered.

* * *

The Hotel Tanganiyka had seen better days — none of them very recently. From the second Egide's taxi had lurched to an uneven stop in front of the once-white plaster walls, Jinnah had an uneasy feeling about the place. It didn't help matters when he was swarmed by another crowd of hawkers, kids, and baggage beggars the moment Egide opened the door for him.

"That will be fifty dollars U.S., sir," said Egide breezily.

Before Jinnah could protest that this was highway robbery, one of the more agile baggage beggars slipped between Egide's massive form and the cab to grab Hakeem's bags and darted toward the hotel doors.

"Hey! Give those back!"

Jinnah hadn't meant to roar, but what with all he'd been through in the past few days, his cry of frustration and rage came out at full volume. It even startled Egide.

"Okay — for you, twenty bucks!" he said apologetically.

Jinnah tossed a double sawbuck at the cabby before pushing roughly through the crowd in pursuit of his bags. Egide gave the bill a glance, dispersed the knot of peddlers in front of his vehicle with a single belligerent Burundian scowl, and roared off back toward the airport.

It took Jinnah only a moment to recover his luggage. The baggage beggar had taken it straight to the front desk and was waiting for him amidst the faded colonial decor, wilting palm plants, and greying whitewashed plaster walls. So intent was Hakeem on his prey that he didn't even notice the large man with the fierce greying beard half-covering his flowing white *kanzu* robe sitting on the threadbare sofa.

"Give me my bags!" he growled at the beggar.

"It is customary to tip the baggage boys a few shillings, sir."

Jinnah looked up and was met with the reserved but steely gaze of the front-desk clerk, an ageless, immaculate man who might have been an African Jeeves. The clerk's dignified manner and firm insistence brooked no argument and the beggar smiled broadly as he held out his hand.

"I haven't got any shillings!" Jinnah protested.

"American currency is also acceptable, sir."

Jinnah was fumbling with his wallet when the man from the sofa appeared by his side and flipped a couple of fifty-shilling pieces expertly into the beggar's hand. The boy skipped out happily, clutching his rhino-emblazoned coins, while Jinnah surveyed his saviour. The man's hands were together in a traditional salaam.

"*Karibu*, Mr. Jinnah."

"*Nafurahi kukuona*, Mohammed Shah," replied Jinnah, his Swahili coming back to him easily. "I'm sorry we have to meet under such sad circumstances."

Mohammed Shah smiled cheerlessly and eyed Jinnah's luggage.

"Which of these contains the remains of my unfortunate cousin?"

Jinnah followed Shah's gaze and froze. Sonofabitch! The aluminum case wasn't there: it was still in Egide's cab and probably halfway to Zanzibar by now. Name of God, the cabby was likely selling the ashes as an aphrodisiac in Stone Town for all he knew. He felt weak and feverish. He coughed and his bowels had a loose, liquid feeling — perhaps it was schistosomiasis after all. To come all this way merely to die of Snail Fever, for God's sake ...

"Jinnahman!"

Whirling about, Jinnah — to his immense relief — saw the massive form of Egide striding across the hotel lobby toward him bearing the precious aluminum suitcase. His hands shook slightly as he accepted the case from the cabby and, muttering a silent prayer of thanks, passed it in turn to Mohammed Shah. The elderly man ran his own trembling fingers over the smooth, hard surface and whispered an Islamic benediction.

"*Innaa Ilayhi Wa Innaa Ilayhi Raaji'oon.*"

Jinnah, of course, knew the words by heart: "Verily we belong to Allah and will return to Allah." He was moved as he turned to Egide.

"Thank you, my friend — or should I say, my driver, hmm?"

Egide smiled and shook Jinnah's hand.

"I am at your service, Jinnahman," he rumbled.

Jinnah handed his new employee fifty U.S. dollars.

"Then you can start by giving Sayyid Shah a lift back home if he needs it."

"I must return to the mosque and would be most grateful for the ride," replied Shah. "You will honour us with your presence this afternoon, Mr. Jinnah?"

"I have travelled halfway around the world for the privilege, my friend. *Asalaamu alekum.*"

"And upon you peace, Mr. Jinnah."

Having finally delivered Kabir Shah's remains safely, Jinnah felt immensely relieved — and immensely weary. He was too tired to even banter with the front desk Jeeves as he received his room key and firm instructions on which wing he had been ensconced in. He almost walked right past the two men at the hotel bar just a few steps from the elevators. They were sitting on high barstools, nursing what looked to be identical gin and tonics. One was a tweedy-looking Brit with thinning hair and the perpetual sunburned tan indicative of a transplanted Northern European. Business-type, a shilling a dozen in Tanzania, and Jinnah wouldn't have even registered that much had it not been for the man he was sitting next to. Immaculate, blond, buff Eastern European Mafioso clone. And strangely familiar. Hakeem took this all in with a single weary, wary glance and continued on to the elevators. It was not until the wheezing, groaning device had carried him unwillingly to the third floor and the wrought-iron grates of the aged doors has squeaked open that Jinnah placed him. In a flash of memory as clear as a surveillance picture, he saw the man's face outside a very different bar two continents away. It was one of the two suits he and Clint Eastward had bumped into in front of Fogduckers.

"Holy shit!" he gasped.

Surely he was wrong? What would Blondie be doing here in Tanzania? Surely the son of a bitch hadn't followed him all the way here? Or had he? A number of scenarios instantly formed in Jinnah's head. None of them were pleasant. He fumbled with the room key and was shaking badly by the time he managed to get the door open, his bags inside, and his butt on the bed. The glory of the view of the garden courtyard of Hotel Taganyika was lost on him as he shivered on the bedside. He thought of having a cigarette — he'd brought a pack, hoping hourly to get a text or email from Sanderson reporting that Frosty had caved and he could fill his lungs with the satisfying deep-blue smoke. He even managed to somehow wrestle the bag containing his darts onto the bed. He was over fifteen thousand kilometres away from the newsroom, for God's sake! Frosty would never know. He scrabbled at the catches on the case, cursing as he tried to remember where he had hidden his suitcase keys, then stopped. He looked around. Frosty may not be watching, he thought, but News God was. The fickle deity that ruled the fate of all good reporters was omniscient. It would be very bad journo-karma if he lost the bet with his supervising editor and lied about it. News God would be angry, and if Blondie had really followed Jinnah to Tanizania, he needed all the good karma he could get.

"Sonofabitch," he muttered, resignedly shoving another piece of nicotine gum into his mouth.

"Bismillah hir-rahmaan nir-raheem …"

The words of the imam floated in the air and filled the courtyard of the Mosque Yousef Alihaji — a small but elegant structure where the Faithful had gathered to pay their last respects to Kabir Shah. The remains Jinnah had so reluctantly brought to Tanzania were now wrapped in a white cloth. In front of the funereal bundle was a picture of Kabir and a beautiful young woman. Jinnah had been puzzling over her identity as he stood amongst the men at the front of the crowd of mourners. As the prayers rolled on, he risked the odd glance behind him to where the women stood at the rear. It was right on the edge of propriety, but he tried to disguise his surreptitious snooping by rubbing and twisting his neck in a manner he hoped would be suggestive of a stiffness brought on by a series of long flights.

It was at the point where Mohammed Shah was casting glances of his own in Hakeem's direction that Jinnah spotted her. It was difficult to tell because of the veil, but he was certain the young woman in the very front rank of the female mourners was the same as the smiling woman next to Shah in the photograph. Up to this point, Jinnah had been obsessing over what possible connection Blondie, Fogduckers, and the unnamed Brit had to this business and kept coming up with blanks. Even softly rubbing the Phoenix Club biker buckle in his pocket had failed to conjure the necessary insight. Now a new mystery had presented itself and part of Jinnah's mind was telling him to forget everything, bail now, and get back to Nairobi where a new life as the King of Burger Palace was awaiting him. But his inherent instincts, which had been lying low the past few days, were finally over their jet lag and screaming that this was important: possibly the key to the whole crime. Well, now was not the time to start interviewing people. But Jinnah knew he would get a chance, and soon, so he tried to focus on his duty to the charred dead before grilling the living. He closed his eyes and whispered along with the imam as he intoned the Takbeer.

"Oh Allah! Forgive those of us that are alive and those of us that are dead; those of us that are present and those of us who are absent; those of us who are young and those of us who are adults; our males and our females. Oh Allah! Whomsoever You keep alive, let him live as a follower of Islam and whomsoever You cause to die, let him die a Believer."

The funeral banquet following the rites of internment was sumptuous. Tables were laden with all kinds of foods — many of them favourites from Jinnah's childhood — and the small room off the side of the mosque was crowded with friends and relatives helping themselves to the feast. But Jinnah's nervous stomach was closed and he was completely obsessed with his pursuit of the mystery woman in the photograph. In Vancouver, it would have been a simple matter, but here, with the women veiled and the husbands protective (not to mention the brothers, uncles, and others who were always close at hand), his search was in a cultural bind. Try as he might, he could not spot the woman he'd glimpsed in the courtyard. After his fourth attempt to look deeply into a veiled young woman's eyes (an attempt that he had hastily aborted when the woman in question caught his eye, looked away, and moved pointedly closer to her husband), Jinnah abandoned his indirect strategy. He decided that, time and circumstances being what they were, a full-frontal approach was called for. He spotted Mohammed Shah and placed himself between Kabir's cousin and the banquet table.

"My friend," he said quietly. "I must ask: who was the young woman in the photograph?"

Mohammed Shah looked at Jinnah for one of those brief eternal moments where the reporter knew the man was sizing him up, deciding if he could really trust him and whether or not to take him into his confidence. It was one of those intervals that proved Einstein's theory that time was a relative construct conclusively, for Jinnah felt he had aged ten years before Shah replied.

"How much do you know about my cousin?"

"A great deal about his business — not much about his personal life," admitted Jinnah. "Is this woman a relation of some kind?"

Shah turned to face Jinnah squarely, put his hands on Hakeem's shoulders and leaned close, speaking very softly.

"It is a delicate matter, Mr. Jinnah. After Kabir's first wife, Armaan's mother, died in Canada ... well ... my cousin came home for a year. He secretly remarried here. The love of his life."

Jinnah saw the whole thing flash in front of his eyes like one of Caitlin Bishop's exclusive news pieces (with, of course, much more taste and depth than one normally associates with TV news): Kabir Shah in the courtyard with his veiled bride, the woman from the picture, the funeral transformed into a wedding.

The guests crowding the happy couple.... The implications were staggering.

"You mean he had a whole other life over here?" Jinnah whispered hoarsely.

Mohammed Shah nodded and continued to stare Jinnah in the eye, as if challenging him to say something: pass judgment, throw stones, flowers ...

"Does Armaan know?"

This was probably the right response. Mohammed Shah straightened up, turned to face the crowd of fellow mourners, and said in a normal (if somewhat formal) voice, "Now is not the time to discuss this. I'll talk to the family to see how forthcoming we can be with you. We want Kabir's killer caught, of course, but — there are other considerations as well. Come to my office tonight."

Jinnah smiled and salaamed.

"You will excuse me until then, Sayyid Shah."

Jinnah walked out of the gathering like a man tied to a great wheel of fire, not knowing the exact nature of the flames tormenting him. As he left, the dark, soft eyes of a young woman who had been hiding behind a knot of male relatives followed him on his way out, silently and secretly fanning the blaze consuming his mind.

"Can you believe it? The old guy had a teenage bride!"

Egide's cab hit a crater that sent Jinnah shooting up to the Mini's roof, giving him a sharp smack to the head, which he took to be Allah's way of rewarding him for speaking ill of the dead. The Burundian shook with laughter, adding to the taxi's general rattle and roll.

"Maybe that's what really killed him!" he chortled.

Egide's mirth was cut short by the gleam of headlights reflecting off the rear-view mirror. His smile vanished.

"Jinnahman," he growled. "We're being followed."

Jinnah whirled around in his cramped automotive womb and stared out the back into the black African night. He was instantly blinded by the highbeams of a vehicle behind them.

"Are you sure?" he asked, rubbing his eyes and willing his cones to transform into rods.

"This white guy's been on our ass for a half-hour," snapped Egide. "At the speed I'm going, any self-respecting African would have passed us by now. He's driving a Land Rover, you know."

"White guy?"

Jinnah's eyes might be blind, but his mind had a sharp, clear image of Blondie and the Brit seated at the hotel bar. Could it be one of them? Both? Or someone else?

"Sonofabitch!" muttered Jinnah.

"Don't worry. I'll lose him."

"Lose him?" piped Jinnah, who was familiar with the operational limitations of an Austin Mini — especially compared to a Land Rover. "In this hamster-driven toy?"

But Egide had made a few modifications to his vehicle to accommodate his weight and outrun the local constabulary, bandits, and poachers. He floored it and the Mini took off like a rocket.

"Name of God!" cried Jinnah. "What are you feeding those hamsters? Crack?"

Egide grinned silently as he kept one eye in the rearview mirror, watching as their pursuer matched every swerve he made along the rough, winding road barely lit by a sullen half-moon. Jinnah pulled out the Phoenix belt buckle and stroked it like a holy relic. He was about to plead/order Egide to slow down when they came around the corner and face to bumper with a herd of cattle in the moonlight.

"Perfect!" cried Egide, speeding up.

Perfect? How could this be perfect, unless Egide had always dreamed of dying in a high-speed collision with a cow? But before he could articulate this sentiment, the bulky Burundian hurled his vehicle through a gap between two cows just big enough to accommodate the Mini. The herd, startled, closed ranks and stampeded up the road in the opposite direction. Through the rear window, Jinnah caught a fleeting glimpse of the Land Rover screeching to a halt, frozen in a sea of mooing cattle, soon lost in the swirling red dust plume that was the flag marking their escape.

The curious thing about a bar is the intangibles that give you comfort. The goal of any bar, anywhere in the world, is to make the customer feel at home. Whether it's the decor or the service, something aside from the universal affect of alcohol on the central nervous system has to make a direct connection with whoever is sitting on the chair/barstool/sofa. Jinnah thought he had found it in the bartender's store of light banter and the Black Dog Indian scotch behind the Hotel Tanganyika's bar. The fact that the TV was tuned to CNN International helped. Almost all the news was from the U.S. point of view about Africa and the Middle East, but it was close enough to home for him to feel thankful. As he sipped his straight double and fought the overwhelming urge to light up, he scanned the hotel lobby for signs of Blondie and the Brit. He thought of phoning Manjit, but decided to wait until his nerves were not quite so shot. He tried to breathe deeply: yes, he was far from home and might be in danger. Yes, his unreasonable pursuit of a killer might endanger his own financial hopes and dreams. But Jinnah was comforted by the thought that at least here he was miles ahead of any competition: his pain was in exact proportion to the lead he had on the pack and Caitlin Bishop. News God, being a jealous deity, decided to punish him for his presumptuousness. Just as he finished the single of his single malt and started on the double portion, CNN let blast a fanfare that Jinnah recognized all too clearly.

"And now for a CNN International Exclusive ..."

Jinnah sat bolt upright, spilling drams of the eighteen-year-old whisky onto his knuckles. They burned his skin silently as he watched the screen fill up with the CXBC logo (and the disclaimer that this was a CNN International Affiliate, in association with Candle Communications, in very small print near the bottom of the frame). The Black Dog was biting his master as Caitlin Bishop's carefully crafted visage came into view underneath a superimposed legend: "Breaking news in pizza oven murder."

Jinnah had just enough time to take in the background — the B.C. Supreme Court building in downtown Vancouver, ground floor, right in front of the elevators — before Caitlin started her stand-up. The piece unfolded like a well-rehearsed scene from a play that Hakeem had seen many times before, but never so beautifully choreographed. There was not a single competing microphone in sight as Caitlin began.

"The bizarre nature of this murder has attracted worldwide attention to this Vancouver courthouse as accused pizza oven murderer Armaan Shah ..."

At this precise minute the doors of the elevator on the left-hand side of the shot opened and Armaan appeared in handcuffs, escorted by two nameless sheriffs and the scowling figure of Bains.

"... pleaded not guilty to charges of first degree murder and offering indignity to a corpse ..."

The bastards leading Armaan had even held him still long enough for a nice, slow close-up of the poor bugger. Then, as if as by some pre-arranged signal, Armaan had disappeared down another elevator as Caitlin wrapped up her stand-up.

"But police and the Crown say the case against this young man accused of killing his own father to get at his untold wealth is strong. Caitlin Bishop —"

Jinnah snapped as the channel was changed to the more rewarding image of the latest cricket results. It was too much of a test for Vancouver's toughest crime reporter. He had to know what was happening on the home front.

"*Bili tafadhali*," he croaked as the tail of the Black Dog gnawed at his throat.

In his room, Jinnah paced back and forth, satellite phone crooked in his shoulder. The pack of cigarettes on the bed beckoned to him. No, he would be strong. Manjit's voice would be more soothing than any hit of nicotine. If he could *hear* Manjit's voice — the space-time continuum and/or stratosphere weren't cooperating.

"Hello? Hello!" he barked down the delicate electronic device as if it was a long, hollow tube. "Manjit?"

"Hello?"

His wife's disembodied voice had a profound impact on Jinnah. He felt like laughing and sobbing simultaneously — his stress was as indecisive as Sanderson dithering over his lede. But he held it together. It wouldn't do to let Manjit know he was scared to death. He needed her calm reassurance, not her alarm.

"My love!" he said, voice thick with a false bravado. "Are you all right?"

"Of course ... why do ... Jinnah?"

Sonofabitch. So much for wasting the shareholders' money on communications technology.

"Manjit? You're breaking up!"

"I ... fine ... there?"

Sweat composed of water, salt, and scotch broke out on Jinnah's forehead. Name of God! Maybe it was the concrete shell of the hotel. The phone had to work better on the balcony where it was open to the sky. He took a step toward it, spied the cigarette pack on the bed, stopped. No. No. Frosty would kill him — what was he thinking? Someone was already trying to kill him! This would be the equivalent of a last cigarette before the firing squad. Even News God wouldn't begrudge him that. He scooped up the pack and stepped out onto the tiny balcony.

"Manjit? Are you still there?"

"Jinnah, you will never believe it ..."

Ah! That was better. Faint, but strong. The exact opposite of his nerves at the moment.

"Has anyone called from Nairobi?" he shouted. "Have I any messages?"

"Hakeem, there's no need to yell at me!"

"I am sorry, my love — the connection is bad."

Jinnah cursed inwardly in several languages at once. The last thing he wanted was to upset Manjit.

"Your cousin called," Manjit continued. "But that's not the important thing —"

"Not important?" Jinnah cried, forgetting the danger he was in, the Shah case, Caitlin Bishop, and the *Trib*'s imminent demise. "What could possibly be more important?"

"I found out what was making everyone sick!"

Jinnah closed his eyes. Here he was, in mortal

danger, two continents away, his Burger Palace dreams crumbling around him, and his wife was still worried about farm workers. Not that Jinnah was willing to tell her any of this — he simply expected her to know it by osmosis.

"That's great!" he said with a forced cheerfulness. "About my cousin —"

"It turned out to be heroin."

"Say what?"

To Jinnah, it sounded like his wife was on drugs. Heroin? Had the farm workers been shooting up on the job?

"Yes, heroin!" said Manjit triumphantly. "Remember the pesticide being sprayed on the fields?"

"Of course."

"Well, the lab work came back and showed traces of heroin mixed in with the pesticide that Black Sea Imports supplied to the pilot —"

"Black Sea Imports?"

Jinnah's mind put his imminent death, the collapse of his financial future, and even his nicotine cravings in the cerebral equivalent of the trash folder. Black Sea Imports. Blondie. The RCMP probe. Fogduckers. Neurons that had lived lonely, separate lives were starting to network.

"How did you trace the pesticide to Black Sea Imports?" Jinnah demanded, wriggling his shoulder to get a more comfortable position.

"I didn't!" Manjit laughed. "Ronald did. He even confronted them —"

"You're kidding!" Jinnah guffawed. "Ronald?"

"Hakeem, Ronald has owned the front page in your absence."

This was too much. Ronald Sanderson owning the front page of the *Tribune*? *His* front page? Surely this was a sign that the end was near.

"Manjit, that's great!" he said, feigning enthusiasm. "But I need to know about the message from Nairobi!"

"Well, your cousin ... and it ... bad news ..."

"What? Say again?"

Jinnah didn't really need Manjit to repeat the fragment he had heard. Talks had been at a delicate stage when he landed and he knew in his heart that without him at the table, his cousins would never have the acumen, the diplomacy, the sheer nerve to seal the deal. He started shaking. Name of God, what a day.

"... franchises ... legal action ... some representative ..."

"Manjit? You're breaking up again!"

Fuck it. He needed a cigarette. And to change positions. Maybe this open sky policy was overrated. Perhaps the signal in the heavens had shifted inside. In a complex and semi-spastic physical action, Jinnah simultaneously bent down to reach for his cigarettes and lighter while taking a step toward the balcony door — all the while fiddling with the hefty phone crooked in his left shoulder. At exactly that moment, the tip of the satellite phone antenna disintegrated and the glass of the balcony door shattered in a shower of shards. Jinnah instinctively hit the deck and rolled inside through the fragments into the shelter of his room. The phone lay on the balcony's tiled floor, and even through the pounding of blood to his ears and the echoes of the explosion of glass, Jinnah could hear Manjit's voice floating from the device.

"Hakeem? Hakeem? Are you all right?"

Jinnah's last coherent thought was that maybe smoking wasn't so hazardous to your health after all. Then the darkness took him.

Chapter Six

Jinnah came to with a start. He glanced at the ancient clock radio on his bedside table. He'd only been out for a minute or two. Had he dreamed the whole thing? His position on the room floor and the glass fragments embedded in his back suggested not. Someone had definitely tried to shoot him. His satellite phone, now quite mute, sat on the balcony deck. It could stay there as far as he was concerned. Summoning up his year of basic training, he crawled on his belly to the door, reached high to open it, and half-staggered out into the hallway. The hotel had an ancient winding set of stairs and alcoves suited to an earlier era when guests might wish the discretion of not meeting the person coming down the hall. This suited Jinnah perfectly — especially as he heard someone climbing the staircase just below him. He managed to stumble into an alcove just as the someone hove into view. It was the pasty-faced Brit, Blondie's friend, carrying a heavy briefcase. It didn't take much imagination for Jinnah to visualize the components of the sniper's rifle within its confines. Sonofabitch! The bastard had missed his mark and was now trying to finish the job at close range!

"Mr. Jinnah!" the Brit cried as he pounded on the door. "I know you're in there! You can't hide forever —"

Like hell I can't! Jinnah flung himself down the stairs, half rolling, half falling down the tight, winding well for what seemed an endless three floors. At the lobby level, he managed to straighten up rather unsteadily. The pay phones. He must risk them. To get there he had to cross the lobby. Legs wobbly, face full of mental Novocaine, he was halfway through the domestic terrain when he spotted Egide at the front desk. He was having an intense discussion with a middle-aged French couple.

"*Mais nous n'avons pas voulu voir Zanzibar!*" shouted the wife.

"*Au contraire, Madame!*" Egide countered. "*Tout le monde doit voire Zanzibar avant mourir!*"

A small part of Jinnah's brain was amused by the prospect of saving the huge Burundian from this slim French woman. The rest was completely taken up by his desperate need to escape. And the haven he must flee to.

"My friend!" he cried in Swahili, grabbing Egide by the arm. "Take me to Mohammed Shah!"

Egide took one look at Jinnah's face and abandoned his fare from Zanzibar in a heartbeat. Throwing one massive arm over Jinnah's shoulders, he hustled the reporter out of the lobby to his waiting cab.

"What's the matter, Jinnahman?"

Jinnah quickly and somewhat coherently told Egide the gist of what had happened. It wasn't the first time his life had been threatened (or even attempted), but he was mildly surprised at how businesslike he was about it.

"So why are we going to Shah's place?" Egide asked calmly.

Good question. Jinnah didn't know. His inherent instincts told him he would be safe there. But he wasn't about to admit it to Egide.

"I need to talk to him!" he snapped, hoping he had ended the argument.

"Office or home?" asked Egide.

Sonofabitch! Jinnah hadn't thought of that.

"I will take you to his office."

Say what? He might be a man who had just been shot at, he may not be lord of his own African Burger Palace, but Jinnah was not about to let some Burundian cabbie boss him around.

"It's late!" Jinnah snapped. "What makes you think he will be at his office?"

"Simple, Jinnahman. Bad things happen in threes. I get no fare, you are in danger. Mohammed Shah will be at his office. It is already written."

Jinnah didn't have the strength to argue. A million thoughts were racing through his head. The dark, warm African night was a perfect incubator. What the hell had just happened? Had the Brit really tried to kill him? How did Blondie figure in all this? Why did Black Sea Imports ring such an alarm bell? And how on earth could Ronald Sanderson possibly own the front page in his absence? Jinnah put it down to the impending collapse of journalistic standards in general, the demise of the *Tribune* in particular. The Germans had even thought up a word for it: *Zeitungtote* — a sure sign of doom and the cause of considerable *angst* among mere mortals like Sanderson. The thought — strangely satisfying — lasted him all the way to Mohammed Shah's office. To Hakeem's surprise (and Egide's triumph), the lights were on and the door was open. Despite the shattered state of his thoughts, Jinnah had just enough prescience to know something was wrong here too as he walked inside.

"Mohammed? Sayyid Shah?"

Mohammed Shah was there, standing in the middle of a sea of papers, overturned office furniture, computer discs, and potted plants. Even the heavy mahogany desk had been tossed on its back. The phone — an absurd dial telephone from another era — was on the floor and off the hook. In his white robe, Shah was like an iceberg in the middle of a sea of rectangular pack ice.

"You're okay?" asked Jinnah.

Mohammed Shah shrugged.

"Me? I am fine. My cousin, I am not so sure...."

Jinnah glanced at an overturned chair. He flipped it around and guided Mohammed Shah into its confines. That satisfied the part of him that was compassionate. The nicotine-starved, nearly murdered part of him, however, was now fully in control.

"Who tossed the place?" he asked in a hard voice.

Mohammed Shah looked puzzled. Jinnah recognized the symptoms of genuine shock. No, no one had staged this. This was the real thing.

"I don't know. I came here to check something and I find this."

Jinnah squatted in front of Shah and put his hands on the man's knees.

"Mohammed," he said slowly. "Listen. You must have some idea what they were after, hmm?"

Mohammed Shah looked at Jinnah with a piercing glance that told the reporter he had finally dissolved any wall that had been between them.

"Kabir's new will. It's missing."

Jinnah was working on shorthand. Will. Kabir. New. Motive. Name of God....

"Cutting Armaan out?"

Mohammed Shah nodded.

"Armaan has control of the pizza business, but the rest of the portfolio ... it goes to Narinder."

Narinder? Who the hell...?

"The young woman in the photograph?" Jinnah cried. "Mohammed Shah, you must tell me everything!"

Mohammed Shah was willing to talk to Jinnah — up to a point. He was, after all, a lawyer. He rose slowly and straightened a chair.

"Mr. Jinnah, I suppose I must ask you first if you think Armaan is guilty."

Shah had hit the very heart of the matter. Jinnah did an instant recapitulation of everything from his own suspicions to Armaan's confession to Caitlin Bishop's news piece. Did he really think the young man was guilty? Mohammed Shah filled the vacuum that Hakeem's non-answer had created. He put the telephone back in its cradle and straightened a potted palm as he spoke.

"Do you really think a son could do such a brutal thing to his father?"

Jinnah had covered cases where sons and daughters had done worse — well, almost worse — to their parents. For him, it wasn't a matter of capability, but character. Did Armaan have enough of a beast, such blinding hatred for his father that he could murder him in such a gruesome fashion, whether he knew about a new will or not?

"Look, Mohammed," Jinnah said, trying to work the facts through his discombobulated brain. "Kabir Shah was last seen alive in his office at Commonwealth Pizza. Someone arrived. He let them in without a struggle, so he had to have known him, or them. Witnesses have described a well-dressed Indo-Canadian businessman. What we have to determine is was this man sent by Armaan or *was* he Armaan, hmm?"

"Do you think the same hit man took a shot at you tonight, Jinnahman?" Egide had entered the office so softly that Jinnah had not noticed his Burundian bulk behind him. Mohammed Shah, tidying a stack of papers, looked at Jinnah, eyes wide, the shock gone.

"Shot at you?" he asked quietly.

"Yes, yes, yes." Jinnah waved his hand in the air to dismiss the connection. "But this was a white guy —"

The words were hardly out of Jinnah's mouth before his near eidetic memory replayed the tape of the interview with the Pizza Punks. Had they actually *said* a well-dressed Indo-Canadian man or had he …

"A sharp dresser? Like me?" he asked.

Derisive laughter.

"Oh yeah. Just like you."

The dude, the sharp dresser, the Jinnah-wannabe — he wasn't necessarily Indo-Canadian. He could be as lily-white as the Brit — or Blondie. He had simply assumed, let his ego get in the way of the facts.

"Listen, Mohammed — if the same guys who tried to kill me did your office, what was their motive? Tell me what the family was holding back!"

Mohammed Shah looked at Jinnah, pursed his lips, and looked as if he had tasted a particularly bitter fruit. He opened his mouth to tell Jinnah everything, the truth, and Jinnah's inherent instincts told him that he was doing so against his better judgment. But Sayyid Shah didn't get the chance. The tense night was split by a sound that echoed louder and more ominous than a rifle shot. The phone rang. Jinnah nearly jumped out of his sweat-encrusted skin.

"*Mwana wa Bitch*!" he yelped. Mohammed Shah gave Hakeem a disapproving look as he lifted the receiver as carefully as his trembling hand would allow. His expression changed quickly from suspicious to baffled and finally astonished. His head cocked to one side, he held the instrument out to Jinnah.

"It's for you," he said. "It's your wife."

How the hell — of course! Jinnah had left Mohammed Shah's office number with Manjit as one of the emergency contacts before he had left. She had tracked him down pretty damned fast. She might make a reporter yet. He took the phone from Mohammed Shah with a mixture of pride and dread. Mustn't upset her. Manjit must not know.

"Manjit my love!"

"Hakeem, what's wrong?"

Manjit's voice crackled over ancient circuits, but Jinnah recognized the tone instantly. Busted. Okay, downplay the seriousness of the situation.

"Nothing, my love — just some communications problems."

"It sounded like your phone exploded. I heard a bang!"

"Just dropped the damn thing from the balcony," Jinnah lied smoothly. "Listen, darling, I'm a little busy at the moment —"

"Hakeem, I don't wish to alarm you ..."

Alarm him? What in the name of God could Manjit say that could possibly alarm him? He'd just been shot at, he was in a ransacked office thousands of miles from home, and for all he knew the guys who were trying to kill him were out there in the darkness, waiting for him and Mohammed Shah to walk out of the office and into their gun sights.

"... but we have been getting calls again."

Jinnah went rigid. His own petty problems dissolved into the black African night. Manjit had managed to trump him — again.

"What sort of calls? Hang-ups? Threats?" he demanded.

"Both," said Manjit calmly. "The last one, a male voice, asked if I knew where my son was —"

"Manjit, call Graham! Get protection! Where is Saleem?"

A very small part of Jinnah's brain, the one most closely linked to his testosterone, derided him for this outburst: mustn't upset her! The wife mustn't know! Wimp ... Manjit rescued him from further subconscious criticism.

"Hakeem, Saleem is right beside me. Bains is having coffee with us."

Jinnah closed his eyes. He could see exactly what was happening here. Still, if he could get out of this place alive, he might be able to solve the murder and protect his family. Indeed, finding Kabir Shah's killer was the only way to achieve both goals.

"Manjit," he said, mastering his emotions. "I am abdicating."

There was a second of silence. Jinnah could only pray Manjit could grasp the meaning. There was, after all, the very real possibility of their conversation being monitored.

"Long live the king," replied Manjit. "Take care over there. All is well here."

Jinnah's heart glowed. Smart, beautiful, and able to recall agreed-to code phrases even under extreme pressure! Now that was a wife!

"My love to Saleem," he said, switching to Punjabi.

"*Mai tennu pyaar kardi aan*," replied Manjit, her voice trembling oh-so slightly.

Then she was gone. Jinnah turned to Mohammed Shah.

"Sayyid Shah," he said. "I have to go home."

Over the course of his career, Jinnah had used the phrase "with military efficiency" a few times to describe operations that had been carried out by ordinary people working in extraordinary situations. Having been pressed into military service himself as a youth in Kenya, he had some personal experience to bring to the term. But he had never seen anything so much like clockwork as the operation that had unfolded with Mohammed Shah and Egide as commanding officers. A scant hour after leaving Shah's office, he found himself dragging his luggage down the stairs of the Hotel Tanganyika (accompanied by a porter for safety's sake) to meet Egide in the lobby. The big Burundian was on the pay phone and just hanging up as Hakeem and his escort entered the room. Egide was all business as he grabbed Jinnah's bags while simultaneously flipping a tip at the bewildered-looking porter (who had never quite comprehended why the guest had insisted on carrying his own bags when he was there to provide the service).

"I'm trying to arrange a flight for you tonight," Egide whispered in Hakeem's ear. "I'll load your bags. You check out."

Egide moved like the force of nature he was and vanished out the doors, leaving Jinnah in the no man's land between the pay phones and the front desk. A matter of a few metres. Jinnah scanned the terrain. All clear. Taking a deep breath, he started toward the front desk. At that moment, the pasty-faced Brit appeared from behind a potted palm, brandished a briefcase, and nudged Hakeem into one of the many alcoves honeycombing the hotel.

"Thinking of checking out are we, Mr. Jinnah?"

Frantically, Jinnah assessed his position. He was out of sight of the front desk and lobby and there was no sign or sound of Egide. Yet he was in earshot of the indifferent front desk clerk. Surely this chap didn't mean to kill him right here? Unless he had paid the clerk off.... Thinking quickly, Jinnah decided to give the Brit what he hoped he was expecting from a son of the subcontinent: Peter Sellers.

"I am begging your pardon, sir?" He smiled bravely, sounding like an extra from *The Party*.

The Brit didn't miss a beat. He was quivering from his thinning brown hair to his sensible (but, as Hakeem noted, distinctly unfashionable) shoes as he jammed his briefcase into Jinnah's midriff.

"We have some unfinished business."

Name of God! Perhaps he meant to finish the job right here and now.

"I am minding my own business, sir — so should you be!" Jinnah cried, raising his voice just enough to be heard in the lobby but not so much (he hoped) to provoke the Brit to violent action. Being heard was one thing. Being heard and dead quite another.

"You leave me no choice, I'm afraid."

In a single, sudden movement, the Brit jerked his briefcase up to chest-level, right under Jinnah's chin. Hakeem was frozen — was this to be a James Bond job with knives shooting out of the case? Or perhaps a noxious gas? No — the Brit didn't have a mask on and the only noxious gas was being produced by Jinnah's own digestive system. This was it. He was for it now. Paralyzed, he could only watch as his assailant snapped open the briefcase latches, flipped open the cover to obscure his view, and reached inside to draw out ...

It took a second before Jinnah recognized the weapon being waved under his chin. It was bright, white, and had multiple edges. It was something more deadly than a dagger — at least, to the man who would be the king of an African Burger Palace chain. Jinnah blinked, looked again, and gasped. It was worse in its own way than he had imagined.

A sheaf of papers. Legal-sized. Bearing official-looking stamps from multiple national courts. Sonofabitch ...

"We know what you're about, Jinnah, and I think you'll find that the courts have closed your little loophole," said the Brit firmly. "This is a cease and desist order."

"Did you say cease to exist?"

The portion of Jinnah's mind that was working in sync with his bowels to avoid social embarrassment was considerable, but he still had enough on the ball to run through what he knew of this pale pest. He had seen the Brit sitting next to Blondie and assumed they were together. But had they been really? The bar had been crowded, they had not actually spoken to each other in Jinnah's presence. Had he been wrong? A non-lethal scenario broke out into his jumbled consciousness. The scenario was given strength by the Brit's laughter.

"Cease to exist? Good one!"

The Brit suddenly put his hand in his coat pocket and, with a lunging movement, brought an object under Jinnah's nose. Perhaps he really was in for it after all ... but it was just the Brit's business card.

"Nigel Weatherall's the name. VP African Operations, Burger Palace International."

Weatherall held the card up to Jinnah's myopic eyes at just the right distance for him to glimpse beyond it. Passing by was a flash of dark suit and blond hair. Blondie? He needed to see more. Assuming that Weatherall was armed with no more than his legal papers and business card, he nudged the man forward out of the alcove.

"Mr. Weatherall, sir!" he began, full of bluster ... and stopped. Someone else had just entered the lobby, and from his new angle Jinnah could see the black-draped form of Narinder gliding toward the front desk. And Blondie. Oh, this was getting too complicated.

"Look, Mr. Jinnah," said Weatherall, anticipating Jinnah's counterattack. "Stay out of Kenya! No matter what your lawyers may say, we have the territory locked up."

Jinnah was hardly paying attention. He was focused on the drama unfolding behind Weatherall. Narinder Shah had made it to the front desk to the indifferent attention of the clerk. She was being watched by Blondie, who had retreated into the lobby's general waiting area and was pretending to read a worn copy of the *International Herald Tribune*. Jinnah did some mental math fast and furious. Need to rescue Narinder and himself from Blondie over the resistance posed by Weatherall squared. He instantly came up with what he hoped was a winning formula. The equation was completed by Weatherall, who took Jinnah's stunned computative silence as an admission of defeat. He lowered the briefcase bar and brandished a colour brochure.

"Now, of course, if you want to buy an authorized franchise, I'm sure we could come to some, ah … arrangement."

Weatherall had added the missing factor. Jinnah seized upon it.

"Mr. Weatherall!" he cried in full Sellers. "You are mistaking me, sir!"

Weatherall looked baffled. Jinnah plowed ahead, gently but firmly shoving the brochure back against the pasty-faced Brit's chest.

"I am not the man you are after at all," went on Jinnah. "My goodness gracious me —"

"No?" said Weatherall, flummoxed. "But I thought —"

Narinder was engaging the clerk in conversation. Blondie was watching surreptitiously. Jinnah's timing would have to be perfect. He grabbed Weatherall by the shoulders and spun him around.

"Sir! You make a very gross assumption! That big blond man over there — do you know him?"

"Why, no — I haven't had the pleasure —"

That was the variable in the complex equation. Weatherall and Blondie *didn't* know each other. Well, given this, it was time to change that. Jinnah pointed the Brit by the shoulders at his golden-haired nemesis.

"That gentleman there, sir, he is the one to be acquiring franchises, oh yes."

"Is he really?" sputtered Weatherall. "I am so sorry —"

"Oh, yes, my goodness gracious me! I am just being his front man. He being a very big good man in fast food outlets. Worldwide. Pizza. Kentucky Flying Chickens —"

Jinnah gave Weatherall a gentle shove and launched him toward Blondie. It was all the impetus the eager legal beagle needed. Jinnah's heart leapt (and Peter Sellers stopped spinning in his grave) as the Brit sped toward his East Bloc stalker. Giving Weatherall a couple of seconds' head start, Jinnah timed his run toward Narinder at the front desk. She turned just as he approached, and their eyes locked.

"Mr. Jinnah —" she began.

With a finger to his lips, Jinnah took Narinder by the arm and led her toward the exit. He just caught a glance of Weatherall on the way out — to his delight, Burger Palace's franchise enforcer had backed Blondie into a corner and was waving a fistful of brochures in his face, effectively covering their escape. They slipped out the front door to find Egide waiting, cab in position and door open. Jinnah and Narinder piled into the back and Egide sped off into the night.

They had gone some distance before Narinder brought a briefcase up onto her lap and flipped it open. Jinnah was surprised — he had not registered the fact that Narinder was carrying what had appeared earlier this evening to be a deadly weapon. As she leafed through the neat files within, Egide's voice boomed from the front seat.

"Jinnahman! You need to give me your ticket if I am to get you a different flight!"

This hit Jinnah square in the pocketbook. He had booked the cheapest possible return flight to Kenya for this side-trip to Tanzania.

"My ticket is non-refundable and unchangeable," Jinnah confessed.

"This is Africa, man! Everything is changeable. I will look after it."

Jinnah was about to protest that there were limits, even in Africa, when Narinder slid an envelope into his hands and spoke for the first time since they had climbed into the cab.

"This is a copy of the new will. Take it with you to Canada," she said.

Jinnah considered the document in its frail paper wrapper. The reporter in him wanted to open it right then and there to see why it was worth Blondie's while to come all the way to Tanzania and try to kill him. The human being in him (a weakness encouraged by his wife) won out, however.

"Narinder, you are in danger here. If they came after me, they'll come after you."

"Don't worry, Jinnahman!" Egide trumpeted from

the front seat. "I have been retained as her personal bodyguard. She has my life."

Well, that was something. Jinnah didn't know which to admire more — the Burundian's sense of duty, his guts, or his entrepreneurial spirit.

"You'll be safe with Egide," he said to Narinder.

"No one will be safe until the murderer is caught," said Narinder.

She turned her face to the window and the blackness. Jinnah sat with the envelope containing Kabir Shah's new will on his lap, coiled like Matilda's Horned Viper, as they drove silently into the night.

The scene that unfolded at the Morogoro Airport was vaguely reminiscent of *Casablanca*, only there was no question as to who was getting on that plane — alone. Jinnah would have cheerfully tossed Ingrid Bergman, Humphrey Bogart, or even Claude Raines off the flight to get a seat the hell out of Africa. The same battered Hawker Siddeley sat on the tarmac, engines running as the last few passengers straggled aboard. Jinnah's stomach was a churning vortex of acid. What the hell was taking Egide so long? The Burundian was still at the ticket hut, arguing volubly with the airline official across the counter. He took a deep breath and tried to think. Okay, best-case scenario, I am getting out of here alive and with a scoop that will be worthy of the *Trib*'s last front page. It will be fantastic — my prose, Frosty's headline —

Jinnah's production line came to a screeching halt as the spanner called "graphics" flew into the works. Sonofabitch! How was he going to tell the world about Kabir Shah's secret Tanzanian bride without having a picture? Narinder was still beside him, briefcase in hand, silently contemplating the plane as its engines gradually gathered speed. Well, if she was willing to give him the will ...

"Narinder," he said above the general din of the tarmac. "Do you by any chance have a photo of yourself that I can use? It may come in handy in Canada."

Jinnah was relieved when the woman dropped her eyes modestly and smiled shyly.

"Why, yes," she said, fumbling with her briefcase. "You have seen it before."

Narinder's slender brown hand held a small photograph out to Jinnah, who instantly recognized it as a smaller copy of the one that had been front and centre at the funeral. He looked at it closely one last time before reverently sliding it into his wallet.

"Kabir must have loved you very much," he said.

Narinder looked at the ground.

"We had a ... unique relationship."

"He seems to have been a unique man."

"He wanted the best for me, you see. He paid for my degree at the London School of Economics."

Jinnah was astonished. Not many Tanzanian businessmen could boast of such generosity.

"All along he was grooming me to take over his businesses, you see."

Jinnah no longer needed to read the will stuffed inside his jacket pocket. His inherent instincts told him exactly what was in the document. And why Blondie had gone to such lengths to get it. Name of God, he hoped Armaan was still alive by the time he had a chance to phone Graham.

"I knew Kabir would not live forever —"

The words came out in a half-choked sob. Jinnah was relieved in more ways than one when Egide appeared suddenly at their side, waving a ticket at him.

"I cut you a deal, Jinnahman!" he crowed, handing him the ticket. "Non-stop to Vancouver."

Jinnah stared first at the ticket, then at the Soviet-era aricraft that was supposed to be his lifeline.

"Non-stop? In that?" he squawked.

"Of course not!" laughed Egide. "Just as far as Port Moresby."

Port Moresby? In New Guinea? Jinnah's eyes resembled that of the Madagascar aye-aye.

"Don't worry — after that, you change again in Guam and it's straight home to Vancouver."

Jinnah's look could not do his feelings of horror and distaste justice, but it was close enough for Egide to throw a consoling arm over his shoulders.

"Look, Jinnahman — your route via Nairobi, London, and Toronto must be known for this blond man to follow you. Who knows who will be waiting at any of those airports, eh? This way gets you home faster and safer — well, faster anyhow."

Jinnah was rooted to the tarmac. Name of God! It was a choice between an uncertain death in an airport washroom in Heathrow or the fate of Amelia Earhart. God, he needed a cigarette! Egide grabbed his bags and nudged him toward the plane.

"And at no extra charge!" Egide shouted above the engines' roar (as if this was the clincher). "Hurry!"

Jinnah hurried. He made it to the plane just in time for Egide to slip the baggage handler a few shillings to load his bags before shutting the cargo bay doors. The foot of the rickety aluminum stairs into the turboprop beckoned, as did an impatient flight attendant at the top. Jinnah heard a soft cough behind him and turned. Narinder was there beside him, her black dress a sharp contrast to the harsh, unnatural runway lights. Hakeem was at a loss as to how to say goodbye. He extended his hand — she had been all business up to this point. But to his surprise and pleasure, she threw her arms around him and hugged him fiercely.

"Mr. Jinnah — thank you!"

"Thank you," Jinnah mumbled into her head scarf.

Well, maybe it was a bit like *Casablanca* after all. Jinnah softly put his hands on Narinder's shoulders and fixed her place.

"I swear to God, I'll do everything I can to find your husband's murderer, Narinder."

Narinder looked at Jinnah as if he had asked her to get on that plane with him. Her face was mingled with frustration, grief, and pride.

"Husband? I'm not Kabir Shah's wife! I'm his daughter!"

It was only then that the contents of Kabir Shah's will really became clear to Jinnah. And the deadly web that he had embroiled his family in hit home. And there was nothing, absolutely nothing, that he could do about it until he got home. If he got home alive....

Chapter Seven

Jinnah had to admit, Narinder looked good sitting in the middle of the vast oak table. She was certainly the centre of attention of every person in the room — all men, as it turned out, which would have mortified her and Mohammed Shah. Fortunately, it was only her picture on display on the light, bleached wooden surface. Hakeem had tossed it there like a photographic hand grenade a few moments ago. The resulting shockwave had silenced Armaan and his lawyer. Even Graham was keeping his mouth shut. Impressive as the first few seconds of quiet had been, however, it was now well past the uncomfortably long mark. This was getting him nowhere fast and Jinnah was facing more than one deadline today.

"Well? What do you think of your sister, Armaan, hmm?"

Graham glared at him. As far as he was concerned, Jinnah was here on sufferance. This session in Armaan's lawyer's office was officially off the record — the only way the reporter could sit in on what should have been a police interview. Hakeem had joked that he was there "as a friend of the corpse," but Graham had strongly advised him not to share this witticism with the bereaved son and his litigious legal counsel. Jinnah had shown uncharacteristic restraint and followed his advice. He knew he was the only one in the room with the goods (most of which he had carefully withheld from Graham in advance of the meeting); he had the whip-hand and he was taking full advantage of it. Armaan sat across from Hakeem and Graham beside his lawyer, whose receding hairline appeared to retreat with each new revelation.

"This is what you and your father were arguing over, isn't it?" Jinnah pressed his advantage. "You knew he had disinherited you in his new will."

Armaan looked up from the photo on the table and into Jinnah's eyes. For a moment, Hakeem really felt for the poor young man. He must be in roughly the same headspace as Jinnah himself; not sure what time zone he was in, still in shock over recent developments, and terrified for his own life. The fact that Jinnah was also certain he had contracted a rare African blood disease gave him the slight upper hand in the competitive oppression session — that and the fact that Hakeem's family was now in danger as the result of this foolish young man's actions. He plowed ahead remorselessly, heedless of Graham's glowering.

"Narinder is the reason you killed your father, right?"

"I didn't even know I had a sister!" Armaan shouted.

The lawyer put a hand on his client's arm.

"You don't have to say anything, Armaan —"

"I didn't kill my father!"

"Then who did?" asked Graham quietly.

That was a conversation killer — far more effective than any hand on the arm. Jinnah, fighting fatigue, jet lag, and every symptom of dengue fever, ignored Graham's ill-advised interruption and carried on with his planned interrogation.

"You don't know anything about your sister? Let me enlighten you. Your father remarried quietly in Tanzania a few years after your own mother died. But your stepmother died in childbirth before Kabir could introduce her to the Canadian half of his family. The child was a girl, but that didn't matter to Kabir. He needed an heir — a successor. He gave her every chance to succeed, hmm? While you were partying and flunking out at UBC, she was doing double-honours at the London School of Economics. No blond boyfriends for her — she worked nights to pay her rent even though she didn't have to. By the time she got back to Tanzania with her MBA, she was ready. She took over your dad's Tanzanian business empire. And what did you do with your shot, Armaan?"

Armaan was shaking, staring at Narinder's picture with an indecipherable expression. Jinnah knew he was close to breaking. He glanced at Graham, who gave him a barely perceptible nod. Craig might not like the format and Jinnah taking the lead, but he did want results. That's what Jinnah had promised. He was on the home stretch to deliver....

"She never let him down. Not like you."

This broke the trance.

"I was trying to save his business! It was a good offer."

They had already established that Armaan had been trying to cut a deal to sell the pizza business. But Jinnah knew something his interview subject didn't.

"A good offer? You were selling out your own father!"

The lawyer leaned forward and tried to whisper something into Armaan's ear, but the young man shook him off like a terrier.

"It wasn't so much a sale as a merger. You gotta understand, Jinnah — my dad, he couldn't see beyond Main Street. This was a chance for us to go global! It was going to be an international corporation. I was going to be the CEO —"

Jinnah laughed, stopping Armaan in his tracks. It was time to lay out some of the information he had pieced together with the help of Mohammed Shah via a series of emails and a very long flight between Guam and Vancouver. It had been the voyage over the Pacific, staring out over the ocean like a giant GPS picture, which had given Jinnah the insight into what Blondie and the boys were after in leaning on Armaan and others in Vancouver. That and the words of Mal Singh, who had warned about the new kids from the East Bloc who were into serious shit.

"Beyond Main Street? Your dad could have had a

seat on Wall Street if he'd wanted to, for God's sake! You were blind, weren't you, Armaan?"

Armaan turned his blazing eyes down to the table, as if willing Narinder's photo to vanish in a puff of smoke.

"I don't know what you're talking about, man."

Jinnah knew he had the boy now. Time for another flash grenade. He reached into his bag, yanked out a stack of papers, and tossed them on the table. Armaan risked a quick glimpse at them, then turned his head away.

"You've seen this before, haven't you? It had never occurred to you, had it? So many clues staring you in the face: the Kabir Shah Foundation for Youth, the charitable works your father bankrolled but never took credit for. He underwrote cultural festivals, bailed out his fellow Main Street businessmen when everyone started moving out. And you never even asked yourself how he could do all that with the proceeds from a single pizza parlour? It was the public tip of a very private, very large corporate empire. You had no idea how big it was — until Blondie showed you how the old man had been holding out on you. The two halves of an empire — business and personal."

The corporate profile of Shah International Holdings, with offices in Vancouver and Dar es Salaam, sat like an enormous white elephant on the table. Armaan closed his eyes. Jinnah saw the pressure of the thin flesh holding back the flood of tears. Well, damn the torpedoes — or was that damn the dam busters? Whatever — he was close to victory. He hit the detonator without remorse.

"But your dad wouldn't go for it, would he? Why would he turn everything he had worked a lifetime to build over to a gang of hoods? Especially since there was no golden parachute for the old man! So you killed him —"

"No! They did!"

"Armaan!"

The lawyer had put a hand on Armaan's shoulders. The young man shrugged him off, half-standing.

"No! I have to tell the truth!"

There are moments when you can hear your own blood pumping in your veins, when things slow down, when the fan slowly turning over your head stops making far too much noise for your shattered nerves and the entire world falls away. This is a moment in eternity, where all that matters is the sound spilling out of a man's mouth, and unlike all the background noise that has come before and will come afterwards, this moment holds the clear, shining truth. Jinnah had been present during similar occasions, but never had it mattered to him so much. Armaan wasn't just defending himself; he was potentially delivering Jinnah's own family.

"That night ... Dad was in his office. I begged him to take the deal. We fought — God, how we fought! He called me a coward. He said if I wouldn't stand up to them ... well ... he would ... I ran out. The rest you know. God...."

Armaan had tears in his eyes. But he was not breaking yet. Jinnah had to do it. He remembered

Manjit and Saleem's safety and, without regret, tossed another photo onto the table: the surveillance photo shot outside Fogduckers.

"They?" Jinnah asked, voice metallic. "These they?"

Armaan looked at the photo and his face hardened.

"Yes. Mallak. Chung."

"Walter Chung? Black Sea Imports?" asked Graham.

Armaan tapped on Chung's image.

"That's him."

His finger traced over to the heavy-set blond man bursting from his suit.

"That's Karel Mallak. CEO of WP Global."

Jinnah was somewhat surprised. The CEO himself had taken a shot at him in Tanzania? Talk about your hands-on executive....

"What's WP?"

Graham elbowed Jinnah in the ribs none too subtly. He knew he had strayed onto RCMP territory, but he didn't care.

"Warsaw Pact. Based in Odessa. Big exporters in the agri-business."

Jinnah could not help but laugh. The poor, naive schmuck.

"I'm sure Sergeant Graham here can add a few more details to that corporate profile, can't you, Craig?"

Graham didn't like being called "Craig" in front of a suspect and he didn't like having off-the-record chats with young men the Crown had charged with murder. But he obliged. Armaan's lawyer was going to read all about it sooner or later. He only hoped it would be in the disclosure documents sent to the defence in advance of trial and not on the front page of the *Tribune*. And that Capulet wouldn't convince his super to bust him down to traffic enforcement patrol when he found out he was, metaphorically speaking, in bed with Jinnah.

"WP specializes in smuggling AK-47s and other former Soviet military equipment to the various warlords operating in Afghanistan and Pakistan. In return, they get paid in heroin — an especially pure form that's known on the street as East Bloc Blonde. It's responsible for at least a half-dozen overdose deaths we know of."

Jinnah watched Armaan closely. None of this seemed to surprise him. He must have known — or guessed — the WP's true colours, but he'd been in too deep to turn back.

"You see now, don't you, Armaan, hmm? Your dad's business interests were perfect for Mallak. Things were getting too hot for the traditional route between Karachi and the Middle East. He needed a new way to get the heroin into Canada. One that went through Africa and Tanzania then over the Pacific. Much easier, far less fuss over the war on terror, officials that were easy to bribe. And a host of companies from Dar es Salaam to Vancouver to cover his tracks and launder his money. How does it feel to be in bed with a drug lord and terrorist?"

Armaan was looking up and coming across guilty as he sputtered.

"I didn't know any of that!" he protested. "I never thought they'd really ... then, when I came back ... I found Dad —"

"On the floor?" Graham finished the sentence.

"No. In the oven."

There was a significant exchange of looks on both sides of the table. The glance between Graham and Jinnah was one of grim satisfaction. Now they were getting somewhere. The look between Armaan and his lawyer was more complex — it was one that would determine how much farther things would go. Clearly, Armaan had crossed the legal Rubicon. There was no turning back now.

"I knew Mallak and the WP had done it. I didn't know what to do. I panicked."

"Why didn't you tell the police?" Jinnah asked.

"Mallak said I'd end up the same way."

Jinnah grunted. It made sense. Graham, however, was less convinced.

"Makes a nice story," he said, paused, then leaned forward across the table and added quietly, "Prove it."

Armaan looked at his lawyer, who tried to keep a composed face. The younger Shah was not the easiest client in the world to deal with and it had taken all of his legal skills to get Armaan bail after he'd been charged with such a gruesome killing. Very costly, very restrictive bail. He took a deep breath and his composed visage subtly transformed into that of a card-cutter from Vegas. Time to deal....

"Sergeant, I think it would be helpful if you quite unofficially laid out a possible scenario in which my client could be given some ... ah, *guidance* as to how he could best cooperate with authorities to convict the real murderers and clear his name. We will, of course, expect a promise of immunity for his cooperation. And some relaxation of his bail conditions."

Despite everything, the jet lag, the fatal case of Pacific coral worm poisoning he had certainly contracted during his pit stop in Guam and the threat to his family, Jinnah felt the fierce glow of triumph burning in his weary bones. He was over the first hurdle of what promised to be a very long day. Now he had to face something more dangerous than the Warsaw Pact, more deadly than Tanzanian Laughing Disease.

Frosty and the *Tribune* newsroom were next.

"You can't be serious! You want me to hand my pizza oven murder scoop to Caitlin Bishop?"

Jinnah's howl — much anticipated and the subject of a few side bets as to length, volume, and level of invective — split the newsroom as well as Frosty's delicate head. As grateful as she was to have her sometime protégé back with a real news story to sell at the afternoon meeting, the senior assistant city editor didn't need this kind of agro right now — especially since she thought she had explained the new reality to Hakeem quite clearly. She closed her eyes and tried again — slowly.

"Jinnah, there is no guarantee that CXBC will pick up the story ..."

"Hah!"

"... or that Caitlin Bishop will be assigned to it ..."

"How can you possibly send our city list to CXBC in the first place!" cried Jinnah, his decibel level reaching alarmed Malagasy aye-aye proportions (and simultaneously enriching several deskers).

"For the last time, it's not the city list. It's the 'shared news coverage strategy briefing note.' And it's orders straight from the top."

"A top that has sold us for thirty pieces of silver to Candle Communications!"

Jinnah was expressing the view of the majority of the traditional newspaper people in the room. But these were in the minority. Most of the *Trib*'s staff were of the opinion that the proposed takeover of the paper by Candle Communications was the inevitable result of media convergence and a foregone conclusion — if they were lucky. The math, apparently, was quite dodgy, and advertising revenue streams, paid classified linage, and subscriber demographic information were far more important considerations that a mere city list. Why not sacrifice a few exclusive stories for job security and the chance to become part of Canada's largest media empire? None of this cut any ice with Jinnah, who could see the fruits of his sweat and blood being squandered by corporate politics.

"I have not survived an assassination attempt in Tanzania, threats to my family, and the contraction of several deadly tropical diseases to meekly stand by and tell CXBC that —"

"That we would be pleased to share our news-gathering intelligence with our potential partners in order to ensure it receives maximum exposure over multiple media platforms, isn't that right, Mr. Jinnah?"

As usual, Whiteman had silently crept up behind Jinnah. Somehow, the bastard had some sort of management cloaking device that rendered Hakeem's early warning brass hat detection system useless. Sonofabitch!

"Whatever happened to 'A *Tribune* exclusive?' What about the value of a true scoop?" Jinnah demanded, whirling on his tormentor. "We used to lead the news, Whiteman, not drink everyone else's bathwater!"

"And just what would this scoop that puts us so far ahead of the so-called competition say, Jinnah?"

The newsroom fell near silent as Whiteman and Jinnah squared off. The betting line was two-to-one that Jinnah would refuse to cooperate and that the editor-in-chief would suspend him. But Jinnah was quick on his feet. He knew exactly how to handle this dog: throw him a bone. First, of course, he would tease him a bit.

"Why don't we just haul Caitlin Bishop in here and tell her to her face, Chief?" he demanded. "She'll be on air at five while we suck wind until six a.m. with the early edition —"

"Come come, Jinnah," chided Whiteman. "We can always post your story on the website at 4:45 p.m. That is, if you have a story by then."

Jinnah ignored the obvious insult. He had to play this just right. He knew Whiteman was counting on him to dazzle the CXBC brass with a kick-ass exclusive. Well, he couldn't file a story if he was dying. He removed his glasses and rubbed his forehead.

"I don't feel so well," he whined. "I may have been bitten by the brown tree snake in Guam after all —"

"In which case, you would already be dead," said Whiteman. "Jinnah, I advise you to tell me what you hope to file today."

Jinnah looked at Whiteman, then at Frosty. It was a bit like being back in Armaan's lawyer's office. The subtle nods and winks. Only this time, Jinnah knew exactly how the interview would unfold.

"You can't expect me to share the fruits of the bitter tree of experience with so callow a youth as Caitlin Bishop!" Jinnah blustered. "If she gets wind of the operation, she'll blow it!"

"Jinnah," said Whiteman, smiling for the first time. "There is no guarantee that Caitlin Bishop will get anywhere near the story. In fact, one of our own may be asked to report on it, live from the field."

"I'm not going on television —" Jinnah cried (further enriching a few select news editors who were in on this particular action).

"You are not on the list of convergent journalists, Jinnah. I was referring to our current network star."

It was at this point that Jinnah became conscious of Sanderson hanging about shame-faced near the city desk. This was too much to be borne.

"You want to give my warehouse bust to the paper's dog reporter?" roared Jinnah. "What qualifies Ronald to do a stand-up on the biggest bust since Annie Hawkins-Turner?"

"Steady on, Jinnah," whispered Frosty.

"Mr. Sanderson has enjoyed a great deal of success working with our colleagues from CXBC in your absence, Jinnah. He was especially popular doing live reports on location concerning a certain health-related issue involving Black Sea Imports."

Okay, Jinnah had been prepared for a lot, but Sanderson as the next Anderson Cooper was too much.

"Is this true, Ronald?" he sputtered.

Sanderson blushed, looked at the floor, and muttered "I have call to make," before fleeing the room. Apparently, the call was that of nature. Leaving Jinnah to goggle at Whiteman's scarcely suppressed smirk of triumph. Okay, enough of the management dog chewing on Jinnah's professional pride. Time to feed the paper poodle his bone.

"You want my stand-up, Whiteman? Here goes: they were heroin pushers and pizza oven murderers. But a joint operation by the Vancouver Police and the RCMP have sliced and diced a new, sinister organized crime syndicate last night —"

"How late last night, Jinnah?"

"How am I supposed to know that, for God's sake?" cried Jinnah. "It's not as if the cops have handed me the timetable —"

"I assume you will push the first edition deadline."

"Look, this is huge, Chief! And it's all ours —"

"For the moment, Jinnah, for the moment."

Frosty could see every vein in Jinnah's forehead throbbing. Jesus, maybe he *had* been bitten by the brown tree snake. Time to steer the discussion away from an alpha-male pissing match to something resembling a story meeting.

"We're pretty sure the warehouse bust will go down in the afternoon, right, Jinnah?"

Jinnah looked down at Frosty, sitting at her terminal, as if she had just sprung fully formed from the earth. He'd been so intent on Whiteman he'd forgotten all about her. But he had the sense to take the opening she was offering him. Carefully, carefully....

"Yes. Capulet has agreed to give us a head's up. We should get there on time to see them slap the cuffs on Chung and start hauling goods out of there. Full access. Exclusive — in recognition of our good work on this file, hmm?"

Jinnah studied Whiteman's face the way a code breaker would pour over a cipher. But unlike other *Tribune* editors that had preceded him, Whiteman could not be read with any accuracy. The key to his predecessor, Conway Blacklock, had been the degree of contempt with which he glared at a reporter pitching a story. Slight disdain and condescension (an expression Jinnah was all-too familiar with) almost guaranteed the front page. With Whiteman, it was like being stared at by a calculator. The editor-in-chief turned to Frosty.

"Ms. Frost, I assume you have put this tale of perfidy on the shared news coverage strategy briefing note?"

"Of course, Chief — at the top."

"Very good. Then put Mr. Sanderson's name next to it and send it to CXBC."

"Right, Chief."

"You're kidding me!" Jinnah shrieked, breaking the aye-aye decibel barrier. "You can't take my story from me!"

"*Au contraire*, Jinnah. The Black Sea Imports story has been Sanderson's all along. He broke it. You wouldn't want to poach on it, would you? Unless, of course, there is some direct tie-in with the pizza murder?"

Jinnah stopped dead. Sonofabitch. The bastard had cut right to the chase and called his bluff.

"It's just a theory at the moment! All will become clear at the warehouse bust, Chief!" he whined at volume. "Graham is working on it —"

"Are they going to arrest anyone for Kabir Shah's murder at the warehouse?"

Jinnah was in full backpedal mode.

"Not as far as I know. But there's a link —"

"And can you provide details that Ms. Frost can put on the shared resources list, Jinnah?"

"Not at this moment in time, actually —"

"Then I suggest you stay in the office and make some calls while Mr. Sanderson covers his well-deserved scoop, Jinnah."

Whiteman turned briskly on his heel and marched off. He was Caesar, unmovable as the Pole Star, and he had spoken. He also had a pretty good idea how his decision would motivate Jinnah. Perhaps he wasn't so much Caesar as Machiavelli.

There was near-silence in the newsroom as Whiteman walked calmly into his corner office. The betting line was on a Jinnah tantrum that would make Caligula look rational. But Jinnah was about to lose some of his closest friends on the rewrite desk vast amounts of money. He took off his glasses, rubbed his eyes, and said, "I'd better help Ronald with that call."

Before Frosty could say a word, Hakeem was out the door, down the hall, and in the men's room. Sanderson was nowhere in sight. But the vague retching sounds from the corner cubicle were unmistakably West Coast in their accent — strained, but polite. Jinnah sidled over and leaned against the thin metal door.

"Ronald! How's the call going?"

"Go away!"

"Are we still talking to Ralph on the great white telephone? I'm so sorry —"

"Jinnah, what do you want?"

"My story, Ronald."

"I never asked to be assigned to the warehouse bust, I swear!"

"Ronald, Ronald, Ronald — it's your story. Well, yours and Manjit's. Go for it."

There was a tense silence. It was broken by the flushing of the toilet. From the sounds within, Jinnah could tell that Sanderson was making himself decent.

"Jinnah, you can't just hand me your story like that! Whiteman had no right —"

"Whiteman has no clue, my friend."

A fumbling at the metallic door and a sliver of Sanderson appeared in a long, narrow crack. His fair face was flushed and even his reddish hair appeared more crimson.

"Explain!" he demanded.

"Yes, please do."

Jinnah turned his head, amused, while Sanderson uttered a squeak and slammed the door shut. There was a frantic scrambling as the cubicle was bolted shut.

"Frosty, this is the little boy reporter room. This is a balls-only zone, hmm?"

"I have more balls than most of the boys on city desk put together, so cut the crap," said Frosty, advancing on the corner cubicle. "Ronald! Get out of there! I refuse to carry on a conversation through a stall door."

"Frosty, this is a violation of a city bylaw! Not to mention the employees' code of behaviour! Please leave!"

Frosty rolled her eyes as she leaned up against the now-groaning cubicle door.

"You wanna see a violation of a city bylaw? Watch this...."

Frosty pulled out a small rectangular package. Jinnah's eyes lit up.

"Want one, Hakeem?"

"Surely not in here!" cried Jinnah in mock indignation. "Are these menthols?"

Jinnah thought Sanderson would rip the door down bolt and all. He and Frosty leapt to one side to avoid falling into the stall as it sprang open. Ronald, looking every inch the prefect from *Tom Brown's School Days*, burst out of the cubicle full of self-righteous wrath.

"You're not smoking in here!" he cried.

Sanderson's worst suspicions were confirmed visually by the sight of Jinnah and Frosty manoeuvring long, slim, white cylinders in their mouths. Cylinders with red tips....

"Cinnamon, actually," said Frosty, chomping off the end of her smoke and chewing it appreciatively. "Like it?"

"Best candy cigarette I've ever had," said Jinnah, sighing. "Now what in News God's name is so important that you're willing to give Ronald here a heart attack? And break every corporate rule regarding mixed-gender urination?"

Ronald glared at his two colleagues chewing and sucking on their substitute smokes resentfully.

"I was not having a heart attack —" he protested.

"No. More a brown trousers episode," said Frosty. "Look, Hakeem, I saw what you did in there. Spill."

"I'll have a hard time matching my deskmate here."

"Jinnah!"

Ah! The voice of the aggrieved senior assistant city editor who knows she's going to have to juggle stories on deadline and perform a professional sleight-of-hand to ensure the *Tribune* can't be blamed for having a ball-busting exclusive. Jinnah wanted to hug his sometime-mentor.

"Bottom line? The warehouse bust is the sidebar. The real action is later on tonight when Armaan nails his dad's murderers."

There was a mixed reaction to this pronouncement. Frosty merely gave a satisfied grunt. Sanderson's emotions were much more complex, mingling relief with resentment and a vestigial sense of professional pride.

"But you said —" he began.

"Give it a rest, Ronald!" snapped Frosty. "You know exactly what's going to happen with Armaan, don't you, Hakeem?"

"Not exactly. But shortly after the warehouse bust, he's going to have a little chat with Mallak and the other real masterminds behind the WP organization. Graham and his boys will record it, move in, and arrest them. They haven't got a clue, the WP."

"And do you have a clue where this will take place?" Frosty asked.

"No," admitted Jinnah. "Graham won't tell me."

"Oh, come on, Hakeem! As if he'd tell you!" Sanderson said.

"Ronald, I deserve to be in on this sting!"

"Police don't usually invite the media into a sting — that's why it's called a sting."

"My friend, there would be no operation if not for me," Jinnah cried.

"If not for the Burger Palace sting, you mean?"

"That's unfair!"

Frosty placed her considerable person and gravitas between the two jostling journos.

"Cut the crap! Jinnah, why didn't you tell Whiteman about the other half of the operation?"

"Simple. If I plead ignorance, you still have a page one layout that has a main and a sidebar and lots of art. When I get the goods on Armaan's sting of Mallak and the WP boys, all you'll have to do for second edition is to flip the stories. Ronald gets the glory along with Caitlin Bishop for the first edition. But, as I am led to believe, there is no requirement to advise CXBC of breaking news, hmm? That ought to keep Caitlin Bishop busy while I get the real story."

Frosty grinned as Sanderson did his guppy fish imitation. The plan was simple, elegant, and she guessed that Whiteman suspected as much. Perhaps the chief did have some newsman in him after all. Cunning dog.

"Let's get this straight," sputtered Sanderson. "I'm going to cover a heroin warehouse bust, the biggest story of my career, just to decoy Caitlin Bishop so Jinnah can write the real line story in defiance of corporate policy? And make me look stupid on network television as part of the bargain?"

"Ronald! Nicely summarized! If only your news stories could be quite so succinct."

Sanderson's mouth formed a pout. This was the moment of truth. Was Ronald a true newsman or was he one of these convergent, cross-over divas? Jinnah glanced at Frosty. Her face was a study in controlled contempt — something Hakeem could relate to.

"Well, I just wanted to get it clear," said Ronald, blushing again. "If we could kick CXBC's butt — do you know where they put my last story on Black Sea Imports? Just before the sports!"

Jinnah laughed. Even in broadcast, Sanderson had managed to have his story put on the TV equivalent of City One. But Frosty looked very grave.

"Listen, boy reporters," she said. "We are once again trying to commit journalism in the face of corporate convergence. No matter what happens, no matter what goes down tonight, we have to swear that we won't tell Whiteman or any of our superiors what the real City List is. Okay?"

Jinnah took what remained of his candy smoke out of his mouth and put it in his right hand. Holding it out in front of him like Hamlet's sword, he said, "I swear."

Frosty did the same with her chewed confectionery.

"I swear."

Both Jinnah and Frosty looked at Sanderson, who resembled the proverbial ungulate in the 500-watt lights. Frost slipped him a candy cigarette from her pouch. Ronald looked at it as if it were the *nicotinus verite*.

"Swear!" said Jinnah and Frosty simultaneously.

It was as if Ronald had been waiting for this peer-pressure moment his entire life and wondering what had taken so long. He bit the butt end of his candy smoke off and put his hand over the mini-forest of candy stalks.

"I swear."

The beauty of the moment lasted less than a second. The door to the men's room opened and Clint Eastward, photographer extraordinaire, walked in and froze solid.

"I can come back —" he faltered, faced with what could only be some weird city desk Satanic bathroom rite.

"Ah, Clint Eastward!" cried Jinnah. "Let me make your day...."

The warehouse was quite unremarkable — that was one of the features that had made it so attractive to Walter Chung and the WP. Just down from the Vancouver docks, it was tucked away in a cove on Burrard Inlet, facing east toward the rising sun. A typical concrete and corrugated tin roof structure, it didn't have the biggest capacity for goods, nor the smallest. Chung and Mallak had thought it perfect for their operations and they had been right — until Manjit and Sanderson had started making life difficult for them. It was discreet, out of the way. Of no interest to anyone.

Not this afternoon. The front of the warehouse was cordoned off with the ubiquitous yellow and black crime scene tape and the media — who had been tipped by local residents who had spotted the unusual level of activity and other correspondents tipped by their colleagues' Twitter feeds — sat in front of it, just like at Commonwealth Pizza, anxiously waiting for someone to emerge.

Inside the warehouse Sanderson was trying his best to understand the guttural utterances of Superintendent Capulet as he followed him from space to space. It was made more difficult by the protective clothing and masks they wore while negotiating the warehouse's labyrinth. Around them, Ronald could see open barrels full of white powder. RCMP specialists wearing hazardous waste gear even more skookum than their own moved to and fro, carefully sorting pesticide from heroin. In the corner, Sanderson noted two workers in handcuffs waiting to be dragged out before the media gauntlet outside. They would have to wait until Chung was taken out the back way, however. Chung looked a bit dazed, but still had enough on the ball to spot Sanderson and shoot him a withering look.

Ronald's discomfort was covered by the snap of Clint Eastward's camera. One of the Mounties had quite helpfully piled bags of heroin on top of one of the pesticide barrels. Even a visual illiterate like Sanderson could appreciate how nicely the image captured the story and he grinned. No wonder Jinnah was hooked on crime: this was a rush! Of course, it couldn't be like this all the time, but it sure beat Parks Board committee hearings. It took him a moment to realize Capulet was saying something through his mask.

"This is East Bloc Blonde, deadliest heroin in the city. Killed at least a dozen users on the Downtown Eastside. Also made all those agricultural workers sick —"

Sanderson rarely interrupted an official in mid-speech. But he couldn't help doing so now. Jinnah didn't have a monopoly on vanity, after all.

"So they were smuggling heroin inside pesticide barrels?" he asked, hoping for the positive, colourful quote that so often enriched a Jinnah story.

Ronald couldn't understand why Capulet was craning over his left shoulder as he answered quite slowly and hesitantly. Didn't he know the details of his own bust?

"Well, not every barrel contained heroin. But the one that got shipped to the spray company by mistake did. It got mixed with pesticide and …"

Sanderson became aware of a commotion behind them. At first, he thought Chung had made a break for it. But it was worse — much worse.

"Get a shot of those guys! And the horse! This is great!"

Sanderson reluctantly turned his head to see Caitlin Bishop and a cameraman entering the scene like they owned the place. And pissed off that they were late. Caitlin spotted Capulet and made a beeline for him.

"Superintendent Capulet!"

Capulet grabbed the media relations officer who had been hovering around the edge of the proceedings and spat into her ear.

"What in the name of Jesus Christ Almighty and all the saints above is that blond pit bull doing in *my* crime scene?" he demanded.

"*Tribune* request, sir," quavered the MRO. "You know how they're pairing with CXBC now —"

Capulet cursed, said a few words entirely off the record of what he thought of said news resource sharing arrangements, and tried to compose himself. Letting Sanderson in under controlled conditions was one thing — you could practically guarantee the results. Adding Caitlin Bishop and CXBC into the equation didn't even begin to cover all the negative possibilities. What the hell was Graham thinking? Couldn't he keep his media pack under control? Besides, he did have a grudging respect for Jinnah, and they wouldn't be here without his persistence. What had this blonde done, aside from make his life difficult? She and her cameraman weren't even wearing masks!

"I'll have a statement for you and the rest of the media outside, Ms. Bishop."

Before Caitlin could enlighten Capulet about shared story resources, how she should be getting *exactly* the same access that the *Trib* had been granted (with a veiled shot at Sanderson about how she had laughed when her news editor had suggested letting

Ronald handle the live hit), the superintendent disappeared around a pile of pallets. Caitlin's pursuit was cut off by two haz-mat officers in full gear who barred her entrance. Fuming, frustrated, she whirled on the last man standing: Ronald Sanderson.

"Ronnie! Nice to see you."

"Ronnie" Sanderson wasn't fooled for an instant. Even as an intern, Caitlin had disliked him, especially after he'd had the audacity to edit some of her copy to what he considered CP standards. He still had Jinnah and Frosty's admonition ringing in his ears to make sure Caitlin suspected nothing — nothing! He managed a wan smile.

"Caitlin. It's been so long —"

Sanderson's attempt at nonchalance was shattered in mid-sentence as Caitlin's eyes narrowed into a single focused beam of suspicion that cut right through his West Coast mental armour — which was about as thin as a layer of bladderwrack.

"Where's Jinnah?" she asked. "Why isn't he here?"

To the reasonably detached eye of Clint Eastward, it appeared that Ronald had been spitted upon a pike, or, perhaps, insect-like, impaled by a pin: still alive and wriggling for life, but completely incapable of escape.

"He's busy," Sanderson stuttered, turning bright red. "Besides, this is my story!"

"Really? Did you give Manjit a 'files by' at least?"

"How did you —"

"Jinnah's busy? Busy with what?"

Sanderson was rescued from further professional abuse (and from committing any further indiscretion) by Eastward, who alertly dragged him away toward the rear of the warehouse where a row of refrigeration units were being attended to by Mounties operating forklifts.

"Are you always this smooth with the ladies?" he asked.

"That's no lady," protested Sanderson. "Unless you consider Medusa a model of femininity."

"Sure turned you into stone. C'mon, get to work —"

Eastward shoved the still-blushing reporter toward the nearest forklift, which was shifting one of the large freezers lining the back wall.

"It's not as if I can ask any questions!" Sanderson shouted above the whine of the forklift's propane-powered engine and the general din inside the building.

"You don't have to say anything, just look intelligent," said Eastward, snapping away. "Need some pics that say '*Trib* exclusive.' Y'know, our man behind the scenes, on the spot —"

The spot was suddenly occupied by Capulet, who was coming toward them, looking furious. From his vantage point, Sanderson saw Caitlin — alerted by some instinct or, perhaps, the snakes in the back of her hair — do a perfect pit bull pirouette, spinning around and grabbing her cameraman in a single, fluid movement that left him gaping in admiration. No wonder Jinnah had mentored this mouse. He had glimpsed her inner gorgon.

"Superintendent Capulet!"

The convergence of Capulet, Caitlin, and Sanderson was hardly harmonic. More like a three-car pileup. The superintendent was obviously desperate to get them out of the area, Caitlin was bent on getting some quotes, and all Ronald wanted to do was to get back to the office without having been exposed to a fatal level of carcinogens. Caitlin's cameraman, Kevin, and Eastward recorded the whole scene as the Mountie on the forklift desperately tried to manoeuvre around the tiny, milling media knot. Eastward was impressed by Sanderson's efforts to take control of the spontaneous mini-scrum. And dismayed at the ease with which Caitlin managed to run over him.

"So would it be fair to say —" Ronald began.

"Is heroin the only thing this Warsaw Pact deals in?" Caitlin cried, cutting him off.

"I can't comment," said Capulet. "Look —"

"With respect to —"

"How are the drugs distributed? Through the biker gangs?"

"I will have a statement for you later outside!"

Through all this, Capulet had been moving them slowly away from the freezers, but Caitlin (trained by an expert in Jinnah) had been blocking, side-stepping, using Kevin's bulk to slow the superintendent's progress, with the effect that the small scrum was lurching unpredictably forwards and back, side to side, rather like a news-desker leaving the Off the Record Club after closing time.

"So you deny any link between this and the gang-war between the Young Lions and the Phoenix Club?"

"Look, Ms. Bishop, I have nothing more to say to your wild speculations. You've been allowed inside a very big bust. What you see is what you get —"

Capulet, like a Mountie muskox, made his move to burst through the scrum's weak link: Sanderson. But Eastward was right behind his reporter and damned if the *Trib* was going to be the scrum-buster. With one hand, he grabbed Ronald's belt through his protective overalls and held him in place. Capulet, his way checked, staggered right and the scrum followed. Unfortunately, that was just where the forklift driver had banked on getting a clear path to the doors and, to avoid running over his superior officer (he could have cared less about the media), swung his machine wildly to the left. The freezer on the forks swayed, tilted at a fatal angle, and both forklift and load toppled over with a metallic crash, just missing Caitlin. She was in perfect position to see the freezer, now on its side, burst open. Its contents spilled out in plain view. Not small packs of frozen goods, not even sides of beef, but a single large, dark form covered in silver frost. For all their training, both Caitlin and Sanderson froze for a moment. Not so the lensmen, Eastward and Kevin, who were framing, focusing, and recording digital images even as the unidentified cargo hit the floor.

Sanderson was so shocked that he forgot everything: Jinnah and Frosty's warnings, Caitlin's suspicion and insults, and the fact that he had been, up to that point, covering the most enjoyable story of his life. His eyes were riveted to the object that had slid out into the floor and was now being documented for posterity. It was a human form, clad in black leathers, and a quick glance at the frozen figure's midriff revealed to the educated eye a wide biker belt without the buckle. Capulet didn't need to see the missing motif. Even the weeks of freeze-dried death couldn't hide the corpse's identify from him. He stared at the spectacle with a multitude of thoughts running through his brain. Only a very small part was occupied by a mental note to never, ever take media management advice from Graham again. Overall, there was a sense of sadness and grief. He'd genuinely liked the young man.

"Jesus H. Christ on a popsicle stick," he said softly but clearly through his mask. "We just found Moe Grewal."

And he didn't give a damn if Caitlin Bishop put it all over the early news.

Neither did Jinnah. The warehouse bust was big, of course, but his inherent instincts told him that if he could somehow get in on the Armaan sting, the pizza murder would trump the heroin bust. He knew the two halves of the big picture and that Chung and Mallak were the link between them, but the fine details were not quite clear. How Mal Singh and Moe Grewal fit in was still uncertain. There were too many possible scenarios and he needed the real goods — like a confession — to secure the ball-buster he knew was waiting for his fingers to pound out on deadline.

The problem was, Graham would not budge. All he would tell him was the sting would take place "in a secure location." Which narrowed things down, but he couldn't be in a half-dozen places at once.

"Look, Hakeem," Graham had said on their last trip together on the Aquabus. "You know I can't let you in on this. Too many things could go wrong."

"But I deserve it!" Jinnah had howled. "Without me, you wouldn't even be in a position to make this bust!"

"The Crown will think bupkis of that and you know it. You want Mallak to walk because I let the media in on the operation and compromised the integrity of the confession?"

"Then deputize me for a day! I can be a cop for a night if it delivers me a killer front page about a pizza oven murderer!"

"Jinnah, I can't let any media near this one —"

"Including Caitlin Bishop?"

The words had been spat out as a challenge. Graham had been equal to it.

"*Especially* Caitlin Bishop. She doesn't even know it's happening, which, by the way, puts you miles ahead of her."

"That's good, my friend," Jinnah had grunted. "Because it's not really me you need to worry about when it comes to media ruining your operation, hmm? Besides, I could practically write the story now, you're so predictable."

"What do you mean, predictable?" Graham had growled.

Jinnah had laughed.

"You use the same script every time, Craig. How many stings of yours have I covered? Five?"

"Four," Graham had corrected him, a little sulkily.

"You always let the guy with the wire enter the location, wait until he gets the suspects to incriminate themselves, and then you swoop in with flash grenades blazing, screaming 'This is the Vancouver Police — freeze!' And you tease me for writing User Key One and Two stories! You need a better script writer. For a small fee —"

"I do not always use the same M.O.!" Graham had cried, insulted. "Each script is unique, Hakeem."

"Is that so? Then how is this one going to differ from all the others, Mr. Robert McKee?"

In the end, Graham had grudgingly given Jinnah a general outline of what he had hoped would unfold for his zed copy. With police in discreet attendance, Armaan would confront Mallak at an agreed-to location. Mallak was a suspicious sort, so Armaan would not be wired. Instead, they would rely on parabolic microphones to pick up the conversation. It would be semi-public, which would lower both sides' sense of anxiety.

"And how are you going to get around Mallak scoping out the area beforehand and putting his goons in a perimeter that excludes parabolic mics?" Jinnah had demanded.

Craig had simply smiled and gave Jinnah a patronizing "You leave that to the expertise of the Vancouver Police Department."

Jinnah knew Graham had a bag full of surveillance tricks and his task, currently, was to figure out what sort of "semi-public location" would afford such a combination of security and ease of access. He was so focused on the Google map of Vancouver on his screen that he missed the first ring of his phone. With a start, he looked at the call display. Ah-chah!

"Ronald!" he snapped. "How's the bust going?"

The voice that wafted over the phone had a distinct gasping, guttural quality about it — a semi-breathlessness that Jinnah was well-acquainted with.

"Hakeem, they found Moe Grewal's body in a freezer down here."

Jinnah sat bolt upright. One of the missing pieces of the puzzle had finally dropped into place. Smiling, he could afford to be generous.

"Great work, Ronald! By the way, have you been throwing up?"

Sanderson didn't dignify this with a direct response. But his next question was on the verge of regurgitation.

"Jinnah, please don't tell me I have to doorstep his widow! I can't —"

Jinnah could have been as cruel as Caitlin Bishop or Frosty, but he liked Ronald. After all, you didn't get many frozen corpses at Parks Board meetings. Sanderson had not only done his job, he had exceeded expectations. *We must be compassionate*, he thought.

"His next of kin? No, no, no, Ronald! You leave them to me."

It was busy at Fogduckers. Mindy was at his usual table on the Phoenix Club side of the green line. Bindhu, a Kali look-alike with eyes like the Indian Ocean, was chatting him up about the latest movies and funny videos she'd seen on YouTube. He was only half paying attention, if that. Jinnah wasn't the only one with inherent instincts. Mindy's had kept him alive through a lifetime of gang politics. Now he knew something big was going down; it was ugly and there didn't seem to be a way out for him and his members. Shit — he was almost willing to reach out to pretty little Billy and his Young Lions, make some sort of common stand, to prevent catastrophe. But pride, face, and honour stood in the way.

"So, like, we're looking at this Manmohan Waris bhangra video and then my girlfriend says, 'Holy shit! Kareena Kapoor just walked into the club!' And I said, like, no way —"

Whap!

Mindy had already subconsciously registered someone behind him before a hand slammed a hard metal object down on the table in front of him. It was thanks to his instantaneous assessment that he was in no immediate danger that Jinnah was still alive and smiling as the biker turned his head a fraction and saw the reporter's face looking down on him. He might also have unconsciously recognized the fact that the bar had gone almost silent, save for Bindhu's constant commentary. Jinnah helped himself to the chair opposite Mindy.

"Ever ask yourself how that Young Lion's buckle got in that pizza oven?" he asked calmly.

Mindy fingered the buckle on the table. He knew exactly who had given it to Jinnah. And why. He looked at the reporter with an expression that said "I'm listening." Hakeem took advantage of the rare opening.

"The Warsaw Pact killed Moe Grewal. When they murdered Kabir Shah, they planted Moe's buckle in the oven as a warning."

Mindy had been through his share of police setups and assorted bullshit. But this one hit home as the real thing. Still, it wouldn't do to look shaken.

"Moe's still missing in action, man," he said, feigning disinterest.

"His body's just been found in a freezer. In a warehouse owned by the Warsaw Pact."

Jinnah let the words ripen in Mindy's mind. He was here all by himself, no one but Frosty knew of his whereabouts, and one wrong word could get him killed. But he knew in his core he was right and the truth gave him courage. That and the certain knowledge that, if he blew this, his family would never be safe. Mindy bristled, brushed Bindhu aside, and whistled over across the Green Line at Billy. Jinnah saw the diminutive gang leader get out of his chair and head toward them. He only had a few seconds to further prime the pump.

"The WP went after one member of each gang, hmm? Provoke a war. Make it easier to muscle in on your turf."

"We don't do that shit, man," Mindy said, spitting the words out. "We don't touch horse or any of that heavy crap."

Billy appeared at the table, looking quizzical. Jinnah pulled something out of his pocket and threw it down on the table over the belt buckle. It was the best letter of discipline that Whiteman had ever given him.

"That's an ad sheet of your legitimate businesses. That's what Mallak's after. A little numbers, a little grow-op. Small-time shit. But your legit operations? Worth their weight in horse to him. A dozen respectable fronts for laundering and distribution. Am I right?"

Billy and Mindy exchanged a look. The way out was presenting itself.

"What do you need from us?" asked Mindy.

Jinnah pulled out his notebook and microcassette.

"Everything you've got on Karel Mallak. On the record. Names, dates, and everything."

There was only a momentary hesitation. Mindy and Billy knew a guardian angel when they saw one — a saviour who would wash away their petty sins in the eyes of an insatiable media that needed bigger villains than themselves. It hurt their pride somewhat, but Billy had the acumen to ask for the guarantee.

"Listen, man, we tell you, you go to print, and we got no idea if the bastard is going down. Wassup with that?"

"I give you my personal guarantee that nothing — nothing, hmm? — will be printed or broadcast unless Mallak and the boys are in the bag," said Jinnah, almost convinced of his sincerity.

"Not good enough," said Mindy. "We need insurance."

Jinnah ran through a whole range of possibilities. The sight of Bindhu sulking not far off settled him. He reached for his cellphone.

"Clint? Jinnah. Code red. Fogduckers."

Jinnah hung up. He had no idea if Eastward would

figure it out. But if any of the *Trib*'s photographers could, it was him. Meanwhile, he had teeth to pull.

"So, tell me, when did Mallak and Chung start leaning on you, hmm?"

"You guarantee this asshole's going down? Tonight?" asked Billy.

Jinnah nodded. "With your help, Billy. Mindy."

It was with considerable relief Jinnah saw the barely perceptible nod between the two men and Mindy and Billy started spilling over each other to save their lives.

"Mallak's a seriously twisted dude, man. Have to be to slice and dice someone like a pizza," Mindy began.

"And flash-freeze Moe," interjected Billy.

Slowly, among the usual invective, ass-covering, and braggadocio, the story came out. It was clear to Jinnah that Mallak had used exactly the same formula that had worked so well with the Shahs on the bikers: divide and conquer. Paint a pretty picture of easy wealth to hook them, then a little muscle to reel them in. And although he hadn't intended to, Hakeem was acting as a mediator between Mindy and Billy, who were discovering they were in the same boat.

He glanced at his watch and winced. He was late! Mustn't miss the main show. He clicked his microcassette off and flipped his notebook shut.

"My friends, my thanks. Your story is safe with me."

Jinnah pushed his chair out, preparatory to taking his leave. But Mindy and Billy were faster and before Hakeem could so much as crouch forward in his seat, the two gang leaders were standing on either side of him.

"When did you say this sting was going down?" asked Mindy, fingering Mal Singh's belt buckle in a thoughtful and somehow menacing manner.

"You never said where, either," added Billy, using his trim-the-nails-with-the-switchblade intimidation tactic.

"I didn't and I don't know," said Jinnah, for the most part truthfully. "Now if you'll excuse me —"

Jinnah tried to stand, but Mindy pushed him firmly down into his chair.

"That guarantee we talked about?"

Mindy left the question hanging in the air. Jinnah would probably have disgraced himself professionally if the door had not opened at that moment. All eyes swung around to see the lean, laconic form of Clint Eastward, camera bag prominently displayed on his arm, saunter into the bar.

"There's you insurance," said Jinnah. "Eastward stays here until you hear from me."

Mindy and Billy looked at each other. Another subtle grunt and nod.

"Pictures are okay, but no identifiable faces," said Mindy.

"Yeah, make it artsy," added Billy.

Name of God, thought Jinnah as Eastward sat down and slung his bag in an empty chair. *What are biker leaders coming to?*

"Clint, my friend," he said. "Keep my chair warm for a few minutes, hmm? I have to check something out."

"Ah, you know I'm on overtime, Jinnah."

"Fantastic! I'll get Frosty to fill out the right form for Lumsden."

Jinnah grabbed Mindy by the shoulder and said softly, "Let him take all the art shots he wants and I'll be back in a couple of hours — three, tops!"

"Okay, but if you skip, *yaha apanē antima sanskāra*," replied Mindy.

Jinnah, finally free, walked hurriedly toward the door.

"Hey!" shouted Eastward. "Where you going?"

Hakeem saw the pouting and petulant Bindhu standing, unattended, beside the bar. He whispered something in Punjabi into her ear, and before Eastward could protest further, she was draped all over the photographer's lap.

"So, like, I hear you're a fashion photographer," she purred into his ear.

Jinnah, his escape covered and the hostage for his good behaviour in place, fled as swiftly as his dignity would allow.

The argument had been going on for several minutes, which in broadcast time is an eternity. By Caitlin's personal clock, it transcended eternity. By Kevin's, it was unpaid overtime and he was not happy.

"I don't care if Jinnah's van is in the parking lot," he said for the tenth time. "Tell me why I should go in there."

Caitlin was on the point of screaming. Kevin was starting to sound like the station news editor. It had taken a lot of convincing to get him to agree to let her stake out Fogducker's while someone else cut her piece for the evening news. She had finally won by painting him a grand conspiracy theory and she was damned if a mere camera operator was going to ruin everything she'd worked for by wimping out at the last moment.

"We're going to ask the bikers in there why Moe Grewal's body was found in a Warsaw Pact warehouse. And Jinnah's van being here confirms there's a link between whatever happened to Moe and Kabir Shah."

"Even if there was some connection, I don't see what we're going to get out of that bar aside from a beer-splattered lens and our tires slashed."

"Kevin, if you weren't ready to go inside Fogduckers when I asked you to come down here — quite voluntarily — then why did you agree in the first place?"

Kevin was not about to admit to his more base motives for agreeing and was formulating some sort of business-like retort when Jinnah exited the bar. Caitlin was, if possible, even more furious.

"Jesus, Kevin! Shit or get off the pot!"

But Kevin had been a camera operator for any number of divas. He had the keys to the van and he wasn't about to squander his advantage.

"Which pot do you want, Caitlin?" he asked. "Jinnah or the bikers. Choose."

Caitlin only dithered for a second. Choice one: navigate a domestic terrain that Jinnah had already been through. That could be good or bad. Choice two: follow Hakeem, likely only back to the *Tribune*, and lose the opportunity at hand. If Jinnah *was* headed back to the *Trib*. If ...

"Sonofabitch," Caitlin muttered.

The peninsula of Stanley Park thrusts out of Vancouver's downtown core into the waters of Burrard Inlet like a broad arrowhead. The concession stand of Lumberman's Arch is set on the top of a slope that rises from the shoreline, facing the North Shore across the inlet. Its public space has the virtue of being easily accessible by car, but it's also backed by dense woods that can be intensely private. More than one body has been discovered within a few hundred metres of the thick brush and it's a favourite spot for business transactions that are best kept from public view. The area is especially discreet when black and yellow "Caution — Construction!" tape bearing the coat-of-arms of the City of Vancouver and the logo of the Vancouver Parks Board is strung across the few entrances to the arch's pathways. Polite Vancouverites without clandestine motives stay away, leaving the dark woods deserted. But are there are sidetracks, mostly made by the wildlife that teems in the park, and the skillful can find their way through the latticework of deer trails and rabbit runs to almost any spot in the seemingly impenetrable brush.

Graham had made doubly sure that his team had made it unseen into their positions surrounding the small clearing in the woods to record the meeting between Armaan and Mallak. The network of unmarked cars, plainclothes bike cops, and foot patrols had been supplemented by aerial observation from what appeared to be a traffic helicopter reporting (rather persistently) on a stall on the nearby Lions Gate Bridge. Everything had come up clean, and when one of Mallak's WP goons had arrived to check out the rendezvous site earlier that afternoon, they'd escaped detection. The policeman had done everything he could. Now, standing beside his squad car parked out of sight on a maintenance road several hundred metres from the action, Craig knew it was time to set things in motion. All he needed was the all-clear from Pizza Hut. Right on schedule, he heard the soft, crackling voice in his ear.

"Central dispatch, this is Pizza Hut. We have the appetizers. Time for the main course. Over."

Graham winced. The coding language had been Capulet's choice, and as the junior agency, the Vancouver Police had been powerless to override their poor taste. He just hoped their frequency was as secure and encrypted as the superintendent had sworn it was.

"Pizza Hut, this is central dispatch," he said softly into his mouthpiece. "Acknowledged. I'll order the entree. Over."

"Central dispatch, confirm Delivery Boy is on his way."

"Delivery Boy, can you confirm?"

"This is Delivery Boy. On my way. At your door in thirty minutes or your money back. Over."

Graham grinned despite it all. Even over the secure channel, he could feel Bain's neck stiffening as his voice tightened. He didn't like being called "boy," even in code. But he could trust the constable to get the job done. All he had to do was drive from the Yellow Cab central station to Armaan's house, pick the young man up, and bring him to the Lumberman's Arch parking lot. Graham's on-site team (bolstered by several Mounties from the Integrated Crime Squad) would take it from there.

"Roger that, Delivery Boy," the sergeant said with a smile. "Pizza Hut, you copy? Over?"

"Central dispatch, we copy," Capulet's voice, almost as tense as Bains', wafted over the airwaves. "And make sure your Delivery Boy isn't attacked by a pit bull. Do you copy that? Over."

Graham's turn to bristle. He had made a point of cutting Caitlin completely out of anything to do with this operation. Hell, even Jinnah didn't know much about it. From a media perspective, the whole thing was under control. What the hell was Capulet so nervous about? Didn't he trust him to do his job? Then he remembered his last conversation with Jinnah. And regretted not putting a tail on both the battling cop reporters.

"Acknowledged, Pizza Hut. Over and out."

Pizza Hut was covering his butt. Graham kicked himself for not covering his own. God only knew what Caitlin was up to out there. Or Jinnah. Especially Jinnah....

* * *

Jinnah was sitting in the Satellite-Guided Love Machine, parked at the head of a quiet side road off Southwest Marine Drive. His position gave him full command of a wide stretch of high-end street that boasted more mansions and millionaires per address than anywhere in Vancouver. It was also just the right discreet distance from the Shah estate to make Hakeem confident that he was outside of any security perimeter Graham may have set up around Armaan. Now everything depended on spotting the vehicle Craig had picked to spirit the young man to the rendezvous with Mallak. That and said vehicle turning right and heading east from the Shah driveway toward the main north-south arterial route of Granville Street. He'd consulted his past experience, his inherent instincts, and muttered a quick prayer to News God before committing himself: this was his one shot. But all the portents pointed to somewhere in Stanley Park — likely Lumberman's Arch. And this was the fastest route from South Vancouver on the Fraser River to the park on the inlet. Not that anything was moving too fast — traffic wasn't exactly crawling but going at a pace where the determined observer could still get a good look at whoever was behind the wheel or in the back seat of a passing vehicle. He was nervous. Far more nervous than he'd ever been on such a stakeout, but then, his personal stakes were higher than ever.

What if he was wrong? What if the rendezvous was somewhere toward the University Endowment Lands to the west, equally discreet-yet-accessible? He'd miss the car carrying Armaan completely. No story to beat Caitlin Bishop. Manjit and Saleem's lives at risk. Worse, Sanderson would have the front page all to himself. Cursing fluently in Swahili, he pulled out his battered pack of smokes and fingered the thin plastic wrapping that sealed it. No, he couldn't. Frosty would find out somehow. And News God wouldn't like it. Switching his invective to Urdu, he jammed the cigarette pack (which now resembled pouch tobacco) back into his pocket.

News God rewarded Jinnah almost immediately. A second later he spotted what he'd been looking for: a Yellow Cab — chosen by seven out of ten police departments as being completely ubiquitous and therefore exactly the sort of car that screamed "police decoy vehicle!" The traffic had sped up just enough for him to miss the driver but it was the back Jinnah was concentrating on and he recognized Armaan's profile instantly. The Satellite-Guided Love Machine sprang to life as Hakeem gunned the engine and nudged aggressively into the flow of traffic. The BMW he cut off honked and the aging baby boomer behind the wheel gave him the finger. Jinnah just smiled and waved in the rear-view mirror.

"Man, if that upsets you, don't you dare drive in Mumbai," he chuckled to himself.

Jinnah was glowing. His guess had been right. He was just two cars behind the Yellow Cab and he knew he wouldn't lose the taxi, especially in this semi-gridlock. So far everything was going according to Craig's script. But then why were his inherent instincts tingling? What could possibly be wrong?

"Shut the hell up!" Jinnah snapped at his instincts.

The inherent instincts went into a corner of Jinnah's mind to sulk. They would soon be in a position to come out jeering: "Told you so!"

Armaan was not blessed with inherent instincts. Even if he had been, he was too much of a mess to have paid any attention to them. It was getting dark by the time he looked at the rear-view mirror and realized with a start that the driver wasn't Constable Bains, but some dark-skinned guy with tinted glasses and a ball cap.

"Where's Bains?" he asked, a little startled but not alarmed.

"Sick," said the driver. "Ate too much curry at lunch. I'm Constable Witek. Nervous?"

"No," Armaan lied.

"It's all gonna be fine, kid. You want some music?"

"Ah, sure."

Witek put on one of the local South Asian radio stations and music mixed with chat and ads in a mélange of languages filled the cab. Armaan sunk back into his seat, desperately trying to remember all the coaching Graham had given him about how to act, what to say, and how to get Mallak to incriminate himself. He was so self-absorbed that they were almost over the Lions Gate Bridge and on the North Shore before he noticed anything.

"Hey! We missed the turnoff for Lumberman's Arch!"

"Different route," said Witek. "Standard procedure.

Gonna circle around and come back through the park like we came over the other side of the bridge."

"But Graham said —"

"Relax! Sarge can't tell you everything. You're in good hands."

Armaan remained leaning forward, staring at Witek and the approaching exit to the North Shore. He glanced at his Rolex. Weird way of doing things, especially since they were supposed to be at the rendezvous in about five minutes.

"I hope Graham knows what he's doing," he muttered as they sped along Marine Way.

Graham knew exactly what he was doing. Especially when Bains radioed from the Shah estate, trying to sound cool but barely suppressing the alarm in his voice.

"Central dispatch, this is Delivery Boy. Chicken's fled the coop. Over."

Graham had gripped the mic with such force he nearly split the plastic casing.

"Say again, Delivery Boy, over?"

"Confirm missed delivery," said Bains, voice quaking. "Competing firm got here first. Over."

There was a finality that Bains gave to the word "over" that made Graham's skin crawl. If what Bains had said was true, Capulet would blow a gasket, his career was over, and Armaaan ... he was over too. Hand shaking ever so slightly, Craig punched the worn mic button.

"Confirm Delivery Boy. Package not in sight? No idea of delivery address? Over?"

"Confirm, over."

"Ten-four. Return to home base. Over and out."

Graham took his finger off the button and closed his eyes. Shit. Shit. Shit-shit-shit-shit-shit-shit-shit …

Often when Graham closed his eyes at times like this, he saw lights, stars — even beautiful colours. All he saw at the moment was black. It was with real effort he got back on the blower to his unit.

"Team, stand down. We have a problem. Repeat, stand down. Prepare to redeploy. Over."

"Babes in the Woods leader to central dispatch. Redeploy where?"

Graham heard the voice of Corporal Lyall over the radio from his cover deep inside the bush surrounding the rendezvous. A number of flippant responses went through his head. Given all that had happened, the sergeant couldn't guarantee their lines were as secure as he had thought, so he contented himself with a simple "TBD, Babes in the Woods leader. Over and out."

TBD. To be determined. Apparently on the roll of a dice.

Chapter Eight

Jinnah had already rolled the dice and as he had followed the Yellow Cab bearing Armaan to his date with Mallak thought he'd come up sevens. But when they missed the turnoff to Lumberman's Arch, his inherent instincts had started chanting "Told you so! Told you so!" By the time they were over the Lions Gate Bridge and driving along Marine Way, they were in full snotty child mode, sneering "Nyah-nyah-nyah-nyah-nah-nah." Unless he'd been wrong, which his exaggerated ego grudgingly allowed. When the Yellow Cab had swung suddenly to the right into the old Harrow Works, his heart leapt. This had been his third choice on the discreet rendezvous depth chart. An abandoned shipyard with plenty of crumbling outbuildings and works to hide in. Brilliant! But it would never do to follow the cab into the yard. No matter. Jinnah knew this neighbourhood well: he'd been the one wearing a wire once or twice (not to mention a rolling tape recorder) on this very spot. He sailed past and went two blocks before turning right, going to the end of a short block crowded by woods and derelict buildings — testaments to the decline in West Coast shipbuilding — before pulling over in the mud and killing the lights.

Using his cellphone as a flashlight, Jinnah made his way from his van down to the water. There was a bush-lined path that would lead him into the back door (or, from a ship's perspective, the front door) into the site quite unseen. He blessed the fact he'd worn his sensible hiking boots rather than his Guccis as he picked his way through the mud, nettles, and brambles toward the great rails that opened from the looming dry dock to the salt water of Burrard Inlet. This had once been the place that launched a thousand ships. Now it would sink an emerging empire of drugs and laundered money — if all went well. And Jinnah certainly planned to do his part.

He scrambled up the gravel path that led to the steel-grated stairs of the vast dock that rose above him like a maritime cathedral. It was a short distance from here to the main yard where he was sure the sting was going down, and he reluctantly pocketed his cellphone and groped his way uncertainly in the dark. His glasses were of no use whatsoever and he barked his shins more than once against abandoned machinery and other industrial detritus as he crept along the side wall. With relief, he made it out of the main slipway building and onto the walkway through the gallery of sheds backed by a rotting wooden wall lining the east side of the property.

Jinnah could now see vehicles drawn up in the yard. He crouched behind a crumbling half-wall for a better view. The Yellow Cab was there, facing the water, high beams blazing. A second vehicle, a black Cadillac, was parked pointing in the opposite direction, its headlights mingling with the taxi's, creating a pool of blinding white light, in the middle of which stood Armaan. As Jinnah emerged from the shadows, Mallak said something to the boy and ripped his shirt open. Hakeem frowned. Normally, Bains would have dropped Armaan off at the entrance and let him walk to the rendezvous alone. And it wasn't Bains who got out of the cab to pin Armaan's arms behind his back while Mallak continued to pat him down. Craig certainly was rewriting his usual script. Jinnah assumed that his ploy to get more info out of his policeman pal had inspired Graham to new heights in realism when it came to scripting a sting. This was going to be an exclusive worthy of the *Trib*'s final front page. Well, there was no sense in not getting some kick-ass art to go with it. Time to cash in that insurance policy.

Jinnah hit the speed-dial on his cellphone and crawled backwards away from his vantage point to avoid being overheard.

"C'mon, Eastward!" he whispered almost inaudibly. "I think it's gonna rain...."

* * *

"Totally, Bindhu, totally — you'd be a great model."

Eastward was rather enjoying being a hostage. The bikers were buying him beer, Bindhu was keeping him company, and Lumsden had even agreed to sign his overtime slip on orders from Whiteman himself. The vibe in the bar was kinda creepy, with Billy and Mindy going at it verbally off and on at a table straddling the Green Line, but the photographer had been at worse gigs. Bob Dylan's lifetime achievement party had sprung to mind. The ring of his cellphone was a very unwelcome distraction.

"S'cuse me." He smiled at the aspiring model. "Eastward!" he snapped at the phone.

"I found the sting," Jinnah's voice hissed softly over the airwaves. "Harrow Works, North Van. Get here stat!"

Eastward's mind did an instant situation analysis. Past experience with Jinnah suggested there was no better than a fifty-fifty chance the reporter was telling the truth. Even if he was, it was a long way to North Vancouver and the action — if there was any — would probably be over by the time he got there. Finally, there was this modeling shoot he was trying to arrange. But that wasn't the determining factor.

"I got no wheels, man!" he whispered, assuming Jinnah's volume. "Literally. Lumsden won't authorize the new tires for my car."

"Then take a cab! It's a small sacrifice!"

"What the hell am I a gonna tell Mindy and Billy?"

"Tell them anything. Just don't tell them the location of the sting. Got it?"

"Got —"

The phone went dead. Eastward sighed. Well, this was the alleged reason he was getting overtime after all. Reluctantly, he finished his beer, fished inside his shirt pocket for a business card, and handed it to Bindhu.

"If you want some promo shots, call me, okay? Nice to meet you."

Eastward almost made it to the door before a giant brown paw tapped him on the shoulder. Glancing slowly around, he saw Mindy and Billy staring at him, looking pissed.

"Where do you think you're going, man?" asked Billy.

"Duty calls. Gotta shoot the Canucks game," Eastward said smoothly.

Billy stepped around him and locked the door. Eastward looked coolly at Mindy with the slightest twist of the head that asked "What the hell?"

"You're our insurance for Jinnah's good behaviour," said Mindy. "You're not going anywhere until he gets back."

"I'm sure he'll be here shortly. Listen, thanks for the beers —"

Eastward turned to see that a half-dozen bikers had silently filed in behind Billy. More framed Mindy's bulk. The Phoenix Club leader smiled, handed the photographer a Kingfisher, and put a massive arm around his shoulders.

"Hey, listen — I overheard how you ain't got wheels. Lemme and Billy give you a lift to your assignment. Okay?"

Eastward carefully scanned each hard, brown face in front of him. He took a long pull on the beer.

"Long as you're going my way, thanks," he said.

In the crumbling wooden shed that gave him cover from the sting unfolding before him, Jinnah's sense of time was warping. It seemed to take an eternity to plug his lithium-powered shotgun mini-microphone into his microcassette tape recorder. It wasn't exactly state-of-the-art, but the device could pick up conversations a good fifty feet away. He fumbled to jam the earphone home, cursing as fatigue, nerves, and the overpowering feeling of something gone amiss robbed him of his coordination. Sonofabitch! He knew he should have taken a diazepam before leaving the office. But Sanderson would have found some city ordinance against it, no doubt. He managed to get sound and hit the record button just as he heard the cab driver say "He's clean, boss."

"Good, Witek," Mallak's voice crackled in Jinnah's ear. "Smart boy, Armaan — those transmitters can give you cancer."

Jinnah risked a look over the half-wall. Armaan was even more the deer-in-the-headlights than he had been in his lawyer's office, frantically casting around.

"Now, first things first," said Mallak cheerfully. "Anatoly? Be so kind."

The WP goon Jinnah had taken for Mallak's driver flipped open the briefcase, acting as a human desk. Mallak pulled out what appeared to be legal papers and handed them to Armaan. Okay — this at least was going according to the usual script.

"If you'd be so good as to sign these."

Mallak held out what even at this distance Jinnah recognized as a gold Montblanc pen. Armaan remained motionless.

"I'm not signing anything."

Jinnah nodded. This too was good. In his head, he was already composing his story: Son stings pizza killers. Cooperating with police, Armaan Shah trapped the men who murdered his father. Hmm, not bad....

"It's your dream come true, Armaan. Shah International Holdings will take its rightful place in the global economy."

This was even better. Jinnah could only hope that Graham was getting all this. He stuck his head as far out over the half-wall as he dared. He hadn't really expected to see Graham's team (they were willing to spend more than $19.99 on their eavesdropping equipment), so he was as much surprised as reassured to see the rim of a parabolic mic peeping just over the top of a pile of rusty machinery and old packing cases directly across the yard from him. He breathed an enormous sigh of relief. Now, if only Armaan could get the son of a bitch to really incriminate himself ... yes, after getting Karel Mallak to confess to the murder, the police swooped in and made the arrest ...

"It's not mine to sign over."

Jinnah stopped composing in his head. Armaan appeared to have grown some backbone. He'd better be careful just how stiff those vertebrae were.

"Oh, we know all about your half-sister in Tanzania," laughed Mallak. "A will over there means squat in our courts."

"Unless it's filed here."

"And does your lawyer have a copy, Armaan? Let me see ..."

Mallak fished in the briefcase held by Witek. Jinnah didn't have to read the document Mallak was waving under Armaan's nose to know exactly what it was.

"The one and only copy," said the WP boss. "Straight from your dad's lawyer's office in Tanzania. So sad ..."

Mallak took out a lighter — an old-fashioned silver-cased Ronson, no less — and flicked its flint. The flame leapt up and eagerly took hold of the fragile, thin legal paper. Armaan gave a cry and tried to grab it, but was restrained by Witek.

"You crazy son of a bitch! You're insane!"

"That's just what your father said before he, ah ..."

Jinnah held his breath. This could be it.

"... ended up in the oven."

Jinnah exhaled. Loudly. Shit! Not enough. Still, they were getting there. Surely after getting a *clear* confession, the police would swoop in and make the arrest.

Mallak dropped the flaming will and let it curl and blacken at his feet. He shoved the legal papers and the pen at Armaan again.

"Sign."

Witek released Armaan's arms. Hand shaking, he accepted the pen from Mallak. *Holy shit! He's not really going to* — Jinnah didn't have time to finish the thought. Armaan hurled the pen as far as he could toward the slipway building.

"Go to hell, Mallak!"

"Have it your way."

Mallak gave a nod to his goons. Anatoly snapped the briefcase shut and handed it to the boss while Witek seized Armaan. The two WP thugs tried to force the struggling Armaan into the trunk of the Yellow Cab. Sonofabitch! Jinnah looked over to the rim of the parabolic mic. No movement. Shit! What was going on here? Before he knew exactly what he was doing, he had torn the shotgun mic and earphone out of his microcassette and pocketed the still-rolling recorder in his jacket. He leapt the half-wall and strode across the yard toward the group of struggling men.

"Only after this *reporter* got Mallak to confess did the damn police swoop in," he said, loud enough for the tape in his coat to record what he fervently hoped were not his last words.

Jinnah's congenital cowardice tried to talk him out of all this, but he had calculated the odds. Graham was there to back him up. He probably hadn't moved in yet because Armaan hadn't gotten the goods. His presence would complicate things, yes, but if he could only get Mallak to make a clear confession, all would be forgiven. Besides, the safety of his wife and son were also at stake. If Craig could improvise on his sting scripting, so could Hakeem.

"Mr. Mallak!" he cried with counterfeit confidence. "So nice to see you again!"

The reaction from Mallak and his WP goons was completely professional. Witek whipped out a gun and placed it against Armaan's head while thrusting him forward as a shield. Anatoly covered his boss, who took one look, recognized Jinnah, and waved his henchman back. He stood in the centre of the circle of light casting a long, dark shadow and smiling serenely.

"Mr. Jinnah! Our fearless reporter!"

Jinnah advanced to within a few yards of Mallak. He was just feet away from a man who had tried to kill him. The only thing keeping Hakeem upright was the surge of adrenaline flowing through his body. He fought to keep cool and think straight. Everything depended on it.

"Did you have a good flight back, Karel? Or perhaps you took the bullet train, hmm?"

"Such wit. Your timing is awkward. Unless, of course, I make this a two-for-one deal."

Jinnah could now see quite clearly that while Mallak was smiling, his eyes were as cold as the Siberian steppes. Fighting his rising fear, he set about trying to help Graham get his confession.

"Timing is of the essence, Mallak. We're pushing deadline and I need you to answer a few questions."

"No questions, Jinnah —"

The WP goons looked like junkyard dogs straining on their leashes. Shit! Keep him off balance.

"Then perhaps you'd better listen to the story as is, hmm?" he interjected. "Karel Mallak, big-time entrepreneur, self-made murderer."

Mallak's smile faded, but not to a frown. He looked vaguely flattered. *Psychopaths*, Jinnah thought. He plowed ahead.

"At least two local killings in his international portfolio. Moe Grewal and Kabir Shah. Accurate so far?"

Mallak seemed amused. Buying into the game.

"I'm not demanding a retraction. Yet."

"Has suffered recent setbacks. Hostile takeover of Shah International Holdings and local biker club businesses? Failed. East Bloc Blonde interests? Shut down. Assets? Zero. Long-term investment outlook? Bleak."

Mallak looked like he was about to open his mouth to say something. Whatever it was, it wasn't likely to be good. Jinnah took in a ragged breath and ran right over him.

"Summary? You're a loser, Mallak. A small-time thug from Odessa."

Jinnah had shot his bolt. He dared to glance toward the parabolic mic just visible above the pile. Still nothing. Sweet Jesus, Craig! What do you need? It took a second for Jinnah to register the fact that Mallak was clapping slowly and sarcastically, a cold smile playing about his lips.

"Very clever, my friend. Here's my contribution: a guest column, as you'd call it."

"Keep it tight, we're on deadline."

Jinnah instantly regretted this remark. Mallak's guest column might consist of a lot of incriminating words or a single slug shot at close range and high velocity. For Hakeem could see that Mallak's mask was slipping. His eyes were those of a man who would stop at nothing to get what he wanted. Fortunately, all Mallak wanted at the moment was to hear the sound of his own voice. And it wasn't warm or fuzzy.

"Moe Grewal worked a dangerous game. He tried to play both sides. I believe in backing the house — my house. Moe lost, I won, and put him on ice."

Amidst the fear and the near-panic, a part of Jinnah's mind remembered to rejoice. That was at least one murder confessed to. But there might be more. *Craig, don't jump the gun — unless the gun is aimed at me, in which case jump away.*

"Shah International Holdings was a corporate acquisition. My final offer? Strangulation. I sealed the deal in the oven."

Armaan lunged forward, nearly breaking Witek's hold. He paid for his indiscretion with a vicious blow to the stomach from Anatoly. Mallak gave him a smile about as comforting as Vladivostok in mid-winter.

"You are pressed at the moment, are you not, Mr. Jinnah? All you journalists are having to multi-task, multi-platform, hmm? Do more with less? Let my guest column be no exception to the rule. It will serve nicely as your obituary. *Polozhit'ikh v avtomobil*, Anatoly," he added in Russian.

Jinnah's inherent instincts, which had been sent to the corner for their earlier tantrum, were now screaming at full volume. Name of God, what did Craig need from him? A signed confession? One more glance at the parabolic mic. Was that thing working? Hakeem took a step toward Mallak to force the issue.

"Got everything you need, Craig?" he shouted.

Mallak followed Jinnah's gaze and pulled out his gun. Hakeem stopped breathing. What the hell was going on here? Where the hell was Graham? For that matter, where the hell was Eastward? Had the whole world gone crazy? There was a script, goddamn it....

As Anatoly covered Jinnah, Mallak walked over to the junk pile hiding most of the semi-circle of microphone. The WP boss advanced slowly, gun held out in both hands. Jinnah saw him spot the mic. A nod to the goons. Both Jinnah and Armaan found themselves thrust down on their knees in the centre of the light circle, guns to their respective temples. Jinnah was facing Mallak and watched as the thug from Odessa approached the slender, semi-circular shape that promised salvation. He was bitterly disappointed by the lack of flash grenades, tear gas, police helicopters, and/or rubber bullets with the accompanying loud hailer announcing "This is the Vancouver Police! Put your hands on your heads!" Instead, Mallak actually laughed and waved his gun at the refuse pile.

"You two. Outta there now!"

Jinnah's emotions were complicated as he watched two shapes emerge shakily from the pile in the gloom. Despite the poor light, his glasses, and the perspiration pouring into his sockets (a natural and excusable by-product of having a gun to one's temple, his congenital cowardice assured him), he instantly recognized the slim form of Caitlin Bishop and the hefty outline of her cameraman, Kevin. Mallak grabbed the video camera and popped the digital pack expertly out of the device, pocketing it.

"Roll," he laughed, waving his gun toward the cars.

Caitlin and Kevin moved toward the circle of light. Their eyes were down and they did not acknowledge Jinnah's look. Wise. Mallak was right behind them, looking immensely pleased with himself.

"Witek, Anatoly, these two in the car with me. Those two in the cab. Come on. We're pushing — *okonchatel'nyy srok*? Final deadline. *Toropit'!*"

Jinnah found himself pushed into the back seat of the Cadillac with Caitlin. As the engine revved and words in Russian were shouted, he managed to grin at his former protégé as they lay head to head on the dark, soft cushions.

"Well, this gives a whole new meaning to shared news resources, doesn't it?"

Caitlin said nothing as Mallak jumped into the car, slammed the door, and shouted *"Dvigat'sya!"*

Frosty was on the third-floor balcony, the designated smoking area in the building, wishing desperately she could light up and staring over the cityscape enshrouded in darkness before her. She had chewed through her entire pack of candy cigarettes and was nearly out of nicotine gum. The view faced north and she was gazing over at the lights shining from the shore nestled by the Coast Mountains and wondering quite unreasonably if Jinnah was perhaps somewhere over there when a hand on her shoulder gave her a start.

"I'm sorry, Ms. Frost," said Whiteman. "Sanderson told me I would find you here."

Frosty grimaced. Good old Ronald. The Crimson Weasel.

"First edition's to bed, Chief. Great scoop —"

Whiteman held up a silencing hand. For once, he wasn't wearing his calculator face.

"Frosty, look. I know the warehouse bust is big. But I'm not entirely stupid. I see Jinnah has filed squat and, for him, put up very perfunctory resistance to having Caitlin scoop this angle of the larger story."

Frosty was able to process this in an instant, from the personal appeal of "Frosty" to Whiteman figuring out Jinnah was up to something. The only question was what the hell did the chief want? Because if it was to know what Jinnah was really about, he could suck her candy cigarette.

"Jinnah's working on finding the connection to the pizza oven murder, just like you asked," she replied, voice carefully neutral. "He may file something, he may not."

Whiteman stared out over the lights. There was an open look on his face Frosty had never seen — and didn't like much.

"Frosty, I don't know if I ever told you, but I started my career in Northern Ontario."

Oh, God! Here we go again! Yes, yes, Whiteman. It was still a hot lead type press. This media convergence thing is all new to you and us. You were just a page runner at the time —

"Back then, we were proud of news. News. Stuff we had before anybody. Understand?"

"Yes, Chief," said Frosty, slightly taken aback.

"Have you ever been on a paper that went under?"

Frosty had. Three times. It had hurt. But there had been the consolation that there would always be another newspaper to take its place, to get a job, to get the news out. In this environment, that was not the case.

"Yes, Chief."

"So have I. It may sound naive of me, Ms. Frost, but the single greatest regret I always had was we never told the truth, as we saw it, on our watch. There is a saying I believe you may have heard of …"

Frosty didn't need to hear the rest. She knew the quote by heart. It was not only from the King James Bible, but the style book of every good journalist. "And the truth shall set you free." Still, she was surprised when Whiteman took out a pack of cigarettes, unwrapped it, and pulled out a slender filter-tipped cylinder. He turned to look at her full in the face.

"Nicole, this may be the last edition of the *Tribune* we will ever produce. The talks with Candle are failing. I know it's selfish, but I want to have a hand in the last big exclusive the paper will ever have. Tell me what Jinnah's really up to. I may appear overbearing and corporate, but I'm really a newsman at heart, you know. I'll do whatever it takes to help you."

Frosty stared at him open-mouthed for an instant. What the hell was she supposed to say? How did she know this wasn't some pathetic plea for news intelligence born of CXBC's need for scoops and Whiteman's need to be the white knight who delivered the paper to Candle Communications? Yet he'd been so personal, so unlike his former corporate self — so un-Whiteman. What he did next sealed it. Whiteman flipped the pack so a single cigarette jumped out above its fellows, beckoning to Frosty.

"Smoke?" he asked.

As the two vehicles containing the captives turned and spun their tires in the gravel yard, Caitlin Bishop dared to sit half upright, pull out a deck of cigarettes, and offer one to Jinnah. Mallak, watching carefully from the front, shrugged it off as last rites. Anatoly was still turned toward them, finger on the trigger. Jinnah struggled up into a sitting position and shook his head.

"Sorry. Bad for the health," he muttered.

Caitlin grunted and, looking Anatoly straight in the eye, lit up. The WP goon shrugged a little without loosening his grip on his gun. It was all one to him. Caitlin leaned back in the Caddy's plush upholstery.

"I guess you were right," she breathed out in a cloud of blue smoke.

Jinnah found himself inhaling the second-hand carcinogens eagerly.

"Thanks," he said between drags. "I'll put it on my tombstone: Caitlin Bishop admitted I was right."

Mallak stuck his head between the two seats.

"Unmarked graves don't get headstones, Jinnah. So you and your girlfriend —"

Mallak never finished his threat. He shot forward between Jinnah and Caitlin as the Caddy came to a sudden, screeching halt. Jinnah was almost in the front seat, stretching to see what was up. It was a lot. A row of headlights barred their way. Single headlights. He could hear motorcycle engines being revved. Mallak twisted around and threw himself forward, took a look, and pummelled Anatoly on the shoulder.

"*Razvorachivat'sya! Bystro, bystro!*"

Jinnah could just make out Billy on the lead Harley coming straight at them. The glare of the headlights reflected off both helmets and turbans. Name of God! The entire Young Lions Club must be out there.

Anatoly spun the Caddy around as fast as the big car could move. Jinnah saw the Yellow Cab performing the same manoeuvre out of the corner of his eye. He pressed Caitlin down onto the seat, partly out of genuine concern for her safety, but there was a healthy dose of enlightened self-interest in the shove.

"Jinnah! What the hell —"

"Save it," he whispered roughly. "I think maybe —"

What Jinnah thought was lost as the car convulsed, jolting Hakeem into the roof. He yelped. The two cars were bouncing back into the yard — a dead end. They sprayed gravel and kicked up the dust. But even through the clouds, Jinnah could see another row of single headlights. A flash of light glinted off Mindy's face. The Phoenix Club was there, boxing them in. On the back of Mindy's bike, Jinnah saw a lean, lanky frame with a camera snapping pictures. Sonofabitch. The bastard must have spilled to Billy and Mindy. But Hakeem glowed inside — it was the first time an insurance policy had paid off for him. Now all he had to do was live to collect.

"Rasshcheplyat'!" Mallak shouted.

The two cars split, the Yellow Cab turning left, the Caddy right. The taxi disappeared while Anatoly desperately looked for an opening. Jinnah sat bolt upright, watching the ring of Harley headlights encircling them. They were back where they started, in the middle of the works yard. They lurched to a halt. Mallak opened the passenger side door and crouched behind it, gun in hand. Jinnah didn't mind that. His entire attention was on the WP boss's left pocket, which held the incriminating data disc. He hardly noticed Anatoly jump out of the driver's side, facing the opposite direction of Mallak. The Harley engines roared as Mindy dismounted and walked forward.

"Give it up, Mallak! We got you cornered!"

"Back off or you're the first one down, Mindy!" shouted Mallak.

There was flash of light and Jinnah was relieved to see Clint Eastward snapping away. Whatever happened now, at least there would be a record of some kind.

Jinnah was determined not to be the subject of someone else's User Key One story. He noted Mallak and Anatoly's positions relative to the rear doors. He smiled fiercely as a plan formed. Caitlin sat up, and with Mallak and Anatoly out of the car, they had moment of freedom. Jinnah looked at Caitlin and summoned up every ounce of mentorship from their time together at the *Trib*. His head moved slightly to the left, then to the right. To his immense relief, she nodded in response. She was with him. He counted aloud, quietly.

"One. Two. Three!"

At three, they threw their doors open. Caitlin gave Anatoly a metal frame in the face and he went down. For good measure, she hopped out and stomped her heel on the WP goon's gun hand, making him howl. Mindy's minions were on him instantly, swarming him and pinning him to the gravel yard.

Jinnah had been somewhat less successful. True, he had sent Mallak flying and separated him from his gun. But unlike Anatoly, Karel had the wit to drop, roll, and flee. Jinnah didn't hesitate. He scrambled out of the car and ran after the WP boss even as a blinding white light beamed down from above and the thump-thump-thump of helicopter blades drowned the roar of the motorcycles' engines.

"This is the Vancouver Police! Stay where you are!"

A day late and a dollar short, thought Jinnah as he raced behind Mallak through the sheds and decaying outbuildings in the abandoned yard. Jinnah's congenital cowardice had long checked out, but now his unabashed unfitness checked in. Name of God, why was he even bothering? In this light and with that obstacle course he'd already run through, Hakeem was sure Mallak was a misstep away from arrest. His prayers were answered as Karel tripped over the rusting winch Jinnah had bruised his shin on earlier. In seconds, the breathless reporter stood over his prey, reached down, and ripped the data disc out of the Odessa thug's pocket.

"I'll take that, Karel," he panted.

Mallak said nothing. A wise choice, because Constable Bains was right behind them.

"C'mon, twinky," said Bains. "I got a police sergeant wants to talk to you. Bad."

Jinnah had never been so happy to see Bains in his life. Then, his self-preservation instincts took over.

"Bains," he said, panting. "Do you —"

Bains yanked Mallak up to his feet by his collar.

"Let's go. Hate to have you face the press. If they ever get here."

Jinnah grinned all the way back to the yard and was positively beaming by the time Graham personally slapped the cuffs on Mallak. Armaan was there with Witek and Kevin. And there was Caitlin, standing there without a microphone or camera, but still game. As officers hustled Mallak and his gang into waiting vans, she tried to interview Graham.

"Sergeant! What happened here?"

Graham eyed Caitlin warily. *Jesus. Still trying to get the story first.*

"Your cameraman is quite safe. Billy and his boys rode them off into a ditch. No one was hurt."

"But my footage —" Caitlin began.

Again, Jinnah didn't hesitate. He knew what honour dictated. And the rules of evidence.

"You may want this, Craig," he coughed, handing him the data disc.

"Hey! That's my exclusive!" cried Caitlin.

"That's evidence," Graham deadpanned, turning abruptly to hide the grin spreading over his face.

Jinnah was left with Caitlin on the docks, watching as due process worked its inevitable magic. He glanced at his watch and smiled. Plenty of time for second edition. How long would Craig keep them on ice? Caitlin brought him back to the present moment.

"Well, that was a wild ride."

Jinnah looked at her. Caitlin was less than permed, her Armani suit was rumpled, and she looked more like the scruffy waif he had mentored oh so many years ago. He could almost love her — almost.

"It always is with you."

"You're not having a heart attack, are you?"

"No, just a bit of justifiable angina," lied Jinnah, hitting the stop button on his tape recorder as discreetly as he could.

"You were always good to me. Hakeem —"

Just how good Jinnah had been as a mentor to her was lost with Graham's abrupt arrival. He had Bains in tow.

"Ms. Bishop? Constable Bains here would like to take your statement."

"Statement? What about my live hit! What about —"

"The largest mistrial in Canadian history? You can discuss it with the nice constable here."

Caitlin reluctantly followed Bains, leaving Graham grinning at Jinnah.

"So how'd you find me?" he asked.

"This was my second choice for the sting — User Sting Two. Besides, Capulet had a tail on Mallak."

Jinnah too was grinning, until the word "tail" jogged his vestigial conscience.

"About Manjit and Saleem —"

"We have a couple of guys watching your house, you know that?"

"Craig, I love you and I want to have your babies. Now, there's one last thing —"

Jinnah didn't really need to ask. He saw Clint Eastward sending pictures over his cellphone as fast as he was snapping them, without interference from the bikers or the VPD. This was one exclusive that Candle Communications wasn't going to get. It was an all-you-can-eat *Tribune* news buffet.

"Do you have an official statement, Sergeant Graham?" asked Jinnah, hauling his tape recorder out of his pocket and holding it under Craig's nose.

"We have arrested three suspects," said Graham rather stiffly. "Acting on information supplied by a usually reliable source."

Jinnah let the "usually reliable" slight slide past. He knew Craig would give him just enough of the goods to make both of them look great on the front page. Assuming there was a front page.

By the time Jinnah got back to the newsroom, the place was almost deserted. One or two late-night deskers, the usual contingent from sports — that was about it. And Frosty, of course, holding the fort. Jinnah was somewhat surprised to see her chewing on an unlit cigarette.

"So?" she said. "Whatcha got for the last front page?"

"You're kidding, right?" said Jinnah, sliding into the empty chair beside her.

"Candle has backed out. Apparently our bottom line isn't attractive enough to their shareholders. Unless something dramatic happens in the next twenty-four hours, we cease publication."

Jinnah rubbed his forehead. Name of God! He should have stayed in Tanzania. With Narinder. Who was now a very wealthy woman.

"Hold that thought."

Jinnah grabbed the phone and dialed long-distance.

"What the hell are you doing?" demanded Frosty. "We're pushing deadline here, Jinnah!"

"I am getting crucial quotes and reaction from Narinder Shah," said Jinnah, flipping open a notebook and scrambling for a pen. "And perhaps saving our collective ass."

"Our collective ass has ten minutes to fill a giant hole on page one, Jinnah!"

"Don't sweat it! Hello? Narinder?"

In the end, it was twelve minutes before Jinnah's hastily typed prose was flowed into the top of page one next to a great shot from Clint Eastward. Frosty stared at the story, scanning it one last time. She was grateful that Whiteman had granted her carte blanche and a late deadline for this, the probable last edition.

"Karel Mallak and his Warsaw Pact accomplices appear in court this morning — we mean tomorrow, right? Likely charges of murder, trafficking, and extortion.... Armaan Shah has had charges against him dropped ... dramatic development, cooperating with police, a *Tribune* exclusive, yada-yada-ya ... Are you sure Narinder is flying to Vancouver as we speak?"

"She will be by the time this hits the doorsteps," laughed Jinnah. "She's got a lot of investments here to take care of."

Frosty darted a glance at Jinnah. She highlighted the last few paragraphs of the story.

"Narinder Shah will take her place at the helm of one of Vancouver's largest business empires. The two worlds of Kabir Shah have finally been united. He is at peace in paradise and his soul is free. Jesus, what a load of purple crap!"

"It's backed up by a quote, for God's sake!" cried Jinnah. "Besides, I think I deserve some credit for finding us a white knight at this late hour."

"Well, if Narinder Shah is going to be our boss, you'd better quote her accurately. Does she really have that kind of money?"

"Frosty, you have no idea."

Reilly, the late-night news editor, glanced querulously over his thick glasses and gave Frosty his best "fresh off the boat from the Cove of Cork" routine.

"You're after sending me the new page one, are you?" he asked. "Time is money, Ms. Frost."

"Yeah, yeah!" said Frosty. "Whiteman himself said we could go late."

"Whiteman himself is over at the club and the tab is open. It would be a terrible shame if I didn't get to add a Guinness to his last reckoning."

A final look over at Jinnah, a nod, and Frosty hit the send key. Reilly smiled, gave the purple prose produced by the newsroom's biggest yellow journalist a cursory look, then grabbed his jacket.

"Clear, boys!" he shouted to the two remaining deskers. "Let's go drink up some of that corporate welfare money!"

Frosty and Jinnah were alone in the newsroom. She turned to Hakeem and pulled out another cigarette. She handed it to him and took out her lighter.

"Great job. If it's our last front page, at least it's a ball-buster. Light?"

Jinnah pulled out his own lighter and flicked it on. Frosty followed suit. They were poised to light up right there at city desk. Sanderson would have had an aneurysm.

"So? Is this our last hurrah, Jinnah? Are you going to leave me for some bullshit African Burger Palace Empire?"

"Frosty, Frosty. The Burger Palace king thing is dead. And now that Narinder is adding the *Tribune* to her corporate empire, we both have job security, hmm? Besides, you know I would never leave you for another editor."

Jinnah leaned forward and lit Frosty's cigarette, then his own. Frosty laughed and took a deep drag on the glowing, slender cylinder. Jinnah calmly dropped his dart into a half-full coffee mug.

"I win," he said. "Pay up."

"Sonofabitch!" Frosty laughed, reaching for her purse.

- 30 -